Francis Brinkley

Life of William T. Porter

Francis Brinkley

Life of William T. Porter

ISBN/EAN: 9783337333294

Printed in Europe, USA, Canada, Australia, Japan

Cover: Foto ©Raphael Reischuk / pixelio.de

More available books at **www.hansebooks.com**

LIFE

OF

WILLIAM T. PORTER.

.

BY

FRANCIS BRINLEY.

NEW YORK:
D. APPLETON AND COMPANY,
448 & 445 BROADWAY.
LONDON: 16 LITTLE BRITAIN.
M.DCCC.LX.

TO

THE FRIENDS OF WILLIAM T. PORTER

AND

HIS BROTHERS,

This Volume

IS RESPECTFULLY DEDICATED,

BY

FRANCIS BRINLEY.

BOSTON, *March* 13, 1960.

CONTENTS.

CHAPTER I.

CHAPTER II.

CHAPTER III.

CHAPTER IV.

CHAPTER V.

CHAPTER VI.

CHAPTER VII.

CHAPTER VIII.

CHAPTER IX.

LIFE OF WILLIAM T. PORTER.

CHAPTER I.

WILLIAM TROTTER POR-
TER,* third son of Benjamin
Porter and Martha Olcott,
born in Newbury, Ver-
mont, December 24, 1809,
was of the eighth genera-
tion from Samuel Porter,
who emigrated with his wife
from the west of England
to Plymouth in 1622. Asa
Porter, grandfather of William, was born May 26,
1742, and graduated at Harvard College in 1762.
He established himself as a merchant at Newburyport, where he married Mehitable, daughter of John

---

* Arms of Porter.—Per Chevron sa. and ar. Three church-bells
counterchanged, each charged with an ermine-spot, also counterchanged. Crest, an antelope's head, erased ar., attired or., collated
gu., therefrom on the centre of the neck, a bell pendant, sa. charged
with an ermine-spot ar.

1

Crocker, Esq.* The love of adventure, and the restless
activity of the men of those days in plans for better-
ing their condition, induced many of the inhabitants
in the immediate neighborhood of Newburyport to
seek new homes and larger possessions in the Coös
Country, which was even then celebrated for the fer-
tility of its vast meadows and the richness of its grand
intervals. Col. Porter yielded to the impulse, and
some time prior to 1780, removed to Haverhill, N. H.,
having purchased a valuable tract of land near the
Little Oxbow, on the Eastern bank of the Connecticut River, where, upon one of its fairest and most
graceful sweeps, which his trained eye selected as a
spot susceptible of attractive ornament and profitable
culture, he built a durable and ample mansion, that

---

* He was a direct descendant from William Crocker, who came
from England to this country about 1630. John Crocker was remarkable for his fine form and manly beauty, as well as for great moral purity
of life and character. He was "nimble and blithe as a child, and up
to the time of his death, without the stoop of age; everybody loved
him." Mary, his wife, was a daughter of Thomas Savage, whose
father (H. C. 1659) married Hannah, daughter of the Hon. Edward
Tyng, May 8, 1661. Of the other daughters of Mr. Tyng, Mary married Gov. Searl, of Barbadoes; Rebecca married Gov. Joseph Dudley,
of Massachusetts; and Eunice married the Rev. Samuel Willard, President of Harvard College.

The Crockers are descended from Sir John Crocker, Knight, cup-
bearer to Edward IV., who was from a branch of the house of Crocker,
of Lyncham, in the County of Devon; a name so eminent that there is
an old proverbial distich, or as Prince calls, an old saw, recording its
antiquity:

> " Crocker, Cruwys, and Coplestone,
> When the Conqueror came, were at home."

Worthies of Devon, p. 274.

to this day commands the admiration of the traveller. His removal to a comparatively remote and unsettled part of the country, which, no later than 1754, the Legislature of New Hampshire designated as a region "hitherto unknown," would of itself establish his character for vigorous enterprise.

Here amidst magnificent scenery, grew up a well-trained and intellectual family, whose home was the favorite resort of the cultivated and refined. Col. Porter was a model of affability and dignity; never laying aside the garb or the deportment of a gentleman of the old school, but always preserving his courtly air and address without sacrificing a particle of his self-reliant energy and fearlessness. He is described by one, who remembers him, as "slow to anger, of a forgiving disposition and kind to the poor. In civility and politeness excelled by none." In religion he was an Episcopalian, in politics a Royalist, and as he wrote to Lord Dorchester, "severely felt the resentment of that part of his countrymen which then prevailed, and suffered greatly in his person and property;" in consideration of which he received from the Crown a grant of the township of Broome, in Canada. Indeed, his landed estate was immense, and has been estimated as high as one hundred thousand acres. At one time he owned a large part of Topsham, Vermont, and extensive tracts in neighboring towns. He claimed, also, the town of Woodstock, Vermont, and was offered a crown ($1.10) per acre, to compromise his claim; but with characteristic tenacity of purpose, he refused the offer, and held to

his title until it was ultimately decided against him.
Most of the lands of New Hampshire and Vermont,
about the middle of the last century, and somewhat
later, were held by the Crown, and grants were made
to individuals; though nominally made by the Crown,
in many cases, the names of the grantees were inserted
by the Governor. Col. Porter frequently had a direct
interest in such grants; but more commonly, he purchased the rights of the grantees for a small consideration. One of the provisions of these grants was,
that five hundred acres in each township were reserved to the Governor. Col. Porter became the
owner of many of these tracts, called the "Governor's
Rights," and sometimes, "Governor's Corners." As
an illustration of his persevering enterprise it may be
stated that to fulfil a contract with the British Government for building a bridge at Quebec, he accompanied
his men on foot from Haverhill to that city. He did
not look like one capable of the effort, but he had
hardened himself by keeping up the habits of gentlemen of that time, who accustomed themselves to
robust exercise, and he was therefore able to accom-
plish an undertaking apparently much beyond his
strength, without serious inconvenience. Pride and
policy may have stimulated him to encounter the
fatigue of this journey on foot, since, according to a
French proverb, "Il est aisé d'aller à pied quand on
tient son cheval par la bride;" and though he had a
select stable, he preferred to walk on the occasion as
an encouragement to his men.

In truth his passion for fine horses was not inferior

to his ambition for ample fields. He spared no pains
in purchasing blood of pure strain. Some of his best
stock was obtained of his friend Gov. Wentworth,
that rare sportsman and accomplished gentleman, who
did much to improve the breed of horses in New
Hampshire, at his princely establishment at Wolfs-
borough, on the shores of Lake Winnipiseogee.

Though Col. Porter was a devoted Royalist, he
did not inherit that faith, his father being a zealous
Whig. There is an amusing testimony to the fact in
the records of the Committee of Safety of New Hampshire, as it seems that the son was apprehended on
suspicion of Toryism about the year 1777, and dis-
charged from arrest on giving bond in the sum of
£500 that he would repair forthwith to his father in
Boxford, and not depart from his farm for the term
of one year, except to attend divine service on the
Lord's day. The Committee may have been over-
zealous; at any rate he was ever faithful and loyal to
the new government, under whose protection he lived
and prospered for so many years.

It is a family tradition that during the revolution
business obliged him to visit Boston. He set off in
his own sleigh, which had the arms of England em-
blazoned upon the back. As he drove into town, he
was surprised to find his sleigh an obnoxious mark
of attraction; while vociferous threats soon warned
him of the cause of the unexpected hostility. At first
he was inclined to pay no other heed to it than starting up his horses a little; but multiplied volleys of
missiles and of words admonished him to take counsel

of his discretion, and he stopped at a painter's shop and had the obnoxious blazonry effaced. On his return home, his wife was at the door to welcome him. She soon perceived the discoloration of the back of the sleigh, and with ready intuition divined the cause. She was of remarkable spirit, and entered into the political faith of her husband with all the animation of her character. She ordered her women to bring soap and brushes, and without a thought of the cold air, or too tender regard for her own fair hands, she picked her way on her little high-heels to the sleigh, and never stopped scrubbing until the old Lion and the Unicorn reappeared "fighting for the crown," as fresh as on the day they parted from her loyal eyes.

Arthur Livermore, Esq.,* now of Missouri, in writing of Col. Porter to Mrs. Brinley, says: "He was beyond dispute a man of a good deal of character. I hardly know whether I can with propriety say to you, his descendant, what I have very often said to those who have known you all as I have known you; that Col. Porter has given this proof of having been *thoroughbred*, as we say of a horse, that he impressed upon all his posterity, through several generations, very remarkable common characteristics;

---

* Son of Judge Arthur Livermore, and grandson of the eminent Judge Samuel Livermore. The latter went to New Hampshire simultaneously with Col. Porter, and purchased an estate at Holderness, where, amidst the most romantic lake scenery, he built a mansion-house, which would be conspicuous for stateliness even in these days of ambitious architecture.

marks that distinguish them from all others. This is said neither in the way of flattery nor disparagement, nor with any purpose to be personal. He was from all accounts a gentleman. His associations were with such. His daughters married gentlemen, and his sons, gentlewomen. In person he has been described to me as a spare man, and to have been in the habit of wearing a good overcoat of sable skins on one side and scarlet cloth on the other. He was accustomed to say that it was a foolish thing to try to brave the cold. The right way was to guard well against it by abundant clothing."

By his marriage Col. Porter had six children, John, Benjamin, Mary, Elizabeth, Sarah, and Moses. The daughters were brilliant and accomplished women, receiving their education at Newburyport and Boston.

The Judicial Courts for the northern part of New Hampshire were held at Haverhill Corner, about seven miles south of Col. Porter's, and the attractions of his daughters, his generous hospitality and reputed wealth, brought the members of the bar to his house in goodly numbers; some of them prosecuted their suits with success, for the three daughters married gentlemen of the legal profession; Mary, the Hon. Judge Farrand; Elizabeth, the Hon. Thomas W. Thompson; and Sarah, the Hon. Mills Olcott.

Col. Porter's son Benjamin, so named for his ancestor, Benjamin Crocker, Esq., was born at Newburyport, July 13, 1771, and on the 11th of October,

1800, was married to Martha, daughter of Gov. Peter Olcott,* of Norwich, Vt., and established himself in the law at Newbury, in that State.

The town of Newbury occupies a natural terrace above the broad, rich sweep of the meadows, flanked on the westerly side by a high, wooded, almost perpendicular ridge called Mt. Pulaski, which, in that direction, serves to the village as a kind of *abat-vent* to keep off the keen blasts of the early spring. Towards the other points of compass, the horizon widens into great beauty and grandeur, embracing a chain of hills forming the lower elevations of the White Mountains, which can be traced from the top of Mt. Pulaski, in all their diversity of shape and coloring, until they unite with Mts. Washington and Lafayette; the pale, spectral pinnacles of those thawless snow-peaks being clearly discerned from Newbury as sharply cut against the sky as on the day Noah removed the covering from the ark. Towards the south the prospect lies open to a length of the Connecticut Valley, "the asylum of love and philosophy," as well as of labor and comfort; its velvet carpets of greensward dotted over with groups of majestic trees and grazing cattle, hemmed in by the naked crests of New Hampshire and the undulating ranges of the Green Mountains, and apparently terminating

* Gov. Olcott was of the sixth generation in descent from Thomas Olcott, a merchant in London, who emigrated with his wife, a daughter of David Porter, Esq., of that city, to Connecticut. He brought with him the experience and fruits of successful enterprise, and was one of the founders of the commerce of that Colony.

at the foot of Ascutney, which stands out against the southern sky like the fragmentary walls of some colossal barrier, to guard it from the outer world; its loftiest points kindling into spires of gold, while the soft gray shadows of night are yet lying upon the valley.

Here, among these meadows, blue hills, and wide sky, the lives of William T. Porter and his brothers took their shape and coloring. Their home included the firesides of father and grandfather, so closely were they united by the tenderest of ties, both marked by the same unaffected tone of polite life, enlarged hospitality, love of out-of-door existence, and study of the best authors. Benjamin Porter, their father, was a man of vigorous stamp. A keen observer, a sound lawyer, active and energetic in his practice, with continual opportunities, even in that retired portion of the country, for the display of acumen and learning in disentangling the legal perplexities, and conducting the controversies in which his father had necessarily become involved during a long and busy life in a community where land titles were undetermined, and the conflicting claims of settlers, tenants, and proprietors were the subjects of frequent and protracted litigation. Indeed, his large-heartedness, popular manners, and strict integrity secured the friendship of numerous clients at home and abroad, and the confidence of all who were brought within the range of his manly influence. "He was about the same height as his father," writes one of his neighbors, David Johnson, Esq., still living at the advanced age of

1*

eighty-two, " but more fleshy and of a larger frame, and was what may be called a handsome, well-built man, more familiar in his habits and intercourse with his neighbors than his father. A very active business man, benevolent, free, and open hearted. He had a very charming, lovely, and amiable wife."

Wm. C. Thompson, Esq., a nephew of Mr. Porter, thus writes of his uncle's appearance when in the prime of life: " Both Mr. and Mrs. Porter were very handsome persons; more so than either of their children, and this is saying much. Mr. Porter's form was like his son Ben's, but taller, more active, and muscular. He had a round, frank voice, and, as I remember him when I was a boy, was particularly pleasant and kind to children. He lived in a liberal and hospitable style, inheriting his father's tastes for owning lands, and farms, and capital horses." Mrs. Porter was a beautiful and attractive woman, remarkable for her dignity of character and ease of manners. She had irrepressible buoyancy of temper, united to the kindest sympathies, and a goodness that lives in the hearts of many to this late day, who never speak of her but with tears of reverence and grateful love.

To fit his children for the ends and aims of life, Mr. Porter employed judicious teachers of both sexes under his own roof, until they were old enough to be sent from home to school, and at every opportunity of leisure from the exactions of professional labor, gave them his personal instruction. About this time, 1812, William was taking his first lessons in spelling, under the paternal roof, from one of the most amiable of teachers, who afterwards married William Trotter, Esq., an especial friend of Mr. Porter, and for whom he named his son.*

Mr. Porter was a capital horseman, and was every day more or less in the saddle as his engagements would permit.

In early life he was in the habit of making long journeys on horseback, as was the fashion of the day, starting off for Quebec, Boston, or New York, with less bustle of preparation than in these days of rapid locomotion, although the time occupied in one of those old-fashioned horseback expeditions seems now almost incredible. In one of his letters dated Newbury, Dec. 3, 1798, addressed to his sister Sarah, then at school in Boston, he writes: "To have spent the evening of my return home, after a seventeen days' journey, in the society of my dear sister, would, to say the least, have been happier than some hours of the way. My route mostly by water to Quebec, was as rapid as I could have desired, but my journey home was as inclement as the season. Not an inch without pain, not a step without a groan. Thus for two successive winters I have made this journey (expeditions of little moment at a moderate season), when hardly a human

---

* She is still living to recall with melancholy interest those days of childhood at Newbury. She assures us that William's desire to make a figure in life was in him from the start, for when playfully asked, before he could speak plain, what profession he intended to adorn when he became a man, he invariably replied, drawing himself up with dignity, " I intend to preach to make the peoples dood."

being could stir from the fireside from the severity
of the weather."

In the following allusion to one of his female
friends at Quebec, in the same letter, we get at the
whole heart of the man : "The specimen of your
painting, dear S., so long promised to my friend Mrs.
W., could hardly be dispensed with, considering the
long friendship and thousand civilities to Papa and
myself. I could only renew the promise that my next
visit should bear it to her. Pardon me, ye belles of
Quebec, if I felt more regret at leaving this good,
old, sensible, thoroughbred, Christian, New England
woman than all the fine faces your town can boast;
and were I for the example of some darling favorite of your sex to describe the good wife and
agreeable friend, my pen would point involuntarily to
Mrs. W."

He closes his letter with some wholesome advice,
which is quite as pertinent in these days of ultra refinement in the education of the daughters of the
land as at the time he wrote : " Col. W. tells me that
his daughter already speaks very good French. This
is all ·very well for Miss W., as she is to reside in
town. But I declare, dear S., I do not believe it will
be ever asked of a girl who lives one hundred and
fifty miles from *salt water*, and who reads with propriety, spells correctly, writes handsomely, and com-
poses easily and elegantly in good old English, whether
she pronounces French à la mode. There are in
my humble opinion many other both mental and
personal accomplishments, together with a long list

of domestic attainments, much more necessary in a fine woman's education, although in that of a gentleman it is quite indispensable. I abhor French sentiments and the hideous tone of French novels; but I love the language, and am far from wishing with W. that every French fop in this country should starve because he can do nothing better than lisp his mother tongue."

In connection with Mr. Porter's journeys to Canada in the saddle, we are reminded of several in which he was accompanied by Daniel Webster, while the latter was a law student with Mr. Thompson, (brother-in-law of Mr. Porter,) at Salisbury. In 1801–2, Mr. Thompson was accompanied by Mr. Webster to Newbury upon the occasion of one of the former's visits at Mr. Porter's house. Both Mr. and Mrs. Porter became very fond of him, and perhaps among the many pleasant recollections of Mr. Webster's early manhood which served as an animating relief from his first struggles, and afterwards from the toil of a crowded professional life, none were recalled with keener pleasure than his visits to old Coös during the ten years following his first introduction. In anticipation of their recurrence, Mr. Porter arranged several horseback journeys to Canada, in which Mr. Webster was to participate, and sometimes as his sole companion. The pleasure they derived from the social qualities of each other, can be readily imagined by those who knew and loved them both. The ripe and instructed mind of the elder friend kept charmed and amused by the originality and buoyant vivacity

of that great mind which was destined to give light
to a nation long after the other had sunk to his rest.
In the later years of the life of Mr. Webster he stated
to us with marked emphasis and feeling, that Mr.
Porter was the most attractive social companion he
had ever known. It was during his visits at Mr.
Porter's house that the foundation of a friendship was
laid which became a source of life-long enjoyment to
Mr. Webster. The youthful object of his regard was
the orphan niece of Mrs. Porter, the only child of her
sister, Sarah Olcott, and the Hon. Jasper Murdock.
Upon the death of her parents she was consigned to
the care of her grandfather, Gov. Olcott. At the
time of Mrs. Porter's marriage she transplanted the
beautiful exotic of her family to her own fireside, and
scrupulously provided that she should acquire at
home and abroad those accomplishments which,
united to her eminent personal charms, qualified her
to grace and adorn her own distinguished home upon
the event of her marriage, June 25, 1810, to Hon.
George Blake, of Boston. Many of Mr. Webster's
most interesting letters during his early public career,
were addressed to her, and are contained in the volumes of his correspondence. She died in the prime
of her days, a few months following the death of her
adopted mother.

During the summer of 1817, Mr. Porter first became aware of an incipient affection of the heart,
though only a few weeks previous to the approach
of any symptoms of the kind he said to a friend:
"I am certain I shall live to a great age. Look

at my breadth of chest. I feel long life in every muscle."

Physicians were consulted at the first apprehension, and by their advice he gave up all business, and retired with his family to one of his farms, where he kept up his almost daily exercise in the saddle, until his increasing infirmities obliged him to discontinue it altogether. He was finally induced in the following summer to try the effect of a journey to Saratoga, where a consultation of eminent physicians was held upon his case. Previous to the consultation his letters evince a sanguine hope of ultimate restoration.

Alas! it was not to be. The decision of the physicians was unfavorable to his hopes, and by slow and painful progress, accompanied by his wife and son Benjamin, he reached Mr. Olcott's at Hanover. It was impossible to go any further. Day by day he became weaker, until all expectation of recovery was abandoned, and his parents and intimate friends were summoned to see him die. The event took place at five o'clock in the afternoon of Sunday, August 2d, 1818. His clergyman, the venerable Dr. Shurtleff, of Hanover, and Dr. Muzzey, his physician, both still living in honorable age, testify to the fortitude of the dying man. Dr. Shurtleff has within a short time described to us the closing scene, which in solemnity, calm resignation, and tender solicitude for the family of his love, he had never, in his lengthened experience, seen surpassed.

He sleeps in the quiet church-yard at Hanover, in compliance with his expressed wish, as he foresaw,

that to give his eldest son, then in college, the benefit
of a home, to secure to his other children the advantage of academic training, and at the same time place
Mrs. Porter where she could have the immediate
counsel and protection of her brother, Mr. Olcott, she
would almost of necessity select Hanover for her residence after the death of his parents. Three months
after his death, his father died. In a worldly
view the death of father and son, so near to each
other, was most deeply to be deplored. The former
died in the belief that he had great wealth; but
much of his really extensive estate consisted in
unproductive tracts of land not readily convertible
into money or easily managed. The son had stepped
aside from his profession to embark in various
enterprises of pith and high promise, which his
sudden and long-continued bodily prostration obliged
him to surrender or neglect. His large expectations seemed to warrant his extended operations, and
if five years more of active life had been vouchsafed to him, and the estate of his father been kept
together, his sons, who derived little or no benefit
from the vast landed property of their grandfather,
would have been rich and independent, and spared
the crushing weight of narrow circumstances and disappointed hopes.

"During the summer of 1821," writes Mrs. Brinley,
the youngest daughter of Mr. Porter, "my mother
removed to Hanover, having purchased a picturesque old residence which occupied the highest
site in the village, a few steps from where the

present observatory stands. It was a large, faded, tranquil-looking, one story house, covering a good deal of ground, of no special color, but mellow with the lapse of time and changing seasons, and had been originally built for one of the presidents of the college. The prospect which it commanded on every side was of wide-spread character, full of variety and heavenly beauty. Even as children we were never tired of looking at the distant blue line of sky, the far-off mountains in the north, the long, low ridge of jagged rocky hills in the rear, and the great purple and gold summits of Ascutney, now almost within arm's length, which we believed to be a celestial highway to the battlements of God's home. Directly opposite to us, across the river, were our own beloved hills of Vermont, the hills of our birthright, the hills of the setting sun, piled up into the vast heavens, with all their pastures, forests, brooks, clouds, and busy human life.

"The village of Hanover was just below us, fresh, compact, and shining as a mosaic, with its venerable college, solemn old church, and clusters of white dwellings in a square setting of young elm trees, which lent a grateful shade to the romantic footpaths round the common. A little removed from the village on the westerly side, a narrow, beautifully shaded avenue led gently to the common burying-ground. It was of the genuine New England pilgrim stamp; its monumental tombs and graves abandoned to weeds and nettles and relentless gloom, inclosed by a plain board fence stained with the damps and moulds of time, hemmed

in and choked up by the high grass, rank shrubs, and
matted ivy which trailed over it. A few stunted
trees were scattered here and there, but shrivelled
into lifeless skeletons, as if unable to resist the inexorable destiny written all about them. The situation of the old burial place, however, was beautiful,
upon the verge of a deep gorge between two hills
lined with a thick growth of young forest trees; over-
looking the gently swelling valley, the winding river,
and the purple masses of surrounding hill. At this
day the spot has participated in the general spirit of
improvement of burial places throughout New England, and is not only ' embosomed soft in trees,' but
includes within its limits the wooded gorge which
already enshrines within its shaded depths the sleeping dust of inestimable worth and virtue.

"On my mother's arrival at Hanover, no time was
lost in placing her four youngest children, William,
George, Frank, and myself, at the prominent school
of the town, which was then connected with Dartmouth College, the President of the College being *ex
officio* President of the Academy. This school was
originally established for the education of Indian
youths, and the corporate name was ' Moore's Indian
Charity School,' but for many years it had been open
to pupils of both sexes on payment of a small tuition
fee. The Dominie, Archelaus F. Putnam, (Scholæ
Moorensis Preceptor, as appears in the Dartmouth
College Catalogue,) presided over the destinies of
that institution, only known to me and to the rest of
his pupils by the familiar name of ' *Old Put.*' I

never knew from what part of the zodiac he radiated, who gave him birth, who taught him Greek and Latin, whether he was or was not the namesake of the lineal descendant of the second son of the Judean Governor who was driven out of his dominions for his cruelty; whether he was Orthodox or Heterodox; whether he believed in Simon Magus, who prescribed lively bodily mortification from a notion that it had a happy influence in enlarging the mind, or sided with Hierax, who regarded children, "till the age of reason," as outcasts from heaven, and to be treated as young rebels or sinners; or sympathized with that sect which sprung up in Italy in 1260, taking their name from the Latin *flagello*, and maintaining stoutly that a brisk application of the whip on the shoulders was of equal virtue with the sacraments; but of the personal appearance of the Dominie, I have a distinct impression. He was an emaciated, narrow-chested man, above the medium height, with a pale, rigid face—eyes inexorable and full of danger, though chafed into a sick and pale dimness, with a mouth that vibrated betwixt a snappish irritability and an evident attempt to appear undisturbed, and at times even jocular. With the utmost diligence in our studies, and the closest observance of the rules of the school, it was impossible to escape the humiliating blows of a mahogany ruler, which carried out the bent of his humor from day to day, by capricious hammerings of our sacred persons, that in time threatened to break down the stoutest heart amongst us.

"Instinct and intellect, however, were quickened by its lightning strokes down to their secret springs of inspiration, and vigorous progress was the result in every department. The very atmosphere of old Darmouth at that period communicated a sturdy emulation in both parents and children. Scholarship was the all-in-all creed of the day. Infants were expected to lisp Greek before the appearance of their first tooth—the very air was said to be freighted with Lysbian lyrics, and precedents of rare excellence among the graduates of the college were forever kept before the eyes of old and young. The whole country ringing with the fame of Mr. Webster, and the every-day presence of Mr. Choate, then a tutor in college, in the rich bloom of his personal beauty, with a reputation more circumscribed but not less commanding within its sphere of display than the fame which surrounded him at the day of his death, gave impulse and courage to every young ambitious spirit within sound of the college or academy bell.

"During these years of unflagging industry, William made great progress in his studies; and though often detected with a volume of Dr. Fox, or the Complete Angler, within the leaves of his Virgil, he was considered 'up to his work' in Greek and Latin, and ranked high as a scholar. Out of school at that time he was always reading. He remembered well and accurately what he read, and in the selection of books from the college library, to which he had access, he evinced a characteristic preference for works of stirring action and the biographies of enterprising men.

"In appearance he was very striking, remarkably handsome and tall for his years, promising, if time kept on, to reach the 'supreme pitch' of old Friedrich Wilhelm's Life-guard Regiment of Foot.

"Roughness and coarseness, such as are common even to most well-trained boys, were entirely out of his line. We do not recollect to have ever seen him angry, though he could plant his foot down occasionally in the shape of an opinion equal to the Dominie. His character at this age was the same as when he came to manhood, generous, unselfish, modest, truthful, cheerful, always retaining the credulity and simplicity of a child. An utter inability to pronounce the monosyllable *no* was the only loose screw in his organization. To utter it in good standfast fashion, and thereby cause disappointment and perplexity to another, was as impossible as to add another cubit to his stature. It lay at the foundation of his few mistakes in life, and was the only source of regret that threw a shade over his beaming spirit from his cradle to the grave.

"In 1823 the discipline of the Dominie began to tell unfavorably upon all of us, particularly upon George, whose temperament being sanguine and excitable, rendered him more sensitive and restless under the forcing system than William. George was a manly type of a boy, with blonde complexion, broad forehead, and eyes of rare significance; tall

for his age, with an unmistakable look of determination written all over him. Of more robust
intellect than William, high spirited, not easily managed, thoroughly sweet-tempered, clear-headed, his
character from first to last bore the same impress—
a transparent simplicity, overlying a foundation
of strength and decision. He had an instinctive
abhorrence of chastisement, and rather than run the
risk of being struck, would strain forward like a
thorough-bred, at the risk of life and limb. Those
who were most sensitive to the blows of the Dominie, and could be forced forward fastest, stood always most in danger from them. George had often
won the first fruits of ambition and perseverance, and
was one of the leading advertisements of the school.
The ruler must not relax. Exasperated and worn
down at last, his sleep became disturbed by a kind
of nightmare, which threatened his health so seriously, as to open my mother's eyes, as well as
those of the whole village, to the severities of the
school, and ended in his being sent to an academy at
Haverhill, N. H., where he remained for years, until
transferred to Meriden, previous to his entering
college. His emancipation had the effect to unsettle
the rest of us, and gave rise to a very general idea
that the long-talked-of royal road to learning was to
be sought out for our especial solace. William
shared in the hallucination, and permitted his mind
to run riot with an idea suggested by the life of
Dr. Franklin, which he was then reading for the
fiftieth time, that if he could persuade my mother to

give up the prestige of Alma Maters for him, he
could start off upon the great venture of life in a
printing office without the necessity of going to
school another day. She, however, refused to give
the proposition a single thought, sympathizing very
clearly with the venerable Vicar when Moses proposed to set out in gosling-green waistcoat to face the
snares of a crafty world.

"Soon after this she had the opportunity, during
one of Mr. Thompson's visits at Hanover, to consult him, together with Mr. Olcott, about William's
change of school, and, in connection with the subject, she mentioned his recent proposition. To her
astonishment they both advised her to let the boy
have his way; at all events to let him make the
trial. Time went on. Conversations were held
upon the subject. The uncles argued, and William
urged and promised, until she finally surrendered her
prejudices, and yielded a reluctant assent. Every
effort was made to find the most unexceptionable
office in New England for his novitiate, and it was
finally determined that Messrs. Flagg and Gould's
printing establishment at Andover, Mass., offered the
fewest objections, and held out more advantages than
any other, especially when viewed through the pious
medium of her mind. It was at that time the foun-
tain-head of Bibles, tracts, and religious works. The
conductors were men of well-known exemplary lives,
residing in a theology-imbibing atmosphere, and
where, from the general idea I derived as a child of
the religious character of the place, I supposed that

the Commandments and Catechism could be seen with the naked eye upon the 'pages of the air.'

" He soon after left in the mail stage for Andover; his letters came in due time, informing us of his safe arrival, good health, and agreeable surroundings. The first Thanksgiving festival which came round, he passed in Boston at Mr. Blake's. This was his first and happy experience of city life, under circumstances which he recalled with fresh delight as long as he lived. Twenty-two years afterwards he alludes to that joyous time, and almost with a sigh as he closes an article styled 'An Hour at Old Drury.' 'We plead guilty to a weakness for the sports of the circus which has grown with our growth, and we can laugh at the jokes of Mr. Merryman with as hearty a gusto as when our coats were minus the tails; like the re-perusal of Arabian Nights and Robinson Crusoe, without an effort they carry us back to the days when, if we knew less, perhaps we were more happy.' He repeated his visit to Boston the following summer, and had the pleasure of accompanying Mr. Blake, who was an expert angler, to the cape, where he fished in the celebrated Marshpee Brook, 'the best trout stream,' he wrote in 1840, 'in which it was ever our good fortune to wet a line.'

" His first return to Hanover was in April, 1825, in consequence of my mother's illness. She died on the morning of the 4th of the following month, of rapid consumption, in the presence of all her children, excepting my brother, the Doctor, who was in Georgia. The day previous to her death, with a clear and cheerful mind, as if about to take leave of us for a temporary absence, she distributed tokens of her love, and gave such parting words of direction and encouragement as our age and circumstances required, setting forth to her sons the necessity of every manly virtue to carry them safely and honorably through life. She tenderly reminded us that she was only going away from us for a little time—a little before—going *home*, where there would be no more death, nor sorrow, nor crying ; and then drawing us all closely about her, in words that cannot be remembered, except as they left an impression upon our hearts ' deeper than all love,' she breathed her last prayer for us on earth.

" Religion in her household had been conscientiously taught, but it was her firm, consistent, courageous, silent example, which made an undying impression upon her children.

" However full and diversified the after life of her sons, through all their trials and temptations, pleasures and triumphs of one kind and another, amidst the congenialities of genial and oftentimes hazardous companionship ' bullying in upon them in masses,' they never outgrew the influences stamped upon their souls when under her care.

" We saw her carried upon a bier, and laid by the side of our father, and in a few weeks afterwards we were all cut adrift from the home anchorage forever.

" Benjamin returned to Boston, William to Andover, while George and Frank pursued their preparatory studies for college at Haverhill and Meriden."

2

Dr. Porter, the eldest brother of William T. Porter, graduated at Dartmouth College in 1822. His friend and classmate Mr. Chief Justice Perley, of Concord, N. H., thus writes of him in a letter to Mrs. Brinley, Sept. 28, 1859:

"I was very intimately acquainted with your brother, Dr. Porter. When I entered college as a freshman in Sept. 1818, I found him then a member of the class. He was then, I think, sixteen years old, and had already reached nearly, if not quite, his full stature of six feet. He was then of a slender figure, very erect, and very brisk and alert in all his movements, full of vivacity and spirit; a general favorite in college on account of his amiable disposition, his winning manners, and agreeable conversation. He was not a severe student of the regular college studies; but a keen observer of all that was passing around him, very well informed on general subjects, and wholly free from all inclination to vice or low dissipation. He left college with the reputation of a young man likely to achieve a brilliant success in any department of practical life that he might select. Soon after he left college he went to Virginia, and afterwards to Georgia, and was absent from New England about five years. In Nov., 1827, I went to Hanover to try my chances in the law, and found your brother there, just returned from Georgia, and attending the medical lectures in the college. I saw much of him while he remained there, which I think was about two years, and found him little changed in character or manners from the man from whom I had parted five years before. He had, however, made great advances in general knowledge, and adopted more settled views in life.

"Your father had died before I knew any of the family. Your mother did not remove from Newbury until some time after the Doctor entered college, and I did not become acquainted with her until near the end of my college course. I was, however, well acquainted with her afterwards, and am under obligations to her kindness, which I trust I shall never forget. She had many points of resemblance to her brother, your uncle Olcott,* his wit,

---

* At the time of Mr. Olcott's death, an obituary appeared in the "New York Observer," written by the late Rev. George Bush, of that city, formerly a private tutor in the family of Mr. Olcott, so masterly in delineation, that the Hon. Rufus Choate (a son-in-law of Mr. Olcott) considered it a more faithful portrait than the skilful pencil of any limner could produce. The influence of such a man standing in the relationship which he did to the five brothers Porter, from their boyhood to the hour of his death, was beyond calculation. He was their beau ideal of all that constituted a gentleman in the highest sense of that term. They loved and honored him through life with the devotion of children, regarding a word of commendation from his lips with more delight than from any other human source, while a hint intended to convey a shade of merited rebuke filled them with unspeakable regret. It is impossible to observe the outlines of Mr. Olcott's rare nature without recognizing much of the breadth and vigor which were conspicuous in his nephews, and which at this date are eminently embraced in the character of his immediate descendants.

HON. MILLS OLCOTT.

Died, at Hanover, N. H., on the 11th inst., Hon. MILLS OLCOTT, aged 71. In the death of this estimable man society, learning, religion, share with a bereaved domestic circle in the consciousness of a loss well-nigh irreparable. Few men have been more widely known, few more profoundly loved and respected in life, or more sincerely lamented in death. The pen which would fain pay a becoming tribute to his various worth, finds itself at a loss to present a portrait, which, while it shall appear true to his friends, shall not seem overwrought and extravagant to those who had not the pleasure of his personal acquaintance. Viewed as to native endowments his character was a rare assemblage of high qualities. Every thing about him was cast in moulds which gave forth only elevated and imposing forms. He was emphatically a man of *large soul*. A certain inbred generosity of nature —a lofty magnanimity—an expansive liberality of sentiment—a signal superiority to any thing low or little—shone conspicuous in his habitual bearing, and was abundantly *realized* in its appropriate actings in the various conduct of life. His intellect was remarkable for clearness and acuteness, and though receiving an early direction to the sphere of the *practical* rather than of the *speculative*, yet it was evident that, had circumstances varied the bent of his genius, he would not have failed of eminence in any department of letters or science to which he might have devoted himself. As it was, though distinguished by a refined and elegant his shrewd observation of character, with more vivacity, and a more easy and flowing style of conversation. Her health, after I

taste, yet his converse was rather with *men* than with *books*, and his keen insight into character—his exact judgment—his far-seeing sagacity—his proverbial prudence—while they secured distinguished success to his own secular plans, gave a peculiar value to his *counsel*—which was always readily accorded—in regard to the conduct and affairs of life. In what is technically termed the *knowledge of human nature* it would have been difficult to find his superior. Yet with all the conscious impression and tacit acknowledgment of pre-eminent powers inspired upon those who knew him, no one was ever oppressed by it. He wore his virtues so meekly—he was so " courteously carriaged "—he had such a delicate respect to the feelings of others, even in the minutest points—and was so instinctively studious of preserving their proper self esteem unwounded by the least word or look which could give pain, that the ideal of the *perfect gentleman* could scarcely find itself more adequately embodied than in him.

His love of the domestic circle made him averse to public life, while it availed not to quench his public spirit. Every useful enterprise, institution, and object drew largely upon his sympathies and freely upon his support ; and yet his private charities, no less numerous or ample for his public benefactions, left their record in the grateful memory of relieved affliction and in the tears that were shed on account of the tears that were spared.

The Literary Institution with whose fortunes he was more than half a century connected, whose interests he was ever active in the various capacities of Trustee, Secretary, and Treasurer, in promoting, and whose successive generations of alumni have borne his revered image engraved on their hearts, will feel itself shorn of a pillar of strength in his removal, and the festivities of its coming anniversary will be gloomily damped by the view of his vacant place on the accustomed stage.

In social life he was the model of every thing at once commanding and attractive. His extensive acquaintance with men—his intuition of character—his unfailing store of anecdote—his delicate irony—his power of graphic portraiture—his brilliant but innocuous wit, made his society a rich treat to all ages; and the exquisite manner in which he managed to introduce some hint of practical wisdom that might especially serve for the guidance of the young and inexperienced, was always felt but never can be duly described. With the keenest perception of the eccentric, the grotesque, or the ludicrous in character, no man ever discovered more leniency to human infirmity, or was more tenderly alive to the sensibilities which guarded the weaknesses he would fain correct.

The qualities which we have thus fully depicted as characterizing the deceased must needs command admiration, as they universally did in the subject of them, independent of the operation of any higher element in the midst of these striking gifts of nature. But we have still to advert to the crowning excellence of the man in the spirit of unfeigned piety which adorned the greater portion of his earthly career. His native endowments constituted a beautiful ground for the display of the inwrought graces of the Spirit of God. Having attained to mature life before knew her, was seldom perfect, but she was uniformly cheerful. She was a very religious person, but her piety had nothing in it morose or severe. Her manners had been formed in the best society of her time, and had the ease and simplicity which I take to be the highest proof of perfect good-breeding."

"I have but one positive memory connected with my eldest brother," writes Mrs. Brinley, "in these early Hanover years, and as it gives significance to his after life, I rejoice to be able to recall it.

"A few weeks after he left college, he was in readiness to carry out a plan quite common among graduates at that time, of starting for the South, to engage as a public or private teacher, in order to gain the means of obtaining a professional education easier, earlier, and more ample than could be done at the North.

formally connecting himself with a church, he lived ever after as if intent upon bringing up the religious arrears of his earlier years. Exemplary and faithful in the discharge of every duty, he yet evinced the air of one who, oppressed with the consciousness of perpetual defects, rejoiced mainly in the hope built upon the gratuitous mercy of the gospel through the finished righteousness of the Lord the Saviour. His child-like trust in the merits of Christ was conspicuously coupled with a delightful softening influence upon the stronger traits of his natural character, causing all the more salient qualities of the man to be kept in wholesome check by the restraining graces of the Christian. Humility, simplicity, meekness, continually mantled over his deportment; and if it were possible to detect a fault in his religious character, it would perhaps be in that extreme self-depreciation which seemed to forbid the thought that *he* could venture to assume that position of prominence in good works which every one else was so ready to accord to him. For this reason he was perhaps unduly prone to keep himself in the back ground, when the grace of God would have been more highly magnified by a believing disregard of his own conscious infirmities. But with all abatements on this or any other score, he has left to a mourning family and church the legacy of a remembered example of Christian virtues but seldom evinced, and the peaceful and hallowed calm of his death-bed, in the midst of excruciating sufferings, put the seal of heaven's encomium upon his life, and gave to himself and his friends the assured anticipation of the future "Well done, good and faithful servant."

"The morning of his departure from home, long before the dawn, while sleeping by the side of my mother, I was awaked by his entering the room to take leave of her. He was sobbing aloud, and fell on his knees before her, and for some time both were too much overcome to speak a word. My mother recovered first, and in broken voice gave him much solemn and earnest advice, which seemed to me very much in the form of prayer. As he was about to leave her, she said to him with prophetic earnestness in her voice and manner, 'My son, if I should die before you come back, promise me to take care of my little ones.' He made the desired promise with firm voice and with all the manly warmth and sincerity of his nature. Another farewell embrace, the door opened, and they were separated, never to meet again until the integrity of that pledge had been tested by a lifetime of labor and love in behalf of those committed to his charge. From the day that he heard the tidings of her death, his oversight of us four youngest children, William, George, Frank, and myself, commenced, and though separated from us for nearly two years after that event, his letters were constant and regular, addressed not only to ourselves, but to those who had the control of our training and education. Nothing was too trivial or insignificant to escape his loving interest and scrutiny; and though there were many times during those two long years of absence, when we felt ourselves alone in the world, scattered and separated from each other, yet his fatherly and responsible care kept us all comparatively hopeful and happy until his return.

"We religiously preserved his letters. Their value to my younger brothers was of incalculable advantage, and were read and re-read so often that at this date their fragile leaves hardly hold together, and are never touched without an apprehension that they will exhale in our hands."

In one of his letters to William, while the latter was still at Andover, he writes, "It has gratified me very much to know that you are so well situated in Andover, and that you are contented and happy. I think your profession, if well understood, is one of the very best in the whole circle of those employments which are usually filled by industrious and enterprising men, and one which will insure every honest man a competent livelihood; and to one who improves every opportunity to become acquainted with books, it can scarcely fail of procuring both honor and profit. You seem to have employed your leisure hours to some purpose. It did my heart good to mark the freedom and justness of your remarks on the works you have read. You have only to continue your diligence a year or two longer, and you will have every thing to hope. I am not at all opposed to the course of reading you have pursued; for you have now arrived at that age when the acquirement of a good style is equally important with the acquisition of facts."

CHAPTER II.

In the year 1829, William commenced his editorial life at St. Johnsbury, Vt., in connection with " The Farmer's Herald," and in about a year removed to Norwich, as an associate in the publication of " The Enquirer," where he remained but a short time, and then with a light heart and a lighter purse, he gave a lingering look at the hills of his native State, and started for New York, as the most promising field for the support of such a journal as he hoped to establish.

The Hon. Horace Greeley wrote us a few months ago from New York:

" I came to this city about the 16th of August, 1831, and very soon found work as a compositor at Mr. John T. West's printing office, No. 85 Chatham Street. I here found Mr. William T. Porter at work as a compositor, and I think he officiated as foreman. My recollections of him at that period are, that he was a tall, comely youth, of about twenty-five, very urbane and kind toward those younger and less favored than himself, and a capital workman. He left West, I think, before I did, the work here being very poorly paid, while he was able to command more lucrative employment. At the last end of this year, he and James How, another young printer, devised 'The Spirit of the Times,' a weekly sporting paper, which they brought out on the 1st of January, 1832. I worked for them from the outset, and remember getting the first number to press a little after midnight of Dec. 31, 1831, Jan. 1, 1832. I continued to work on this paper, first at No. 64 Fulton Street, afterwards at No. 45 Wall Street, till September, 1832, when I left on a visit to my relatives in New Hampshire, and my place was supplied, so that I did not work on the 'Spirit' thereafter." *

As the *first* number of the "Spirit" was issued on Saturday, December 10th, 1831, according to Mr. Porter, it must have been the fourth number on which Mr. Greeley was engaged as indicated in his letter; the precise date the author has not been able to verify, as the early numbers cannot be found. The circulation was about six thousand copies; a large number for the new paper, under all circumstances. In a few months it was united with "The Traveller," with Mr. Porter in charge of the sporting department. This arrangement did not last long, and Mr. Porter took charge of "The New Yorker" for a short time —and then of "The Constellation." But as those

---

* As illustrative of Mr. Porter's appreciation of a genuine strong character, he thus alludes to Mr. Greeley as long ago as when the latter was editor of the "New Yorker":

"Mr. Greeley is the friend of our early days, and a right manly, honest editor is he. So eminent are his abilities and so remarkable his industry, that we boldly predict for him a brilliant future; and his career as an editor—thus far since his recent outset, propitious—is destined to be yet more commanding; he will be yet heard in the councils of his country. Into whatever situation he may be thrown, however he may be elevated or depressed in life, he will carry with him right staunch and sturdy honesty, the noblest gift of God."

2*

journals gave a subordinate place to sporting matters, it was natural that his thoughts should revert with affectionate regard to " The Spirit of the Times," *which he originated*, and which was baptized by his brother Benjamin, who suggested its name ; and he soon after purchased the copyright of " The Traveller, and Spirit of the Times " from C. J. B. Fisher, by whom they had been united, and on Saturday, January 3, 1835, Mr. Porter issued the paper with the name it now bears.

He was now in the position which he coveted, and the opening words of a genial address to the " Fraternity," which is full of kindness, attest his satisfaction. " We joy to meet you thus *alone*. It has been our good or bad fortune more than once to be connected with prints over which our control was shackled by the will of others, and where it was inexpedient to give free vent to our feelings to our editorial compeers. To be sure we had our own way, but then, as Col. Hardy says in the play, we hadn't our own way of having it. Thank Heaven, such is not now the case, and we seize the opportunity of making our grateful devoirs to each and all in that spirit of courtesy and good fellowship which harmonizes with our sincerest sentiments."

When he had thus consummated his cherished purpose of establishing and solely conducting a sporting newspaper in the Commercial Metropolis of the country, he was perfectly aware that there existed, in some sections, a marked antipathy to the very name of race-course, and a morbid apprehension of the

ruinous and indefinite mischiefs which were erroneously believed to be its inseparable attendants.

In the Middle States, a tolerant and kindly feeling
for the turf was quite prevalent; while at the South
and South-west, out-of-door life with its various sources
of amusement and excitement, and its promptings to
a zealous, yet rational regard for the horse, the gun,
and the angling-rod, was an ardent passion with agricultural gentlemen of wealth and spirit.

The conflicting opinions of different sections of the
country, were obstacles to the smooth, rapid, and
profitable progress of the novel enterprise. To face
and to correct deep-rooted prejudices, demanded the
aid of a "man of hope and forward-looking mind,"
and in whom should be united a rare variety of
qualities; enthusiasm in the subject-matter, talent,
practical knowledge of printing, and a clear sense
of editorial duty, good temper, sound judgment,
perseverance, honor, and pluck. Fortunately, all
these elements of success were mingled with different
degrees of intensity, in the trustful and generous nature of the gifted projector of the new journal.

It was a novel undertaking, no other American
newspaper having the same specialty, or claiming to
be regarded as reliable authority as to the value and
ownership of animals asserted to be thorough-bred.
These points were becoming more and more important
as the investment in stock was regularly and rapidly
augmenting in most parts of the United States.

Horses were introduced into England at a very
early date; the crown and the people both encourag-

ing the growth of breeds of different, but superior qualities.

In the reign of Queen Anne, (Herbert informs us,) the English thorough-bred horse may be regarded as fully established; the Darley Arabian, son of Flying Childers, Curwen's Barb, and Lord Carlisle's Turk, son of the Bald Galloway, being imported in her reign. Sixteen years after her death, and three years before the foundation of Georgia, the youngest of the royal colonies, twenty-one foreign, and fifty native stallions, some of them the most celebrated horses the world has ever seen, such as Childers, Bartlett's Childers, the Grey Childers, the Bald Galloway, Bay Bolton, Coneyskins, Crab, Fox, Hartley's Blind Horse, Jigg, Soreheels, and Trueblue, were covering in the United Kingdoms; and from some of those are descended almost all our racers of the present day. Six years before this, the first racing calendar was published in England, with nearly seven hundred subscribers. During this period it was, precisely, that the American colonies were planted; and, as might be anticipated, English horses of pure blood were at a very early date introduced. And in those regions where the settlement was principally effected by men of birth, attached to the cavalier party, race-horses were kept and trained; race-courses were established, and a well-authenticated stock of thorough-bred animals, tracing to the most celebrated English sires, many of which were imported in the early part of the eighteenth century, was in existence considerably before the outbreak of the old French war. In the Eastern States, the settlers of which were, for the most part, attached to the Puritan party, and therefore opposed to all amusements and pastimes, as frivolous, at the least, and unprofitable, and to horse-racing more especially as profane and positively wicked, very few horses of thorough blood were imported.

Virginia and Maryland as the head-quarters of the cavaliers—the former State having for a long time refused submission to the Commonwealth and to stout old Oliver—as the seat of the aristocracy, fashion, and wealth of the Colonies, prior to the Revolution— took an early and decided lead in this noble pursuit; and while the love of the sport continues to distinguish their descendants, who are by far the most equestrian in their habits of any other citizens of the Republic, the result of the liberality of the first settlers is yet visible in the blood of their noble steeds.

The emigrants from those States to Tennessee took some of their best stock with them, and thus it became more or less diffused, as population was attracted to fresh territory, and as the boundaries of the Union were enlarged.

It is believed that the amusements of the Turf were introduced into America by Gov. Samuel Ogle, during his term of office as Governor of the Province of Maryland, from 1732 to 1745. David Ridgely, in his " Annals of Annapolis," states that

" The first public horse-racing at, or near Annapolis, is advertised in the Maryland Gazette, to take place on the 30th and 31st days of May, 1745. The purses to be run for by any horse, mare, or gelding, ('Old Ranter' and 'Limber Sides' excepted,) to

carry 115 pounds, three heats, the course two miles." * * *
"How this race came off, we are not informed. From the exclusion of 'Old Ranter' and 'Limber Sides,' we may infer they
were somewhat celebrated in their day." * * *

"1747. On the 29th of September, in this year, a race was
run on this Course (at Annapolis) between Gov. Ogle's bay
gelding and Col. Plater's grey stallion, and won by the former."

"A Jockey club was instituted here about this period, consisting of many principal gentlemen in this and the adjacent prov-
inces, many of whom, in order to encourage the breed of this
noble animal, imported from England, at a very great expense,
horses of high reputation. This club existed for many years.
The races at Annapolis were generally attended by a great concourse of spectators, many coming from the adjoining Colonies.
Considerable sums were bet on these occasions. Subscription
purses of one hundred guineas were, for a length of time, the
highest amounts run for, but subsequently were greatly increased.
The day of the races usually closed with balls or theatrical
amusements."

"On the same ground, some years after, (1767–8,) Dr. Hamilton's horse *Figaro*, won a purse of fifty pistoles. * * * Figaro
was a horse of great reputation; it is stated of him that he had
won many *fifties*, and in the year 1763 to have received premiums at Preston and Carlisle, in Old England, where no horse
could enter against him; he never lost a race."

Between the years of 1752 and 1766, Jolly Rogers,
James, Fearnought, and Partner, were imported into
Virginia.

Dr. John B. Irving in his interesting history of
the South Carolina Turf, written in 1843, says:

"It is upwards of a century since racing commenced in Carolina
as a popular pastime. The earliest record that exists of any public running, appears in the South Carolina Gazette, February 1,

1734. The prize was a saddle and bridle valued at £20. The race was on the first Tuesday in February, 1734—mile heats—four entries. The horses carried ten stone—white riders. This was one of the stipulations of the race. There was also another condition, that the horses should be entered on the Saturday preceding the race. This race took place on a Green on Charleston Neck, immediately opposite a public house known in those days as the Bowling Green House."

Dr. Irving describes the season of 1788 as " a golden age of racing in South Carolina," and says in reference to it,

" Whether we consider the elevated character of the gentlemen of the Turf, the attractions that the races possessed at that time, and for many subsequent years ' for all sorts and conditions of men ; ' youth anticipating its delights for weeks beforehand—the sternness of age relaxing by their approach—lovers becoming more ardent, and young damsels setting their caps with greater dexterity—the *quality* of the company in attendance—the splendid equipages—the liveried outriders that were to be seen daily on the course—the gentlemen attending the races in fashionable London made clothes, *buckskin breeches and top-boots*—the universal interest pervading all classes, from the Judge upon the Bench, to the little school-boy with his satchel on his back—the kind greetings of the Town and Country—the happy meeting of old friends whose residences were at a distance, affording occasions of happy intercourse and festivity—the marked absence of all *care*, except care of the horses—the total disregard of the *value of time*, except by the competition in the races, who did their best to save and economize it—every thing combined to render race-week in Charleston, emphatically the *Carnival* of the State, when it was unpopular, if not impossible to be out of spirits, and not to mingle with the gay throng.

" The best idea we can give of the *moral influence* of race-week, (as exerted formerly,) is to state that the Courts of Justice

used daily to adjourn, and all the schools were regularly *let out*, as
the hour for starting the horses drew near; with one consent the
stores in Broad and King streets were closed—all business being
suspended on the joyous occasion, the feelings of the good people
partaking of the rapidity of the races themselves—in fact, it was
no uncommon sight to see the most venerable and distinguished
dignitaries of the land, Clergymen and Judges, side by side on
the course taking a deep interest in the animated and animating
scene around them!

"With such a stimulus to prosperity and the preservation of
good morals, no wonder that order and sobriety and good fellowship prevailed as abundantly as they did in those days. We
must not omit to notice that in the early days of Racing in South
Carolina, the gentlemen of the Turf, like the ancient nobles, Hiero
and others, never ran their horses for the *pecuniary value* of the
prize to be won, but solely for the *honor*, that a horse of their
own breeding and training should distinguish himself. Mr.
Daniel Ravenel, and many others, of the high-minded turfmen of
those days, expressed great disapprobation at any departure from
the good old custom of their fathers, and did all in their power
to prevent a change when it was proposed. The prize used
to be, not a purse of gold or silver, but a *piece of plate.* Several
of these tokens of success are in the possession of the descendants
of those who formerly owned race horses in the State.

"Such were the races in South Carolina! Let us hope then
that we of the present generation will never feel less attachment than our fathers did to the Sports of the Turf; and that
whatever other changes may occur in our State, no change will
ever take place in the celebrity of our horses; that the animating
spirit of the Chase will in all time to come, continue to call our
youth to the woods, and the rational amusement of the course,
our Sportsmen to the Turf!"

It is not proposed to ascertain the number and
names of the numerous race-courses which have since
been established all over the country, or to give even

an approximate estimate of the value of the thorough-
bred stock, imported or native, as this volume is not
intended for an Index to a Racing Calendar, or a
mere repertory of names. But some reference to the
value of choice animals, and to the pecuniary interests
allied to the Turf, is indispensable to an appreciation
of the motive, independent of personal taste, which
stimulated Mr. Porter to embark his limited resources,
but large intelligence, in this untried field of periodical
literature. A few prices are, therefore, jotted down
from memory, and without regard to date, not as the
most remarkable, but because they happen to occur,
and will give a general idea of the great cost of the
best order of animals. Thus, $10,000 were paid for
Henry ; Zenith and *Magnate* could not be purchased
for $5,000 at 3 years old. *Medoc*, one of the very best
of our native stallions, was said to be worth not less
than $35,000 at the day of his death. *Black Maria*
was sold at public auction, at Nashville, Tenn., for
$4,000 when thirteen years old. *Mary Blunt* sold for
$6,000. *Altorf* for $10,000 at nine years of age.
Rodolph for $22,000. For *Fashion*, $12,000 was
asked, and so on.

Taking into account all the associated interests of
the Race-course, its numberless auxiliaries and surroundings, one cannot fail to perceive the importance
and even necessity of a Journal which should repre-
sent the condition and demands of an interest of such
pecuniary magnitude and so widely extended, and
which received the encouragement and support of men
of the stamp of Col. John Tayloe, John Randolph,

Hoomes, Selden, and Col. William R. Johnson of Virginia; Govs. Ogle, Ridgely, Wright, Lloyd, and Sprigg of Maryland; Messrs. Hampton, Washington, McPherson, Alston, and Singleton of South Carolina; Gov. Williams and Gen. Carney of North Carolina; Gen. Jackson and Gen. Harding of Tennessee; Richard Smith, Major William Jones, and the Messrs. Hall of New York; the Messrs. Stevens of New Jersey, and hosts of other honorable men in all parts of the country beyond our ability to specify in a work of this description. They gave an impulse to the meetings of Turfmen, and laid the foundation of that zeal and success, in the improvement of the breed of horses, which have been so triumphantly displayed.

To advocate the claims of such a cause and the interests of such men, Mr. Porter at once devoted his time and strength.

The increased interest which began to be manifested in regard to the Turf and a variety of out-of-door athletic sports was most grateful to him, and we can easily imagine the satisfaction with which he announced the spirited action of the New York Jockey Club, in the very paper which contained his salutatory address.

Some of its members agreed to run a sweepstakes over the Union Course in the spring of 1838 with fillies and colts then three years old. The entrance to be $1,000, and the forfeit $250. Distance, mile heats. Among the subscribers were Messrs. W. Livingston, R. Tollotson, J. C. Stevens, W. R. Johnson, Jno. C. Craig, S. Ringold, S. Gouverneur,

Wm. Wynn, A. L. Botts, R. F. Stockton, Wm. H.
Minge, J. H. Wilkes, R. L. Stevens, John Heth,
R. Randolph, Wm. Coleman, John M. Botts, A. B.
Meade, Samuel Laird, J. H. Oliver and D. W. Jones,
all gentlemen of the highest respectability and public
spirit.

The transactions in blooded stock during the year
1836, amounted to over half a million of dollars, and
the high prices obtained for that of superior quality,
indicated the fresh impetus which had been given
to the turf in this country by men of wealth and influence.

In the autumn of this year Mr. Porter made a
visit to the pine-clad hills, rich prairies, and verdant
valleys of the south and west, from which he returned with enlarged and enlightened views of
the character and condition of the agricultural dis-
tricts, and a confirmed appreciation of the care and
attention given to the raising of fine stock, whether
of horses, cattle, hogs, or sheep. The number, value,
and improvement of blood horses for the ordinary
purposes of life, or destined for the chase or the turf;
the management of race-courses in the vicinity of the
prominent cities, and their large and liberal clubs, as
well as the whole system of racing, with all its ramifi-
cations, enlisted his acute powers of observation.
Of the many courses, jockey clubs, and associations of the South, he was especially delighted with
the "Hampton Course," at Augusta, Ga., and the
"Hampton Court Stud;" the latter, he says, "rivalling
that of his late majesty, and containing more stock

bred at the Royal Stud, than any other in the Union," and the former receiving its name " in honor of a gentleman whose ennobling talents and public spirit, more than his princely fortune, have placed him at the head of the Turf in Carolina and Georgia." Of *Emily*, owned by Col. Hampton, and out of Elizabeth, by Rainbow, bred by his late Majesty William IV., at the Royal Stud at Hampton Court, and imported into South Carolina by his present owner, he writes with characteristic enthusiasm : " She is a beautiful bay with a star and a stripe, about fifteen hands and one inch, and presents a most striking resemblance to Ackerman's superb colored engraving of the *Queen of Trumps*. Her head is faultless, a perfect nonpareil, and her eye and face beam with intelligence. Her limbs are as finely modelled as those of the fair representative of '*Ion*,' and her beautiful pastern joints remind one of the delicate and well-turned ankle of *la petite Augusta!* Her proportions are almost perfect; her shoulder is broad and oblique, running well back, and she is also very fine across the loins. Her hocks, knees, and feet are also good, especially the first, which come well down to the ground. Altogether she is as game a looking filly as can be seen in a year's travel."

Of *Missouri*, he writes : " She is a chestnut, under fifteen hands high, and very well put up; a small star is her only white natural mark. Her dam was a tip-top *Director* mare. She was bred by Gen. Broadnax of Virginia, and has been thrice a winner since she made her début last spring. While we were examining her in her stable, at Augusta, her owner remarked, 'Give her a name, Mr. Porter.' 'Well,' said we, 'call her after a fine State and a charming woman who bears the same name, and call her *Missouri.*' 'I don't know much about the *State,*' replied McCargo, 'but if you know a pretty woman of that name, why *Missouri* it shall be.'"

On his return from the South he wrote :

"After a surrender of the editorial seat for some weeks, we mount the box, and gather up the ribbons of our darling turn-out. Were we not quite up to the mark in condition, we should fear being distanced upon again entering upon our duties. For a period of nearly seven years, we have held the reins and guided the fleet coursers that have drawn this sheet from the realms of darkness into regions of light, from an inauspicious and gloomy beginning to the enjoyment of a wide-spread patronage. Seven years since, a mere boy, unknown and unaided, we started the project of a Sporting paper. Trammelled by circumstances, retarded by inexperience, we groped our way slowly into those Southern and Western regions of our country, where the sports we advocate were more generally appreciated and more liberally encouraged. To gratify our most earnest desire to visit these portions of the Union, and to make ourselves perfectly acquainted with the gentlemen, the country, and the various interests involved in the Sports of the Turf, we took our leave in November, and most advantageously employed three months in the pleasing survey. What shall we say of the receptions which everywhere awaited us? What shall we write that is not already known of the unbounded hospitality that everywhere pervades that section of the Union, and which was absolutely bestowed upon us in a manner at once so elegant and so bountiful, that the mere acknowledgment of the grateful compliment fills our throat and eyes with the emotion its remembrance must ever excite? From Baltimore to Wheeling, thence to Cincinnati, thence to Louisville, and thence to Vicksburg, Natchez, St.

Francisville, and New Orleans, our journey was chequered by the most flattering attentions. At New Orleans, we had the happiness to renew old intimacies and create new ones in a wide circle of gentlemen who are unsurpassed for their elegant and refined hospitality. Our visit among that gallant throng of friends to the Turf, occurred during their great annual Jockey Club meeting," (of which Judge Alexander Porter was President,) "and long shall we retain the impression of their courteous bearing amid the excitements of the race; their bland and gracious freedom at the Club, and their mirthful reminiscences of the fortunes of the day. On our return, we traversed the entire range of the Southern States, pausing here and there amid hospitalities that often well-nigh allured us to outstay the bounteous welcome we universally received."

In reference to the "magnificent stud" of Col. Hampton, he writes :

"The excess of his choice blood stock, native or imported, whether consisting of horses, cattle, or sheep, is seldom or never sold, but from motives the most patriotic distributed among those of his friends not engaged in breeding, who will rear them with attention. If, as some writer has forcibly remarked, he is entitled to the esteem of mankind who causes two blades of grass to grow where one blade grew before, what amount of commendation does he not merit who thus dispenses a princely fortune in perfecting the breed and ameliorating the condition of the most useful and invaluable of animals, and so materially contributes to the interests and general enjoyment of the community."

During the editor's absence at the South, his brother George, who was his junior by four years, undertook to supply his place; as he had not before wandered far from his chosen path of the law, and had but a very limited knowledge of the specialty of his brother, it was to him a task of great labor and anxiety. In one of his letters now before me, dated February 17, 1838, he writes : "Rejoice with me for my labors are at last over. William is at home again and has now nominally and *actually* relieved me from care and trouble. The first number of the new volume is at last out, and henceforth William will sail his own ship."

George Porter graduated at Dartmouth College in 1831, with distinguished honor, and had, besides his admitted intellectual eminence, quite a reputation for oratorical ability ; one of several prizes which he received for superior declamation, while yet an undergraduate, is in my possession. On the completion of his collegiate course, he commenced the study of the law with George Brinkerhoff, Esq., of New York, and remained with him until he was admitted to the bar, when he opened an office in that city, with ardent aspirations for distinction in his profession. In the autumn of 1836, he was so fortunate as to become a partner of the Hon. Edward Curtis and his brother, Geo. Curtis, Esq., who were engaged in a varied and extensive practice. Preserving his literary tastes and resorting to them as a relaxation from the engrossing cares of his office, he occasionally wrote for his brother's paper ; and as already stated, at one time undertook its entire management ; not only its literary department, but its fiscal affairs fell under his temporary, but exclusive control. With the latter he became so complicated that, in the end, he felt obliged to withdraw from his legal engagements that he might devote himself exclusively to the task of sustaining the fortunes of the "Spirit," at a time of general bankruptcy and discouragement: a fancied, not a real necessity, as we believe; and the more to be regretted on that account. Had he continued in his profession, with one-half the persevering industry which he exhibited while connected with the press, he must have risen to eminence, for he had the elements of success in him to an uncommon degree. His mind was clear, comprehensive, and quick; his power of abstraction and application very great; his manner of speech strong and emotional; while the responsive play of his fine and expressive face, imparted an indescribable charm to what fell from his lips.

The origin of the playful sobriquet, "York's tall son," which first became in 1837 a favorite and familiar title applied to William, adding another to the many memorable cases in which a pointed verbal phrase sometimes becomes incorporated into the popular vocabulary, was the result of a private incident of no interest whatever disconnected from the hero himself; But from its still living hold upon the hearts of those who loved him, as expressive of his lofty stature as well as of his popularity in the city of his adoption, its history is worth preserving, inasmuch as one of his few characteristic letters is bound up with its origin. Some time during the year 1836, Miss Clifton offered, through the columns of "The Spirit," the sum of $1,000 for a Tragedy, "adapted to her histrionic acquirements." This met the eye of the younger sister of Mr. Porter, and prompted her to address a letter to him, dated January 13, 1837, and found among his papers after his decease. She goes on to say:

"You may perhaps be aware that I have long been a worshipper at the shrine of the Muses. They sometimes smile upon me with a friendly spirit of encouragement, and now have deigned to inspire me with the ambitious scheme of winning the prize for the best American tragedy suited to the peculiar genius of Miss Clifton. As you are one of the number selected to examine the efforts of the aspirants, I do not hesitate to commit to your hand the following extracts from my unfinished tragedy of Hophir:

ACT 1ST, SCENE 1ST, *Copenhagen.—An Apartment in Gyneth's Bower.*

GYNETH. Fold up the curtain, Ina,
And let the crimson morn burst on my aching vision.
Sleep has kiss'd his last farewell to me,
And time drags weary off.
　　INA. Holy Mother save thee! mistress Gyneth,
And teach thee patience to endure the frowns
Of fortune. Ne'er repine—
Three more suns must set,
And Gyneth's bosom will thrill
With deeper joy than——
　　GYNETH. How! what! Say you that he,
The Lord of PORTER—will be here?
　　INA. Yes, sweet lady,—
He of six feet lineage, and gilded crow-quill,
Was, by the artifice of a "*Girl Up Town,*"
Releas'd from prison. A carrier-bird
Dropp'd at my feet this morn
These perfumed stanzas, which unsuspecting,
Eagerly I traced:

　　　　"Dear Gyneth, to thy arms I fly,
　　　　　Tho' wardour's tower be steep and high,
　　　　　　And maelstroms fill the air;

3

Not unicorn, or tusked boar,
Shall keep me from my true love more,
　　The brightest of the fair.

For thee I'll curl my twisted crest—
For thee I'll wear my " *yarllerest* " vest,
　　My stiffest collar, too ;
My standard with Propontic fury,
I'll wave on top of Alpine Jura,
　－ Then fleet, my love, to you.

Then haste my pye-bald, gallant steed,
Thro' rushing stream and verdant mead,
　　And make thy nostrils snort ;
While I for love and my ador'd
Poise the tall lance, grasp high the sword,
　　And peal aloud *Le Mort !* "

GYNETH.　Hand o'er the lines,
And let my burning eye-balls trace the hand
Of him I love.　Yes, 'tis true, his own lov'd signet.
Haste thee, Ina, and bid old Gaffer
Set in preparation all things fit, of mirth,
And song, and joyous cheer, to greet
The near approach of York's tall son.　　　　　[*Exit* INA.

SCENE II.—*Moonlight.*

[*Hophir appears on the top of a dilapidated tower.*]

HOPHIR.　Moon,—cold, loco-foco moon, I loathe thy light ;
Thou who dost shine upon the sea and sand
Alike indifferent—who round the rugged world rolls
Rapid on in rotatory revolution,
Like a green cheese upon the deep above,—
Thou marrest all my schemes, betraying moon !
Thy silvery beams disclose my wisest plans.
Shut out thy light—stars hide your rays—
I hate ye—aye, as fervent as I hate
The blue-eyed lord of her whom my heart loves.

Yes! shake ye fountains! freeze ye gelid skies,
I am for Patagonian revels, and the throne—
Beauty and wealth wave o'er me. Speed my aim
Ye powers of air, who live in the blue flame!
On Hophir's brow let fall the crown of gold!
My name is Haynes—I'm off, or I shall catch a cold
Upon this turret—or, perhaps, the jaunders,
Because I've left my wig for curling at that Saunders.

[*Exit* HOPHIR.

"NEW YORK, *April* 3, 1837.

" DEAR SISTER SARAH

" Will hardly credit me when I assure her, that in my card-
rack over my desk is a letter addressed to herself, that was
written weeks upon weeks since; but pity 'tis, 'tis true. The fact
was, after I had taken a deal of pains to write a famous letter as
long as your arm, or my boot, I very promiscuously misdirected
it as Paul Pry would say, whereat George laughed so much, that
I, in a huff, expunged it, by drawing black lines across the face,
and every day since have been thinking of re-writing it. *Entre
nous*, I have now and then something to do, or your dear letter
and charming communication would, despite my carelessness,
have been acknowledged long since. As it is, after frankly
pleading guilty of unpardonable inattention, I throw myself upon
the mercy of the court, after first engaging your husband as my
counsellor, who, I trust, will bribe the judge (with a kiss) to let
the defendant off with a reprimand on promise of future good
behavior.

" You cannot conceive, my darling Sis, of the pleasure your
letter excited in *us*. I say ' us,' for I speak not only for myself,
but for my ten thousand readers. You, of course, have seen it
immortalized and preserved in ' Spirit,' and probably have won-
dered at my gazetting you among the Staëls, the Landons, and
though last, not least in our dear love, the Trollopes of the 19th
century. Such a laugh as *the* Clifton and Dr. Pangloss of all the
Porters had over it! She really screamed over ' York's tall son,'
and vows to embody it in some love-lorn soliloquy. She

declares that not one of the veritable tragedies offered for her
$1,000 prize are comparable with it, and, i' faith, she speaks truth,
for I have read them—a paragraph each—and had I not been
predestined a dunce, I should have caught the infection of their
stupidity. The Doctor—the hearty old cock—strutted about
like a hen with one chick, as if he knew more of the authorship
of ' Hophir ' than he really did. He carried the original manu-
script in his pocket until worn to shreds, and then supplied himself with about a dozen and one over of copies, the which were
crammed one in each pocket, another in his hat, and for what I
know, one in each boot. These he read to everybody, making
a holiday for his scholars, while he himself, like Leigh Hunt's
pig, went up all manner of streets, radiant with the quips and
quirks of the sentimental ' Gyneth,' winning raptures of applause
by the emphasis and discretion, the grace and dignity, the pathos
and feeling, the taste and humor with which he invested the
life-drawn pictures of the amiable princess and chivalrous ' Lord
of Porter ! ' Miss Clifton and myself were about rehearsing it one
night, and should, but that instead of catching her, I was like to
catch a cold, so that throwing aside the maiden delicacy of ' Gyneth,' she opened the portals, let fall the drawbridge, and invited
the ' Tall Son ' above mentioned ' to come in to supper,' when,
what with her oysters and beauty, champagne and wit, pretty
eyes and olives, French rolls, ardent sympathies, and capital cook,
' the original tragedy of Hophir ' was shelved. When the warm
weather comes—some fervid night in the dog-days—she has
promised and agreed to order a tremendous bowl of lemonade,
when we are to rehearse the same with becoming gravity and
spirit.

"R.'s new-born girl is a cherub !—I haven't let her fall but
twice ;—the image of her uncle William, and strange to tell, born
without teeth. I've named her already, just to put her aunts out
of all pain on that account, Frances, Bentimia, Sarah-phina,
Wilhelmina, Georgiana, Seton, Startin, Brinley Porter.

"Now, my darling S., do write me often. The Doctor and
George are so occupied as to give me no assistance whatever, and
with the sole charge of my paper and its thousand cares upon

my hands, cares of which you have no idea—obliged to write on subjects, and *knowingly*, of which I have little practical knowledge, my time is incessantly occupied. My correspondents are immensely numerous, and compel my prompt response, but they are necessary to the success of my paper, which, by the by, is doing gloriously.

" With best love to F., believe me your devoted

"BROTHER WILLIAM."

CHAPTER III.

In the spring of 1839, a meeting of gentlemen took place at the Astor House, for the purpose of infusing fresh life and spirit into Northern Racing, by the formation of a new club for the Union Course; under whose auspices the year commenced with every appearance of a successful season in all sections of the country. A post match, for $20,000, was concluded to come off over the Newmarket Course, in Virginia. Great preparations were made for races over the Course at Trenton, N J., and elsewhere, and a produce Stake with a subscription of $2,000 each, $400 forfeit, two miles heat, to be called "The Hampton Stake," was projected.

Commodore Ridgley was re-elected President; Messrs. John A. King, John C. Stevens, H. Wilkes, and James Foster, Vice Presidents; Messrs. Henry K. Toler, Gouverneur Kortwright, Wm. K. Gaston, and Gerard L. Coster, Stewards of the New York Jockey Club, and its organization was celebrated by a dinner at the Astor House.

Mr. King presided, and eloquently addressed the company upon the object of the meeting. A Club was formed for three years. "The song, the toast, and the enlivening story succeeded each other; and as the circling glass went round, flowing bumpers were pledged to the good men and true of the South and West, and heel-taps discolored no goblets quaffed to the Sports of the Turf."

Mr. Porter was of opinion that there should be a tribunal of some sort, to which the various Jockey Clubs, as well as individuals, could resort for the adjustment of controverted questions, and in a strong appeal in favor of a Turf Convention, he says:

" So desirable do we deem a convention of the friends of the Turf, with a view to the adoption of a uniform code of rules, and the establishment of a Court of Appeal for doubtful points, that we should gladly advocate it with such ability as we could command, had the project not found an able supporter in the gentleman who first suggested it. The proposition is worthy of the most serious consideration of turfmen. The permanent well-being of the turf depends not alone upon one, or two Jockey Clubs or States. The character of all sportsmen suffers by every act of injustice, or by any suspicion of unfair management that may be attached to the most insignificant club or association. The direct method of avoiding the hazard of foul play, and any purpose of it, is the creation of a tribunal, the power of which may be brought to bear *directly* upon all clubs formed, as auxiliary to it, or with an acknowledgment of its jurisdiction; and *indirectly*, as by exclusion, upon all other clubs. There would be no hazard of conflicting jurisdictions, for in associations for the promotion of sport, and the improvement of the breed of horses, there are no diverse interests to be concerned, no sectional jealousies to allay; it is our pride, that in the pleasures of the turf, common sense and manly amusement are the only *ends* of association, and perfect honor the principle of constitution.

"A board of umpires, or a central Jockey Club, which should give law in general questions to the local clubs, could by no possibility be actuated by motives of interest; composed as it would be of gentlemen of the highest moral worth, from different sections of the country, the local influence of an individual, which sometimes tyrannizes in a small association, is neutralized, or stripped of all power save that which integrity of purpose, and intelligence as to means, should ever command.

"To pursue in the details the advantages which would accrue from the formation of an 'American Jockey Club,' would take us beyond the limits we had marked out for this discussion, or trench upon the ground covered by our correspondent in the following, and in a preceding letter. A uniformity of decision as to Betting, general rules governing the Entrances to Stakes, and the Payment of Forfeits, a more uniform Adjustment of Weights, a strict Regulation of Running Heats,—these are obvious and palpable results of a Turf Convention, which should provide us with a constitution for 'The American Jockey Club.' But by far the most commanding consideration upon our own minds, is the respectability and dignity which it would confer upon the Sports of the Turf, in the United States. To the 'Jockey Club' in England, and the consideration commanded by its members in general society, by their wealth, by their intelligence, and by their moral worth, is to be attributed the high and palmy state of the Turf in Great Britain. Racing is the National Sport of that country, and so will it continue to be, as long as its manly pleasures, so natural to man, and especially to the Anglo-Saxon race, shall be hedged in from abuse, or the suspicion of abuse, by an Association of Gentlemen, *sans peur et sans reproche.*

"Will not turfmen be persuaded to give the subject their attention, and commune together upon the practicability and the propriety of the preliminary step—a Turf Convention, to be held next winter at Washington? That city is named by us, because it has been suggested by the originator of the whole plan in his letter from Natchez, because Congress will then be in session, and because general political conventions are to be held there, or at a city still further North, during the approaching session. And may we not further call upon gentlemen, for the expression of their views upon the whole proposition,—persuaded that whatever may be the decision as to the precise plan marked out by our correspondent, a general discussion of the subject will inevitably promote the interests and the respectability of the Turf?"

Contemporaneous with this suggestion, sprung up a controversy upon the question : " Is a bet naming two horses against the field, void, if one of the horses named fail to start?" Here was a case where a common, recognized, appellate tribunal could be profitably appealed to. A correspondent of the "Spirit," J. K. D., assuming as a maxim that a bet must stand in all cases, unless made void by its terms, or one party has no chance to win, his communication elicited this response from the pen of George Porter :

"In reading the communications of 'J. K. D.,' we are reminded of our college days, when we had to battle it with the Moral Philosophy Prof. about 'Edwards on the Will.' The logic of the old divine was too subtle for young minds, and admitting his reasonable premises, he would straightway hurry you into conclusions, accurately deduced therefrom, which revolted your moral sense, though you could discover no way of escape from them. So it is with our correspondent, he maintains his position with such dexterity and cogency, that it appears impossible to dislodge him, though we are satisfied that the position is a false one. We will make one effort more to set ourselves right, both with 'J. K. D.' and our readers.

"The whole argument of 'J. K. D.' is built upon this assumption, that a bet must stand in all cases, unless it is made void by its express terms, or unless *one party has no chance to win.* On this latter clause hangs all the controversy. We give to it this interpretation, that a bet shall stand when the party has the chance to win *named in the bet*, or which was in the reasonable contemplation of both parties. That is, if I bet on a horse, I am entitled to the chance of his starting; if I name two horses, I am entitled to the chance of their both starting, and not one of them; by the expresss terms of the bet, I name two horses, and not one of two. 'J. K. D.' says no; if but one of the horses start, you have a chance to win, and therefore the bet must stand. Here is the sole point at issue.

"The burden of proof lies not upon us, but upon 'J. K. D.' I name two horses, and I am certainly entitled to the two, unless 'J. K. D.' can cite a rule which shall say that one of the two is enough to satisfy the requisitions of the bet. But there is no such rule in express terms.

"But 'J. K. D.' says that the maxim governs all betting, that a bet must stand when there is a chance to win. And yet there is an express rule, that where one horse is betted on, and fails to start, the bet is off. Now, what is the use of such a rule if the maxim of 'J. K. D.' actually governs all betting, as he *interprets that maxim?* It would be plainly useless—mere surplusage.

"We do not insist upon a vague and uncertain rule, but a rule fixed and reasonable, a rule like that which governs all contracts, all transactions between man and man. The bettor should have that chance to win which he reserved by the express terms of his bet, or which is fairly to be inferred from its terms. If I name Mingo in a race, Mingo must start, or it is no bet; if I name Mingo and Post Boy, Mingo and Post Boy, not Mingo *or* Post Boy, must start, or it is no bet. This is reasonable, this is common sense, and this is law, unless 'J. K. D.' can cite an express rule to the contrary.

"There is no need of 'J. K. D.'s' maxim, if he will give it the interpretation for which we contend, and that is the reason why it cannot be found in the betting codes. A bet must stand, *of course*, when there is a chance to win,—that is, the chance named, the chance which each party knows the other betted on,—or, in case of dispute, the chance which a Court or Jockey Club would infer from the express words of the bet, to be the chance betted on.

"Now in what way can I more surely signify my intention of betting on two horses (not P. P.) than by *naming two*,—not one, nor *one of two*, but two? Now the chance on which I bet is the chance of having two horses start; there is no uncertainty about it, no vagueness, such as 'would annul all bets.' Nothing is said in the bet about the condition of the horses, or of the track, nor of the ownership of the horse, and, therefore, nothing is to be *inferred* on those points as being 'the chance on which I betted;' but it is certainly a fair inference, and a clear, undoubted one, that two horses must start. Again we say, the burden of proof lies upon the other side.

"There does not appear to us to be room for much argument here. It is a simple proposition: 'Does betting on *two* horses entitle me to two, or one of the two?' We hold the two, and 'J. K. D.' 'one of the two.' But in the course of this newspaper writing, many cases have been put to illustrate the hardship of the rule, construe it which way you will. These are, of course, but illustrations. 'J. K. D.' has the benefit of the last case, which certainly seems hard, but so confident are we of the security of our position, that we shall rest here, without an effort to suppose a harder case, a more flagrant instance.

"But it is proper, before quitting the subject, to deprive 'J. K. D.' of the *appearance* of an advantage, which he derives from his illustration of a bettor on 'the field.' He says that in the Louisville sweepstakes of ten nominations, the man who names five of them against 'the field' should be in no better situation than he who takes the field. He might just as reasonably contend that a bet was unfair should a man name one P. P. in that stake against the field. There would be no unfairness in such a bet; it would surely show that one of the bettors was a fool. Mark the want of candor in 'J. K. D.'s' argument here. There is a positive, written rule, defining 'the field.' Every bettor is supposed to know that rule, and that by the terms of it, if he back 'the field,' he may be reduced to one horse. Now, because

a man is silly enough to take 'the field' against half the entries
in a sweepstakes *named expressly*, 'J. K. D.' cries out unfairness.
He should rather cry out upon the folly of his field bettor.
What, in Heaven's name, was the need of a rule defining a 'field,'
if naming two or more horses amounted to the same thing?   It
is a term purely technical, like 'Play or Pay,' and as he who
names the field is by rule entitled to one horse at all events, because he stipulates for one horse by the terms of his bet, so he
who stipulates for two horses, or for forty horses, is entitled to
them, if there be any meaning in language, and any man rash
enough to bet against forty *named* horses.

"Since the above was written, we have received another
long communication on this subject, maintaining our side of the
question.   We give place to a portion of it; several heads of it,
however, we omit, as they seem calculated to provoke further
discussion, though really very good.   We thank 'D. E.' for his
assistance, and beg him to excuse us for so abbreviating his article.
'J. K. D.' will likewise observe that we have suppressed the
concluding paragraph of his paper.   It might wound the feelings
of others, and would certainly call out a reply, although it does
not pretend to bear upon the argument.

Mr. Porter, as an act of civility to his uncle, Mr.
Olcott, always sent him "The Spirit."   The following
letter from the latter is so creditable to both gentlemen, that it ought not to be hoarded in private :—

"Hanover, 14*th March*, 1839.

"Dear Cousin William,—

"I was absent when your letter of December arrived, and
Prof. Adams * (after he had ciphered it over and cast out the
9s) deeming it necessary for him to hold it as a voucher against
you, it has not since come under my eye, which is my poor
apology for not having replied to it; this I ought the more

* Of Dartmouth College ; a man of high honor and great excellence
of character; guardian of William and the younger children.　　F. B.

especially to have done—for though this little affair might not figure much in *amount* in Wall Street, it has toed right up to the mark when the time came, as honorably as if it had been done by the Primes or the Rothschilds. In these 'costermonger times,' when not only Burke's age of chivalry towards the sex was gone, but all chivalry in money matters is trampled in the mire, to see old claims that had been dead and buried, ordered to be raised and brought to life again—to direct principal and interest to be paid in full, and see '*paid*' on the letter announcing it—this cannot be a transaction of late years, I think, but must belong to another century—must be a dream of bygone and better days, when at least one's self-respect was worth something to him, if nothing else.

" I am very glad to learn that much success is expected from your paper, and I hope you may realize from it all the fame and money that would be good for you. Your Andover masters little dreamed what they were raising up, when they thought they were preparing you for the *Recorder*.

" It could hardly be expected that one of my age would be much attracted with a heading of 'Fill high the bowl with Samian wine.' I therefore skim over your paper and light upon parts for reading, as the clergyman who divided his sermon into three heads: the world, the flesh, and the devil—and said he should just glance at the world, touch lightly upon the flesh, and hasten to the devil!

" We shall be glad to see you or any of the blood at Hanover, and with hearty good wishes to all of you,

" I remain most truly yours, &c.,
" MILLS OLCOTT."

The " Spirit of the Times " was a coveted and favorite name, judging from the frequency of its appropriation by those who had no right to use it, and the editor thus adverts to this poaching on his domain. The " Boston Morning Post " announced that a new democratic paper had been established in Philadelphia, under the cognomen of "The Spirit of the Times," and very gravely added, "Its name is appropriate." "Can't say," writes Mr. Porter, "we see any thing very 'appropriate' about it, save the appropriation of a good name. This makes the fourth time the immediate jewel of our soul has been pilfered from us by some *Hateful Parkins* in this kind of way. We were first frightened out of our propriety by a great, bloody, anti-Masonic 'Spirit,' in the western part of this State; a Republican Spirit then started in Maryland; then all sorts of Spirits in Arkansas and Missouri; and now the 'deep damnation of our taking off,' is chargeable to a democratic Spirit in Philadelphia. Since the first number of our paper was issued on the 10th of December, 1831, no less than *seven* newspapers have sprung into existence, bearing the same euphonious and elegant appellation. These young 'Spirits' are generally pretty clever fellows; their very name is a tower of strength, and if they follow in the steps of their illustrious predecessor, there's no telling but they may become as popular and respected as their great old grandfather."

The oldest magazine then published in the United States was "The American Turf Register and Sporting Magazine," commenced in 1829, by Hon. John S. Skinner, of Baltimore, for the express purpose of recovering as much as possible of the lost early pedigrees of the magnates of the American Turf, and for the preservation of authentic records for the future. In February, 1839, it was purchased by Mr. Porter, and came under his editorial control. Mr. Herbert, in alluding to it, said, "it passed into the hands of the most able and admirable Turf-writer, than whom the Turf of America has had no more consistent advocate, or more strenuous defender."

The first number of the "*Register*" issued by Mr. Porter, contains a characteristic letter to him from its former editor, Mr. Skinner :—

"BALTIMORE POST OFFICE, 1*st March*, 1839.

" To WM. T. PORTER, ESQ.

"MY DEAR SIR,—Right glad am I to have my favorite hobby —the old ' *Turf Register*,' fall under your care. It was the first of its race ever bred in the United States. Its natural history is remarkable, as it had but one sire and no dam ; when it was foaled it was not certain where or whether it would find food or pasture. It was thrown upon the wild world, without any guarantee of corn or long fodder—but being watched with care, and sent out once a month on short excursions, for air, exercise, and exhibition, the friends of its founder, far and near, who had been previously taught by him to make good crops, most kindly and generously petted and pampered the young hobby,—sending it an ample supply of provisions, until it grew, in four or five years, to be a nag of good size and full of spirit. But, like all things excellent, in this enterprising Yankee nation, in the progress and ' *Spirit of the Times*,' it met its rival ! Passing from one hand to another, it has happily ceased to run the race ' antagonistical ' by being led, where old ' Napoleon ' sends all that he can't beat, into the same stable with its competitor ; here I sincerely hope, both will long live in the best condition. ' *The Spirit of the Times* ' may do the light skirmishing to amuse the crowd, while the more ponderous ' Register ' is reserved for more serious work ; as *Monarch* is held back, for the four-mile day, by a nobler man than any monarch that lives.

" As I have some right to know what will suit the old horse's constitution and temper, should he ever show signs of getting amiss, and you may imagine that his old groom can suggest any

thing to bring him right, you must not fail to call on his and your
friend and humble servant."

This first number contained one hundred and
twenty-eight pages of valuable matter, to which the
new editor contributed an "Introduction," an article
on trout-fishing, which was illustrated by an exquisitely finished picture, the pedigree and performances
of *Harkaway*, and a capital essay on *English Eclipse;*
it was further embellished by accurate portraits of
those horses, and more than realized the highest expectations of the friends of Mr. Porter.

The number for March and April contained a portrait of *Plenipotentiary*, with a memoir by the editor,
and an admirable steel engraving of the *Traineau* of
D'Orsay, full of rich life and movement. The May
and June number was exquisitely embellished by an
engraving called a Forest Joust, and Trout Fishing, and
contained an illustrated article on Fly Fishing by the
editor, with the usual amount of literary and sporting
matter. In this number that distinguished scholar
and sportsman, the late William Henry Herbert, commenced a series of admirable sketches, entitled "A
week in the Woodlands, or Scenes on the Road and
round the Fire," which he published over the signature of "*Frank Forrester*," a celebrated *nom de plume*
originating with George Porter, and readily adopted
by the gifted author.

In the July number there was a portrait of *Don
John*, with a memoir by Mr. Porter; and in that for
the next month appeared a portrait of Mr. Stevens'
Janette, with an editorial memoir, together with a spir-

ited engraving of Landseer's amusing sketch, " Running the thing into the ground," which is archly described by the editor, but closes in this practical vein : " Badinage apart, our engraving is a sly, but well-conceived and pertinent caricature, that will be well understood by those proprietors of race-courses who are in the habit of resorting to ' Mule-races, and Foot-races, and Gander-pullings, and Cock-fights,' to swell the receipts of enclosures devoted to the legitimate *Sports of the Turf.* Wherever the sports of the Turf have been brought into discredit, it will be found, nine cases in ten, that the mismanagement of the proprietors of the course has been the primary cause ; the real friends of the Turf have more to fear from them than from open and declared enemies. Whoever heard of racing being unpopular in a section of country where the courses were managed by men of character and respectability—on the ground of any objection against racing itself? The Charleston races are the most popular, the most fashionable, and the best attended of any in the United States. Race-week, in that city, has been aptly termed ' the Carnival ' of South Carolina—the annual jubilee of the State. The reason is perfectly obvious ; the course and its appointments are under the control of gentlemen of the highest character, and nothing is permitted to interfere with the legitimate sports of the Turf, which are managed with a degree of spirit, liberality, and scrupulous propriety unknown elsewhere on this side of the Atlantic. In Charleston a gentleman feels no more hesitation in enjoying *with his family* the festivities and enlivening sports of the race-field, than he would the attractions of the theatre, or any other rational source of amusement. The consequence is, that the ladies' pavilion during the meeting, and the Jockey Club Ball at its close, are crowded with the *élite* of the beauty, the fashion, and the chivalry of the State.

"The number of gentlemen interested in the success of the Turf in this country, has more than doubled within the last ten years, and it is daily becoming more and more popular. The great practical advantage to be derived from its extension and successful prosecution, are deemed so important in a national point of view, that many of the Governments of Europe are lending it their aid, and keenly watching over its interests. We have nothing here to do but to go on and prosper, keeping in view this single fact, that if the legitimate ends of the Turf are stanchly maintained, it must become at length universally and eminently popular with all classes of society, while its friends will best subserve its true interests and their own, by frowning down those individuals whose malpractices have so long been '*Running the thing into the Ground !*'"

"N, of Arkansas," "Frank Forrester," and other distinguished writers appear in this number, which contained but five selected articles. Among the new correspondents is "*Cypress, Jr.*," the accomplished author of the delightful sketches which were published in the "American Monthly Magazine," under the designation of "Fire-Islandana," and attracted great attention both in this country and in Europe.

The embellishments for the September number were portraits of "Bloomsbury" and of "Deception," with memoirs by the editor; and in that for the next month, he announces that he was making arrangements to give a series of portraits of distinguished Turfmen. The November number contained an illustrated article on "Duck Shooting," by "Cypress, Jr.," the sixth day of "A week in the Woodlands," and other excellent matter; that for December closed the tenth volume of the Magazine, being the first of the new series under the conduct of Mr. Porter; it contained an engraved Title Page—"The Turn-out of the Season" on steel, and an outline of Charles XII. on wood. The editor in his "Address on the close of the volume," said that the Magazine was commenced with little promise on his part, and not with any hope of large pecuniary profit; and in this last particular it seems he was not disappointed; still he boldly purposed to conduct the next volume on the same plan of liberal outlay. A careful Index appropriately closes the volume, to which are added as Appendices, "the American Racing, and the English Racing Calendars for 1839," most elaborately prepared.

The January number for that year gives a highly spirited portrait of *Charles XII.*, winner of the Great St. Leger Stakes, 1839, and a woodcut of a "splint used for fractured limbs of horses."

Among the contents of the February number, are

a memoir of *Wacousta,* by the editor, with a portrait; and a brilliant sketch of " Wild horses fighting," on copper, by Bannerman after Herring.

The number for March, an admirable one, is embellished by a stylish portrait of Col. Singleton's *Phenomena,* with an editorial memoir, and notices of that gentleman's stock. But its chief and attractive feature is Mr. Porter's masterly report of the great race between *Wagner* and *Grey Eagle.* A memoir and an engraving of Col. Hampton's imported mare *Delphine,* with Herald at her foot, is in the April number, with notices of his stock. And so we might go on with all the numbers of this brilliant periodical, which was unrivalled for the high finish of its engravings, the exquisite beauty of its type, and its sporting excellence, until it ceased to exist, Dec. 1844.

The price of a complete set of the Turf Register, ten volumes, was at that time seventy-five dollars. It cannot be purchased at this date for even that large price.

In the April number of the Magazine, 1841, Mr. Porter records the death of one of his especial friends, as well as one of the most admirable contributors to the Register, William P. Hawes, Esq., known as J. Cypress, Jr. His productions were remarkable for their wit and pathos, and classic elegance. He died at the early age of thirty-eight. Had his life been prolonged, his brow would have been encircled with the triple crown of legal, political, and literary merit. It was to the fresh creations of his mind, and to " Frank

Forrester," Pete Whetstone, the author of the "Quarters' Race" and "Jones's Fight," that the Spirit and Register were indebted for much of that fascinating and original literature to which Mr. Porter lent his special patronage and fostering care.

In comparing the communications in the English Sporting Magazines with those which were contributed to American publications, Mr. Porter took occasion at that date to say: "In the purely literary magazines the English beat us a long way. In England, which for more than a century has boasted the most respectable Sporting Magazines, the appropriate themes are somewhat exhausted. The Great Race meetings are necessarily monotonous. To give spirit and the interest of adventure to their sketches, the greater number of sporting writers lay the scenes of their articles in foreign lands. British India and our own country are most often selected; and it is rare that you open either of the Sporting Magazines without finding a bear, a buffalo, or a panther hunt in the United States. It is to the exhaustless supply of material of this nature, the adventurous life of a frontier settler, incidents of travel over prairies and among mountains hitherto unknown to the white man, the singular variety of manners in different States, springing from their difference of origin, of climate and product, peculiarities of scenery unhackneyed by a thousand tourists, to this is to be attributed the greater freshness and raciness of American sketches. In pure turf-writing, England never boasted of an author equal to 'An

Old Turfman.' In plain elegant English, logical deductions and perfect familiarity with his subject, he was superior even to ' Nimrod.' Nor have our Turf-writers all passed away with the ' Old Turfman.' Many still remain, who ever and anon delight and instruct our readers."

In December, 1839, Mr. Porter made another delightful circuit through the South and West, renewing old intimacies and forming new ones at Louisville, Lexington, &c., and everywhere receiving the most gratifying hospitalities. The interests and prosperity of the publications under his care were the chief objects of his journey. Returning fresh from the " Race-Horse Region," he was in fine condition to minister to the tastes of his readers.

Notwithstanding the heavy addition of the Register to his labors and disbursements, Mr. Porter carried out several proposed arrangements for the improvement of the " Spirit," and the first number of the ninth volume came out March, 1839, in an enlarged and attractive form, with a beautiful engraving of Augusta, the celebrated danseuse, in the character of " La Sylphide," and a portrait of Black Maria, by Dick, from a painting by Troye. As the old mare entertained some vulgar prejudice against " sitting for her portrait," Troye directed Bill Patrick, her faithful groom, to ride her out into a paddock in front of his window. This proceeding might be all very well for the painter and the mare, Bill thought, but as for him, he was inclined to sulk after two hours' promenading ; so whipping off his saddle, he incautiously determined to hitch

the mare and "bolt," for which disregard of orders
and lukewarmness in facilitating the progress of the
fine arts, Troye clapped him into his picture in the
very act of committing so grave an offence in the eye
of a turfman, or an artist, as hitching a race-horse to
a tree! Of course he will now go down through all
time as *the* boy who was guilty of so unpardonable a
sin; but for fear his punishment would be greater
than he could bear, Troye, through urgent interces-
sion, was finally induced to remit a portion of the
punishment he had intended, by concealing his face!
This fine engraving was the first of a series of costly
embellishments which the liberal editor continued
for several years.

The price of the paper was raised from five to ten
dollars. No expense or labor was spared to furnish a
journal to be identified with the sporting interest in
America, that should be creditable alike to the editor,
and worthy of the cause he advocated. In answer to
his solicitations for advice upon increasing the price
of the paper, he was assured by the most distinguished
Breeders and Turfmen throughout the Union, of their
hearty support; "make the 'Spirit of the Times'
to the American sporting world," said they, "what
'Bell's Life in London' is to the English—flinch at
no expense in procuring early information, or in im-
proving its appearance and the extent and variety of
its contents, and you will find *Brother Jonathan* will
not be behind *John Bull* in backing his friends."

For the "Spirit" of June 2, 1838, Mr. Porter
wrote a full account of the gallant race between Bos-

ton and Charles Carter—the best four-mile heat, with the exception of Henry's, that had been made in the United States.

The five great match races which have taken place, and which will immortalize the names of the contesting horses in the annals of the American Turf, are those of American Eclipse and Sir Henry, of Ariel and Flirtilla, of Black Maria and the three mares, known as the twenty-mile race, of Wagner and Grey Eagle, and of Boston and Fashion. The two last were reported by Mr. Porter in a style of undisputed excellence. As a turf-writer, he was without a rival in this country, or even in England, where sporting literature had been cultivated for years by men of taste and education.

CHAPTER IV.

DURING the month of March, a new weekly journal was projected and started by Dr. Porter and N. P. Willis, Esq., called "The Corsair," the first number of which was issued March 16, 1839.

The "Doctor" from the first intended to make the practice of medicine the great business of his life; but a removal from Vermont to New York turned the current of his days into unlooked-for channels. As his brothers, one by one, followed in the family procession to that great city, "thistle-down," as he wrote, "never flying faster from the parent stock," an increasing sense of loneliness, and the ever-present obligation not to intermit a parental supervision of the younger brothers, compelled him, as he thought, to plant himself by their side, to guide, encourage and sustain them. While waiting and struggling for professional advancement, he was invited to a Professor's Chair in the French Academy of Mr. Coudert, which he accepted; its duties allowed him sufficient leisure for the indulgence of his passion for general litera-

4

ture, and he soon acquired the reputation of a ready and spirited writer.

When he was at the South, he contracted a permanent friendship with Mirabeau B. Lamar, late President of Texas. They were in constant correspondence, and Gen. Lamar's letters breathe a tone of rare affection and confidence. In July, 1837, he writes, " some say that Houston is about to resign, and that I, of course, will have to act as Chief Executive until the next election. If this be so, I do beseech you, my dear friend, to be certain to come on to Texas in October, or earlier, and any thing in my power to promote your welfare may be commanded. It is a beautiful country, good population, and you not only can acquire with little exertion a good fortune, but can greatly promote the cause of free government and the general happiness of man. Your brother William too—one-half of the talent displayed in his paper, would bring him in Texas four-fold fame and fortune, and be productive of an hundred more of public good." In 1839 he writes, when President of that Republic, " I should be proud to place you where you could serve the cause of our young and high-spirited Republic. Would you be willing to come to this country, and identify yourself with my fortunes?" Specific and honorable appointments were tendered to him when General Lamar became President; but he was not to be moved, though he well knew the immediate and prospective value of all that he relinquished in deference to his somewhat exaggerated and over-refined sense of youthful obligation.

His intercourse with editors, publishers and authors, drew him into an acquaintance with N. P. Willis, Esq., which soon ripened into a lively friendship; Mr. Willis giving him the highest proof of his regard, by dedicating to him his "*Letters from under a Bridge.*" During the summer of 1839, the "Doctor" proposed they should establish a weekly newspaper in New York, which should be an attractive family journal, devoted to literature, dramatic criticism, fashion, and novelty; and at the same time advocate some satisfactory system of legislation on the subject of international copyright. Mr. Willis gave a willing ear to the suggestion, and wrote to the "Doctor," "you are the best man in the country to do it— with or without me." Among the preliminaries to be settled was that of the name of the proposed serial, which was of difficult determination. After sundry perplexing consultations, that of "The Corsair" was proposed by the "Doctor," and adopted. Mr. Willis wrote, "if I had not heard you split hairs and talk like a Professor in a hailstorm, I should never have started on a cruise like ours with you. Your talent is to be the main-stay of the paper, and you are the best off-hand writer I know. You are world-wise, which no other literary man I know is except Halleck."

The first number of an enterprise which started under the most flattering auspices, was looked for with great curiosity, and was esteemed fully up to the highest expectations of its friends. In its external appearance it resembled the London Spectator, and contained twice the number of pages of the Albion. In typographical arrangement it was very beautiful. It ranked high for its selections from the most approved literary sources of the day, its original contributions, its sound and liberal criticism, and its spirited range of observation and scholarship. It was under the " Doctor's" exclusive editorial charge; Mr. Willis being abroad, and contributing very irregularly to its pages. It would be difficult to find a single volume of any American literary periodical with more to commend it to the scholar and critic, or to the general reader desirous of occasional entertainment in the realms of literature. It was discontinued after a year's cruise.

The following letter from Mr. Webster of this date evinces his interest in the children of the friend of his early days:

"NEW YORK, *March* 16, 1839.

"GENTLEMEN:—I experienced so much kindness and hospitality in your father's house, and had so much pleasure in his and your mother's acquaintance, and remember you so well as boys, that I have felt regret at not having found an opportunity of seeing and knowing more of you since you came to manhood. My interest in the family has led me often to inquire after its members, and I have had true pleasure in learning your successful progress in life. If your leisure should allow you to call on me when I may be in the city, or if you should be in Boston, or Washington, when I am in either of those places, I should be very glad to see you. In the mean time, I will thank you to send me your paper, 'The Spirit of the Times,' addressed to me in Boston, when I am not in Washington, and at the latter place during the sitting of Congress. I hear, too, that your brother is concerned in the 'Corsair.' Will you ask him to send it to me? With many friendly recollections, and much regard, I am yours,

"DANIEL WEBSTER.

"Messrs. WILLIAM T. & GEORGE PORTER."

Two months after the date of this letter, Mr. Webster with his family sailed for England, and Mr. Porter in chronicling the fact, added the following paragraphs :

"Like all Americans, of whatever political sect, we admire the lofty genius of the man, his giant powers of mind, his simplicity, his downright honesty. Could he be raised above the reach of party divisions, every man in the nation would reverence him as the legitimate offspring of our free institutions. Humble in his origin, and born in a Democratic State, he caught the inspiration of freedom in his infancy. He has been the architect of his own fortune ; his elevation in life has been the direct result of his own moral and intellectual excellence fostered by our peculiar form of government. In his personal and political character, he represents the dignity of republicanism. But he possesses other characteristics which have especially won our regard and attachment, and impelled us to this paragraph. Mr. Webster is a sportsman, and as such we honor him ; he is one of the best shots in the States ; he is as destructive to woodcock, as to his adversaries in debate ; at English snipe-shooting, he has hardly a compeer. * * * But more than all, Mr. Webster is an angler, an humble disciple of Izaak Walton. Show me the man who loves trout-fishing, and I will tell you who is generous, and brave, and tender-hearted. Such a man is Mr. Webster, and as such do we love him more than we respect him for his greatness and integrity."

The advent of the " Corsair " was announced in the " Spirit of the Times " in this characteristic paragraph :

"*Barclay Street.*—' The Corsair ' will be published about a week hence—say on the 16th inst. The proprietors have taken an office which is nearly opposite those of the ' Albion ' and ' Mirror.' We shall hear no more of Paternoster Row, we fancy, now that four such journals as the Mirror, Albion, Corsair, and

Spirit of the Times have established themselves in Barclay street. A month or two ago, we had another distinguished contemporary with us,—we allude to ' *La Verité*,' a French journal, under the conduct of that distinguished peruquier, GRAND JEAN, who likewise grows hair to any length and of any color, if we may credit the announcements which stare at us from over the way. Whether the literary enthusiasm of the Frenchman has at last gone out ' spontaneously,' or whether, which we shrewdly suspect, he finds wig-making more profitable, we know not; but the truth is, we believe that 'La Verité' has left this world."

There are few who knew William T. Porter and his brothers at the time this playful announcement was written, who will not love to linger with us for a few moments over the recollection of them at that time. With firm health, elastic nerve, and a capacity for great and protracted mental labor, William had succeeded in placing the " Spirit" among the foremost weekly journals of the day, and in a fair way to command a world-wide celebrity. A mere cursory examination of its pages and of those of the " Register," will prove how great was the demand upon his mental and physical resources, and how gallantly he came up to the work; his intellectual efforts for the year 1839, and for the years that he conducted the two publications, not always exhibited in the form of elaborate essays, but in the laborious preparation of memoirs, pedigrees, calendars, tabular statements, and all the other matter of these crowded journals, were not surpassed by those of any other editor in this country. His list of subscribers comprehended a body of talent, character, spirit and wealth, from Hudson's Bay to the Caribbean Sea, from the shores of the Atlantic to the Pacific. With seventy-five out of a hundred of them, he had the pleasure of a personal acquaintance; some, to be sure, as he said, old enough to be his father; a fact to which he took delight in ascribing his success, having relied upon their paternal oversight, sagacious counsel and assistance from the start.

The five brothers at that time were all living in New York, united together by the tenderest affection, and by almost hourly intercourse. As a group of contemporary kinsmen, if they were not all conspicuous enough to make an impression upon their day and generation, they were at least fortunate enough to draw round them an electric chain of close and admiring fellowship of men of worth and distinction, as spontaneous and wide-spread while they lived as it proved sincere when the grave closed over them. "That band of brothers," writes one of their southern correspondents, "united as we never remember to have seen or heard of any other brothers; those five, brave, gallant, good, glorious Porters."

There were certain peculiar traits which were common to them all. An abhorrence of any thing sordid or contracted, an inbred simplicity and frankness, an acute sense of humor, a passionate love of rural sports, an ability to look the inevitable straight in the face, however disagreeable, and make the best of it. In the "Doctor" and William an irrepressible gayety of temperament and a fondness for the society of those they loved, admirably fitted them for the delights of social and convivial intercourse. The "Doctor" was by common consent allowed to have no

inconsiderable share of what Christopher North calls
" the invincible spirit of genius " which inspires a
good talker.   When surrounded by the circle of his
most familiar friends, of which he was regarded the
life and ornament, it was delightful to look into his
fine face, when a topic was started that stirred his
genial nature.   All subjects coming up at such
moments reflected the prismatic hues of his mind,
whether they pertained to the qualities of a favorite
statesman, a criticism upon the book of Job, a race on
Long Island, or the uncorking of a bottle of Chateaux
Margaux.   " Mony a strange story fell down stane-
dead when his tongue grew mute.   Thoosands o' curi-
ous, na, unaccountable anecdotes, ceased to be, the
day his een were closed."

By taking the bits in his teeth at the time he went
to Andover, William lost the advantage of the resources of academic training, and was of course compelled to severer labor than the " Doctor " or George.
Faculty, quick observation, diligence, a retentive
memory, courage and hard work, however, enabled
him to acquire a manly, graceful, unaffected style,
marked often by a vein of downright humor as fresh
and free from all guile as it was characteristic of the
man.   He often recommended to his correspondents
and to editors of papers, desirous of writing effective-
ly, the following advice of Lord Jeffrey, and judging
from his clear and sensible style we have no hesitation
in believing that he adopted it as a guide to his own
pen :   " A man fully possessed of his subject and confident of his cause, may always write with vigor and

effect, if he can get over the temptation of writing
finely, and really confine himself to the strong and
clear exposition of the matter he has to bring forward.
Half of the affectation and offensive pretensions we
meet with in authors, arises from a want of matter—
and the other half of a paltry ambition of being eloquent and ingenious out of place."

No better idea can be had of William's fitness to fill
the place he occupied among his fellow-men, than is
to be found in the general admission that he possessed
to an eminent degree the qualities which he enume-
rates in the subjoined paragraph, as essential to the
position :

"Every editor of a newspaper should have extensive familiarity with literature ; cultivated tastes, thorough knowledge of
men and the world, habits of observation and great facility in
giving expression to his opinions. The qualities of his heart
should correspond to those of his head—he should be honest,
generous and brave. Alas! how few of the craft can pretend
to a tithe of the few requisites we have enumerated. But into
the composition of a Sporting editor should be infused, not only
other ingredients but a double portion of industry, of patience,
of command of temper, and of charity ; verily he has need of
all ! Then too he must be learned in a new walk of science—of
small dignity in the eyes of the multitude, yet entitled to all
respect for its mysteries, its usefulness, the difficulties of its acquisition and the 'exceeding' small number of its adepts! The
Stud Book should be as familiar to him as his alphabet ; families
of horses and their pedigrees should be as well known to him
as his own. He should be intimate with every Turfman and
Breeder in the country. He should number among his acquaintances every Trainer that ever girthed a saddle, and every Jockey
that throws his leg over a thorough-bred. He should be familiar
with race courses and their proprietors, with the constitutions,

4*

rules and decisions of every Jockey Club, and with the standing
of every man connected with the Turf. He should have the
keenest eye for the points of a horse, know the comparative
merits of rival champions, and no one should be able to teach
him as to the capacity of different trainers. He must know the
odds on every horse *in advance*, foresee the result of every race,
and withal, act with consummate prudence in giving expression to the conclusions at which he arrives by the exercise of
his rare capacity and foresight! With all these gifts, super-
natural, acquired or otherwise, grant him good health, good
nature, indomitable perseverance and assiduity, and one would
think he might hope to become reasonably popular as a
Sporting editor."

He was habitually considerate of the feelings and
even the prejudices of others, and with marvellous
tact brought them to his own conclusions as if they
were in fact the spontaneous results of their unassisted
reason. His faculties were clear, acute and honest,
enabling him to see rapidly through a vexed point or
obscure question, and to sift and adjust them not only
to his entire satisfaction, but in his quiet, unpretending
way, as far from self-conceit as his pleasant smile was
from dissimulation, to the cheerful acquiescence of the
parties interested in his decision. The expansive generosity of his mind, his patience, his truthfulness and
entire freedom from the petty motives which often influence men much his superiors in masculine preten-
sion, united to the absolute and sweet frame of his
temper, gave to his judgments the weight of irreversi-
ble decrees.

To give an idea of the literary Exchange in which
he contrived to write during the high noon of his

work-day reputation, and of "the good fellowship which rallied round him there as the centre of magnetic attraction," we again cite the correspondent to whom we have just referred.

"In the palmy days of the Turf, when the North had stables as well as the South, and when such gentlemen sportsmen as WALTER LIVINGSTON, and ROBERT TILLOTSON, and Major JONES, and the STEVENSES, and Commodore STOCKTON made 'The Spirit' office their head-quarters, and when one never could enter its time-honored door without meeting the best company, and having the best conversation that was to be found going in America; in those days, what talent, as well as what good fellowship, used to assemble within those walls, and rally around old BILL, as the centre of magnetic attraction.

"No class of men but had, there, its representative; no branch of talent but had its proficient, from the storming a fortress or throwing up an earthwork, to calculating a lunar, or club-hauling a ship; from construing a Greek Chorus to cropping a pup's ears; from check-mating a first-rate player to cutting down a woodcock under full headway in a brake, or stopping a coot skating at ninety miles an hour down a northeaster; from running a hundred off the spot, to writing a review for the North American, or a poem for BLACKWOOD; from riding a steeple-chase to painting a portrait of Fashion; from rolling a dozen tenstrikes in succession to amputating a thigh in the socket—if you wanted anything done, however strange or difficult, or out of the common way, in the office of 'The Spirit' you were sure to find the man that could do it, and do it *the best*, too, and no mistake!"

It is perfectly safe to say that neither of the brothers had a world-wise value for money. William's purse, however, had a peculiarity which did not belong to that of the others, it being understood that it was devoted to the use and entertainment of everybody but himself. The stanch, but unfortunate gentleman, the broken-down scholar, the poor artist, the despised, even the very offscouring of humanity, had equal right to it as long as it held out the attraction of a sixpence, although the spectre of his bootmaker's head with an unpaid bill between his teeth, vanishing through the door of his sanctum at stated times every day in the week, threatened to deprive him of all natural sleep.

This general suicidal disbursement of what would have contributed so much to his own comfort, always reminded us of that eccentric branch of the finny family which, according to Old Izaak, "cast their spawn on flags or stones to become a prey and to be devoured by vermin and other fishes." Indeed, such was his comical carelessness about money, that if the wealth of the Cæsars had been compressed into a bank bill and placed in his hands to meet his "current expenses," he would probably, in a sudden rapture and enthusiasm over a "hob fly," or the points of a favorite horse, have mistaken it for a pinch of "Mrs. Miller's best," and incontinently demolished it, and upon discovering his misfortune would have regarded it as a capital joke, and dismissed it from his mind with the mild philosophy of Uncle Toby. It is consoling in this connection to take refuge in Paley's idea, that "a man who is not sometimes a fool is always one." "Where in all the world," writes Col. Albert Pike, who knew William as thoroughly and loved him perhaps more devotedly than

any other .acknowledged friend, " was there so pure,
so manly, so generous, so unselfish, so loving a soul ?
Where one so tender, so guileless, so noble, so wholly
free of all stain or taint of envy, malice, ill-will,
revenge, uncharitableness ?   Let every one who knew
him answer, if he ever saw the peer of Porter in all
that constitutes the true, generous, unselfish gentleman, made by God *incapable* of a base action or a
sordid impulse."

In personal appearance the brothers were very
attractive, which added much to the interest of their
social intercourse.   All of them of commanding
stature, compact and well put together with the exception of the youngest brother, who was of medium
height, and built of frailer materials than the others.
Their heads manly, spirited, and gracefully set upon
their shoulders, the regions of wit and mirth conspicuous in the heads of all of them, their features
clear, fine and expressive, and when lighted up with
expansive feeling or flashing a response to some generous emotion, it would be difficult to find five brothers
of equal power to charm and enchain the affections.

In connection with their environment in Barclay
street at this time, we insert the following article
upon " Frank's," a favorite club-house in the vicinity
of the offices of the " Spirit " and the " Corsair," which
will be read with interest by those now living who
can recall the friends and wits who met there nearly
a score of years ago, the eyes of most of them sealed
in dust, and the music of their laughter subsided into
the silence of eternity.

FRANK MONTEVERDE'S IN BARCLAY STREET.

THE HOUSE AND ITS PATRONS.

"During the palmy days of the old Olympic, when Mitchel's 'little box' was the nightly rendezvous of a knot of men about town—fast men of an almost by-gone generation, these 'bloods' were wont to congregate before, or after the play, at a quaint public house on the corner of Howard Street, bearing a mysterious sign-board, representing something like a counterfeit of those engravings we were wont to see pasted on the inside of an imported segar box. This place, designated the Havannah House, at that period was beneath the supervision of a hearty Italian, Francis Monteverde, afterwards more familiarly known as 'Frank,' and nightly were assembled beneath his roof, and particularly within a cosy ante-chamber, motley crowds of actors and patrons, of sportsmen and of fast gentlemen, discussing the merits of the drama, of the turf, and the chase, interrupted only by the monotonous clang of domino pieces, employed in deciding wine wagers, by means of the then novel game of 'rounce.'

"Noted as was the Havannah House, fortune, however, destined Mr. Monteverde to preside over the destinies of another establishment still more famous, and whose memory will be ever treasured, in connection with the celebrated sporting sheet, the 'Spirit of the Times,' as the favorite resort of the coterie of talented gentlemen who delighted to contribute to the columns of that popular journal. Unlike his neighbors, who considered it necessary to migrate to the outskirts of the metropolis to anticipate the emergencies of trade, Frank made a crab-like retrogration and located his hostelry at No. 5 Barclay Street, which he forthwith christened by the title of 'Frank's.' Within a few doors of his resting-spot was located the office of the 'Spirit'— that museum of literary, artistic, and sporting marvels, the Mecca of every Western pilgrim visiting the Atlantic metropolis.

"For over fifteen years, 'Frank's' and the 'Spirit' jogged

harmoniously along the road to wealth and fame, until the irresistible march of improvement dissolved their local connection, and, soon after this inimical divorce, the hostelry of Frank became, as it were, desert in the midst of busy scenes, and survives, in the vicinage of its departed glory, but the shadow of a name. The bond of association had been broken, and the charm of familiarity, which gave so earnest a zest to 'Frank's' liquid combinations, was wasted upon the generation of merchants' clerks and store porters, who succeeded the crowd of 'smilers' following in the wake of the 'Tall Son of York.' Even the original building has disappeared to make way for some palace of merchandise, whose tenants are probably ignorant that they daily tread upon ground hallowed by reminiscences of probably as great a body of wit, humor and talent, as has ever been congregated within any four walls of this progressive metropolis; for 'Frank's' in the zenith of its glory may have been justly regarded as the Boar's Head of a cis-Atlantic Eastcheap.

"There were peculiarities distinguishing 'Frank's' which could be encountered in no other public house in the city; it was a specialty in its very nature, being to the literary man and the higher class of sportsman, a species of intellectual exchange comparable to the mercantile relation that 'Delmonico's' bears to its trading patrons. It was the distinction of 'Frank's' that its habitues were considered almost wholly as gentlemen, as the term was interpreted by the conservatives of twenty years since, meaning thereby men of independent resources, or members of the learned professions. In truth, the frequenters at 'Frank's' despised any thing like mercantile pursuits, for, being gentlemen of education, they treasured a traditional prejudice against that which we are nowadays tutored to designate the dignity of commerce.

"'Frank's' may have been regarded as a natural offspring from Washington Hall, many of its elder frequenters having been former patrons of that tavern, and a spirit of similarity pervaded the conversational atmosphere of both celebrated localities. The patrons of each were decidedly fast men, leaders in sports and pastimes, whose generation is being rapidly extinguished. They were as unlike Young New York as we are to Hercules, our juveniles having imitated the townsmen of former days in naught save their exceptionable vices.

"Let us turn our memory to the contemplation of 'Frank's' eighteen years ago—not a long period, to be sure, but long enough to have bestowed upon New York an entirely fresh population, radically distinct from those who flourished at the epoch of which we treat. Let us seat ourselves in one of the rough arm chairs hospitably placed by the table, covered with newspapers from every part of the world—'The Spirit's' exchanges, and make the acquaintance of the *habitues* at 'Frank's' as they casually visit 'the sanctum,' as the place was familiarly entitled. 'Frank's' was not only a refreshment saloon, but a well-appointed club-house, possessing private retreats, an ample billiard room, and a couple of bowling alleys, which, however, disappeared as that game, to which Masonic Hall was once sacrificed, grew in popular disuse.

"Prominent among the visitors, as a matter of course, stood William T. Porter, the well-known editor of The 'Spirit of the Times,' which paper he is erroneously supposed to have originated, but which was commenced by the late Chas. J. B. Fisher, who, in the imprint of its first issues, announced the fact of its being edited by a brother to the celebrated Clara Fisher. 'The Tall Son of York,' for William counted six feet four inches, perpendicular from his stockings, was remarkable for his general suavity and disinterested philanthropy, his evident mission on earth being, as he contended, to oblige everybody. As an editor he was ever ready to confer favors; as a man, his heart and purse were within the reach of every applicant, for selfishness as well as egotism were unknown qualities to a man of so generous a nature. Mr. Porter was probably the only editor on record who died without enemies.

"Dr. Porter, a fine, portly man, whose cast of countenance reminded one of Martin Van Buren, was a more thoroughly educated man than his brother, and possessed every one of William's good qualities, besides a decidedly superior business capacity. In

by-gone days he had been connected with 'The Corsair,' a literary journal, published by him as co-editor with N. P. Willis, but
at the period of his demise, the Doctor was English professor in
Coudert's French Academy, where, from the amiability of his
disposition, he was regarded by his pupils with a feeling of tenderness rarely bestowed upon knights of the birch and ferule.
In the earlier portion of his life, 'the Doctor,' as he was familiarly, and distinctively entitled, after having graduated with honor
at a medical institution, essayed practice of his profession, but
found, although theoretically an enthusiast in the science of
medicine, his nerves unable to withstand the contemplation of
physical suffering. In consequence of his repudiation of surgery,
he was compelled to devote his attention to belles lettres, and
proved himself in all his productions, to be a superior critic,
finished writer, and clever essayist.

"George Porter, brother of Wm. T. and 'the Doctor,' possessed fine literary acquirements, and by nature was more impulsive, or, if you please, more enterprising than any of the
brothers. He never avoided, while attached to the 'Spirit,' any
kind of severe labor, so that he could get ahead of his contemporaries. In 1842 he left New York, and accepted a leading position on the 'Picayune.' For many long years he labored with
most commendable industry, his peculiar abilities finding a
natural field in the excitement of the Mexican war. His knowledge of Spanish was perfect, and his reports of the progress of
the campaign gave the 'Picayune' a deserved pre-eminence.
George was educated for the law, and in the few years he practised in this city, he secured the reputation of being one of the
most promising young men at the bar.

"Another member of the Porter family—Frank—was for
many years a visitor at the 'lower office,' as William good-
naturedly designated Monteverde's Sanctum. His exterior differed
from the robust forms of his more celebrated brothers, being a
man of comparatively small stature, but in warmth of disposition,
and ingenuousness of character, was well worthy of their relationship. He, too, was a man of letters, and the circle at

'Frank's' missed an esteemed companion, when he was called to assume a situation on the New Orleans 'Picayune,' on which his brother George had been engaged.

"A distinguished personage among the *habitues* of 'Frank's' was a dapper gentleman, whose face bore a bushy pair of auburn whiskers, and was garnished with a perpetual smile. Lord George Gordon, for we had ennobled him from admiration of his patrician qualities, was quite a Chesterfield among us, and his opinions on all matters, especially such as appertained to dress and manners, were to be regarded as pure gospel. George was the very pink of neatness; not a speck of dust was allowed to contaminate his olive-cut-away, not a wrinkle to be observable upon his dainty waistcoat, while his blue neck-scarf, spotted with white dots, after the manner of a Belcher tie, encircled his neck with most faultless gracefulness. But particularly did the jauntiness of Lord George display itself in the style and manner of poising his hat on his head, as well as in the condescending patronizing elegance with which he removed it for purposes of salutation. Still the merits of Gordon were in nowise confined to the exterior man; he had that within which passeth show, and was the Yorick of a thousand dinner parties, which he enlivened by a constant flow of wit, humor and anecdote, for Gordon was a walking encyclopedia of amusing information. The peculiarity of Gordon's wit, its appropriateness, was enhanced by the novel manner of his speech, and the earnestness of his gesture. Once called to the witness stand, the lawyer propounded the usual question as to his profession.

"'Profession—eh?' musingly responded Lord George; 'how we live? Olden time, king's fool—nowadays, dine out.' And he gave a majestic wave of the hand. 'Then,' continued the lawyer derisively, as if annoyed at the retort, 'you live by your wits?'

"'Oh, dear, no!' coolly returned Gordon, 'not at all—not by my wits—want of 'em in others?'

"Another worthy of the same school was Tom Oldfield, whilom Consul of the United States at Lyons, a position he resigned, as he boasted, from the inability of the inhabitants to

comprehend or appreciate his jokes. Tom was emphatically a
fellow of infinite jest, and although he in nowise aspired to the
Beau Brummell qualities of Gordon, he possessed a striking ready
fund of anecdotal humor, rendering him on convivial occasions a
most agreeable companion. Poor Tom! he had experienced his
shares of the ups and downs of a mundane existence, which he
bore with stoical composure. While in London, with leisure
time on his hands, he observed near his lodgings a broker's office,
whose proprietor seemed to be of a nervously suspicious temperament. To worry the individual, Oldfield was wont to plant
himself before the heap of gold in the money changer's window,
and contemplate it, with mysterious earnestness, for hours together. The movement he repeated diurnally, until the patience
of the suspicious proprietor was wholly exhausted from inability
to comprehend a motive for Tom's eccentric conduct; consequently, one day he rushed from his shop door, seized upon his
outside visitor, and threatened that if he caught him again
lounging around his window, he would give him into the custody
of the Police.

"'My dear fellow, don't,' pathetically responded Oldfield,
'don't destroy my last consolation; for, if I wern't to stop here
every morning, I should lose all knowledge of the current coin
of the realm.'

"Still another proficient in conversational knowledge was
Mr. Gwilt Mapelsden, Knight of the Order of St. Louis, and
formerly a member of the Court of some Italian Grand Duke.
He was induced to visit the country by the representations of a
gentleman who died on his passage; and by this misfortune,
Mapelsden was forced to resort to his pen for a livelihood. His
knowledge of heraldry, and an affection for mediæval drawing,
distinguished his publications, which were of a unique order in
our literature. The 'Lays of the Western World,' his 'Shakspeare
Ballads,' and his pedigree of Washington, remain beautiful specimens of a revived taste for ancient illumination, which we could
scarce expect from our Democratic community, to please whose
vanity, as well as to earn an honest penny, Mr. Mapelsden manu-
factured armorial bearings in unlimited abundance.

"Speaking of literature reminds us that 'Frank's' was honored by visits from two distinguished living poets, whenever they chanced to sojourn in our metropolis. Col. Albert Pike, of Arkansas, a noble-looking man, over six feet in height, a remarkable embodiment of our romantic ideal of a frontiersman—has not only composed some of the finest poems in our language, but has wielded his sword in the service of his country during the Mexican campaign. Did we not dislike the bad taste of bestowing comparative titles, we would say that Col. Pike could be designated as the 'Korner of America,' notwithstanding that the veteran author of 'Woodman, Spare that Tree,' lays claim to a similar honor.

"The other disciple of the Muses is a fine-looking, elderly gentleman, reminding one strongly of that which an Englishman, rather than an American, is expected to be, as much from the style of his peculiar habiliments as the polite heartiness of his manner. Mr. Fitz Greene Halleck, the contemporary of John Targee, and the other worthies of Tammany Hall his pen has locally immortalized, still survives the ravages of time, and converses as agreeably as in those days when Dickey Riker judged and Croaker sung, above the turmoil of mercantile life.

"Another relict of a past age was Walter Livingston, 'the last of the white cravats,' who adhered with pertinacity to his cambric neckcloth, ruffled shirt, buff waistcoat, and blue dress-coat, until such a fashion of costume grew to be an eccentricity even with his companions. An enthusiastic admirer of field sports, Mr. Livingston was among the last to desert the Jockey Club, and the appearance of this venerable gentleman on the Turf, until racing gave place to trotting, was ever hailed as a guarantee of the respectability of the ancient pastime.

"As a striking contrast to this vestige of the ancient regime, could be observed the bustling apparition of Col. John Haggerty, who, in his time, might have been regarded as the Beau Nash of the day, so neat and trim his attire, so neatly fitting his velvet faced Chesterfield, so accurately turned over his wristbands a la d'Orsay. And how heartily the Colonel laughed at one of Gordon's jokes, and then ventured upon a relation of his experience, when he fished up a relative in the neighborhood of Holyrood in the Count O'Haggerty, *valet de chambre* to Charles X. King of France.

"Still another beau appeared to us in the person of Captain Marx, vulgarly and contemptuously nicknamed 'the Dandy,' although he labored strenuously, in advance of his time, to elevate the taste of the younger citizens, and to impart that appreciation of appropriateness in costume and appointments which distinguishes a gentleman of refinement. Poor Marx! despite many foibles, he was a man of cultivation and of merit, and was lamented by a large circle of admiring friends. The group is augmented by still another man of ton—Henry Allen Wright, who has a tendency towards the adoption of Canadian peculiarities in the way of manners, conceiving possibly that British provincialisms may be applicable to revolted colonies, in which particular he differs from another patron of 'Frank's,' the dashing Frank Waddell, who, in lieu of being 'King of Bath,' aspired to the sovereignty of Newport, and to the principality of Saratoga. Poetic Frank believed in the criticism of good manners, and conceived that no public demonstration of festivity can be regarded as *comme il faut*, unless the programme has been submitted to his judicial inspection.

"A representative of Knickerbocker gentility has dropped in to inquire for a friend. Mr. Harry Hone, a sturdy specimen of good-humored yeomanry, probably in search of one of his equally stalwart nephews, the Anthons, that the two may exercise with dog and gun on the plains beyond Babylon on the Island.

"The gentleman in fustian shooting jacket, corduroy pantaloons, and preposterously thick brogans, is the sporting writer, 'Frank Forrester,' on his way to his favorite shooting-ground near the Highlands of Neversink, who has stopped in to leave a series of messages with 'Garry,' the bar-tender, who, by the way, was a feature at 'Frank's,' as much from his personal affability, as from the possession of a twin brother Peter, whose resemblance was as puzzling to the 'Barclay Guard' as the two Dromios to the ancient Syracusans. Accompanying Herbert was pretty generally his co-editor, Thomas Picton, who, from having been originally his pupil, maintained ever afterwards a close friendship with his preceptor.

" A gentleman of the same profession frequently made a flying visit about the hour of noon—a fine middle-aged Scotchman, Mr. A. D. Paterson, who, after having been long connected with the ' Albion,' attempted to establish the ' Anglo-American,' as a rival sheet, which experiment alone failed by reason of his sudden demise. Mr. Paterson was an excellent scholar in belles-lettres, and unfortunately left but a few fugitive writings behind him.

" So likewise on an afternoon would drop in Lewis Gaylord Clark, the editor of ' Old Nick,' partially with the view to take a hand in a roll, at ' Graves ' over the way, and partially to pick up a few stray jokes for the next number of his magazine. These contributions were never withheld from him, as the ' Spirit ' and ' Old Nick ' were regarded by all as the only genuine oracles of literature.

" Accompanying Mr. Gaylord Clark, would probably be a slight-made gentleman, excessively amiable in personal appearance, and polished in his manners. Mr. Henry Inman, the portrait painter, was a kind, generous-hearted man, emphatically one of nature's noblemen, as famed for his hospitable urbanity as for the invariable gentleness of his disposition. Although sorely oppressed with a pulmonic disease, which seriously interrupted his professional labors, Mr. Inman was ever a leader in our cheerful assemblies ; in truth, it appeared that the relaxation of an evening, passed in the companionship of men of talent, wit and humor, revived a spirit which otherwise would have morbidly succumbed beneath disease and the pressure of the toil ever attending his works of art. As a man, the loss of Mr. Inman was severely felt by sympathizing friends ; as an artist, our country mourns a painter, leaving no successor and few imitators behind him, for his natural geniality, and affectionate admiration for children, rendered portraits of youth and innocence masterpieces of his skill.

" Still another artist, in formidable beard and a slouch hat of gigantic dimensions, stands before us. It is not the person of

Fra Diavolo, but of Charley Elliot, whose pencil has consigned
more than one of ' Frank's ' celebrated patrons to immortality,
as far as a very high standard of painting can confer immortality
on the memories of human features. Elliot, in a mercantile
method of speech, can be quoted as A No. 1, among his contemporaries of the pallet, and among all ' good fellows ' he is surely
to be honored as worthy of a ' bold stand ; ' therefore, say we,
may his beard and shadow never be less.

" An elderly gentleman, who occasionally penetrated into the
sanctum, was for many years the inseparable companion of Mr.
Inman on his piscatorial excursions among the trout streams of
Long Island ; for the artist, like the immortal ' light of other
days,' Phillips the vocalist, was a profound angler. This gentleman, who, strange to say, has resided for half a century in one
and the same ward in this city, is Mr. Fosdick, more familiarly
styled ' Uncle Richard,' who, after surviving most of his contemporaries, has experienced the ingratitude of Republics in being
defeated as Alderman in that very Ward in which he has passed
of his life threescore years, less ten. In latter years, too, even
the fishes appear determined to imitate the conduct of the poli-
ticians, for although the venerable angler annually continues his
expedition, the recusant finny tribe absolutely refuse to be taken
by other stratagem than the vulgar expedient of silver hooks,
Probably, however, the ' old inhabitant ' has outlived the race
which peopled the streams he frequented in his youth.

" An artist of a different school entered on the scene in the
person of Bob Clark, the animal painter, who had finer natural
genius for this particular line than Landseer or Cooper, and was
for several years about the only delineator of horse flesh possessed
by our metropolis. Bob was a generous, impulsive, yet good-
natured child of Erin, being the son of Sir Jas. Clark, of Dublin,
and the nephew of the celebrated Lady Morgan. Poor Bob !
he had but one vanity, and a harmless one at that—he imagined
himself the best gentleman rider in America ; indeed, so pas-
sionately fond was he of equestrian pastimes when at home, that
almost the only clothing he brought hither was jockey or hunting
dresses.

" Prominently among those visitors addicted to the pastime of bowling, was a mysterious gentleman, Jas. Banks, a particular friend of Porter, who facetiously styled him ' Jim Baggs.' A very powerful and handsomely framed man, he excelled in the exercise ; and on one occasion, it is said, rolled a string with Caleb McNulty, of Washington, for $10,000. On another occasion he flourished before the public as the presumed robber of ' Pomeroy's trunk,' having been arrested on suspicion, as his trunk at the hotel was opened by accident, and found to contain $25,000 in gold, with regard to the possession of which he positively declined giving any explanation. The apprehension and suicide of the real robber relieved him from every imputation of criminality ; but to his dying day this eccentric personage declined gratifying public curiosity as to the source whence he derived the contents of his trunk, but which were in reality the proceeds of a heavy government contract for the transportation of the Southern Mail ; Uncle Sam then, as now, being in the habit of liquidating his liabilities in hard cash.

" Conversing with his friend Gordon, would probably be seen the medical adviser of the crowd—Doctor Warrington, a skilful surgeon and polished gentleman, whose eccentricity evinces itself in the wearing of a white hat of a peculiar construction, which had doubtless been patented by the original inventor somewhere about the year one. The Doctor is at the present moment the popular surgeon on one of the California Steamers.

" Then would come a short, dapper individual, who jumps about, somewhat after the manner one would be expected to assume if treading upon hot coals. This is C. II. Stanley, well known as a chess champion, and as an *attache* of Her Majesty's Consulate. Stanley is a capital companion, with only one fault —a passion for concocting the most villanous puns that could ever emanate from the human brain.

"As a contrast to Stanley we have Isaiah Howe, the advocate in ordinary to every patron of ' Frank's ' who has the misfortune to tumble into legal disputations, a matter-of-fact personage of more than ordinary talent, and a decided propensity to argue with somebody. At this moment he is laying down the law to a

small contented looking gentleman, who glides about the apartment with that mysterious profundity of manner which has been
chronicled as the attribute of the learned Linkum Fidelius—the
'Little Man in Black,' of Manhattanese creation.   In fact 'Mac'
—nobody gives him any other cognomen—is quite as whimsical,
and slightly more unfathomable a character than that antique
celebrity has been represented to us in the traditions of the
Knickerbocker.   Two local personages have entered the saloon
—Harry Mabbett—a perfect epidemic on police mismanagement,
who regulates conventions and committees, and, Joshua-like,
commands the political Sun shining over at least two down-town
wards to stand still, until he chooses to set the affairs of state in
proper motion.   The other is Mr. Peter Chanfrau, brother to the
theatrical representative of Mose, who, after having reaped a
neat fortune by ornamenting the exterior of the human face, con-
templates the measure of their internal living, and has performed
the mathematical feat of converting the almost decimal fraction
of a man into a full blown Boniface.   'Measure for Measure' has
been, and now is, his motto; whether the one measure be by
the yard, or by the sections of a gallon, the other is inevitably
by the standard of cash.

"An Indian curiosity we have in the person of Adams, the
Rocky Mountain trapper, who glories in an Indian chieftaincy,
with an unpronounceable name to match, but is withal an excellent specimen of civilization, having deserted his rifle and taken
to the 'long bow,' in the drawing of which he excels his red-
skinned brethren.

"Next we make the acquaintance of two enthusiastic cricket-
ers—John Richards, whose hearty laugh and boisterous jocularity
ring through the hall, while his younger companion, a tall, wiry,
athletic gentleman, seems inclined to a pensive consideration of
the important subject-matter under discussion.   This latter is
Delancy Barclay, son of the British Consul, who, after having
attained the dignity of an engineer in our fire department, has
turned his attention to the game of cricket, of which both 'the
Governor' and he are most enthusiastic supporters.   In their
conversation they are joined by a melancholy-looking personage,

5

who delivers his opinions with the profundity of a Delphic oracle; for as Hercules was known by his tread, so is 'Cuyp,' the famous bowler, recognized by the excessive gravity of his demeanor. Indeed, a casual observer would be induced, from his personal appearance, to believe him to be a Methodist parson in disguise, for he is seldom known to laugh even at Richard's jokes.

"A knot of worthies in the corner embrace some distinguished men in their own particular sphere. Col. Costar, who has witnessed the changes of half a century, and remains himself as unchanged as the day he first perambulated Broadway; Col. Pride, gay, handsome, robust, just as if he had discovered the philosopher's stone, or at least swallowed a good dose of the elixir of life; Lovell Purdy, as intent upon the encouragement of a racing stud as if he had grown legitimate heir to the 'Napoleon of the Turf,' and Tom Battolle, wild, harum-scarum traveller in many lands, who has determined upon trying his luck at the first new enterprise which fortune, or common rumor, suggests to his notice.

"Then again, 'Frank's' is invaded by the apparition of a bevy of theatrical magnates—not men of extraordinary calibre, but artists of established merit, particularly those who are afflicted with a propensity for scribbling, and find the 'Spirit' an opportune vent for their surcharged emotions. First, we have the poet laureate of the Mammoth Cod Association, author of that spiritual ditty, 'Don't think I'm going to Rail, or' &c.; everjoyous John Brougham, inventor of the Greeley Hat and other divine institutions. After him may come Harry Plunkett, another disciple of Momus, who executes tragedy on the stage, and does up farce upon paper. At another period can be seen the 'merchant vocalist,' deep-toned Brough, who claims admission to the sporting circles by dint of agency for diamond-grained gunpowder, and who has been induced to relinquish 'those scenes I view so charming,' to dispense in wholesale Parr's Life Pills and the 'Illustrated London News.' Between merchandise and minstrelsy he leads a life unequalled by the 'Monks of Old,' and he would be the happiest of mortals were not his nerves shattered by afflictions of gout, slang, and 'nothin' else.' But before him stands another of his tormentors—'Gemotice,' whilom literary editor of an extinguished 'Planet,' but, at that moment, musical *satan* of the 'Express,' who is intensely reading, from proof, a forthcoming *critique* upon the latest opera, each sentence of which gives the vocalist a twinge incomparably more severe than that produced by his hereditary gout. Among theatrical celebrities we moreover notice Harry Placide—a better.'Sir Harcourt' off than on the stage—who has condescended to relinquish his parental government over ducks, chickens, and hens, and has suffered them to roam in wildness over his homestead on the 'island,' that he may shine as a star for a week or two upon the boards of old Drury. Near him can be observed his brother Tom, undeniably the best low comedian on our stage, saving the incomparable Mitchell—whose years alone prevent his identification with his better-known relative.

"Sometimes we are favored, in the summer season, with the presence of New Orleans manager, Mr. Place, likewise a man of portly dimensions, who visits our city to replenish his troupe, and to add to his store of equestrian utensils, for Place, breathing this atmosphere of 'Frank's' and the 'Spirit,' is afflicted with a propensity towards equine worship.

"Speaking of Southern notabilities, here we have Col. Thorpe, a stout, solid gentleman, better known as Tom Owen the Bee Hunter, whose personal appearance gives little token of the possession of that heartiness of humor which characterizes his South-western sketches, particularly 'The Big Bear of Arkansas,' and who is assuredly entitled to a front seat among the American humorists. On the contrary the Colonel, has the look of a solid planter, from whom we should as confidently expect the execution of a joke, as to contemplate his brother, Colonel John S. Du Solle, performing on the *corde volante*.

"Another literary celebrity of the South is George Wilkins Kendall, of the New Orleans 'Picayune,' who has 'seen the elephant' and, during the hunt after whom, acquired some unpleasant reminiscences of the road to Santa Fe. He has ventured hitherward to astonish the nerves of a special party, bound to the Wilderness of the Empire State, where he expects to take down the deer, still tracking the sylvan groves of Hamilton County; after this feat he will hie to Paris, to appreciate that improvement of the fandango, known to the *senoritas* of Mabille and the Parisian Prado, as the *can can*.

"Moreover at times there could be encountered at 'Frank's' pure specimens of the professional sporting race, doctors, trainers, jockies and turfmen proper, especially during the week preceding meetings over the Union Course. Then was a carnival with those who 'talked horse,' and many were the entries booked, and wagers laid for and against horse, time and field. But as these people were but of an ephemeral character, mere birds of passage, who visited the North for the instant, their acquaintance would in nowise amuse the general reader at our day.

"Conspicuous, however, among turfmen, came Alfred Conover, the Nestor of Long Island trainers, who was once charged with the studs of Commodore Stockton, Capt. Sutton, and the Stevenses, when these worthy gentlemen encouraged, in princely style, the most attractive of all field sports. But the memory of those halcyon days has been obliterated, and Alfred and his stables have probably shared the fate of oblivion, according to the destiny of racing.

"We have attempted to carry our readers back with us to the palmy days at 'Frank's'—many of the habitues of whom we have spoken, are already gathered to their fathers, many more are progressing thither rapidly with the stream of time. We have endeavored to preserve a faint reminiscence of the frequenters of a once famous locality, conceiving it a pleasant duty to treasure the memory of familiar faces, before all vanish before the irresistible touch of the future."

CHAPTER V.

WAGNER AND GREY EAGLE.

At no time had the Turf stood higher than in 1839, and the races of that year were of unsurpassed interest; all the horses of note had their sanguine friends, and more than one was believed by his own especial partisans to be invincible. Of none was this more true than of those two gallant animals, (Wagner and Grey Eagle,) whose grandest exploit was incomparably reported for the Turf Register in 1840, by Wm. T. Porter. Herbert states that

" *Wagner* in his five-year-old form, was already a tried horse, of proved speed, courage, and bottom, a distinguished winner, and even, in the high-flown aspirations of his owner, capable to compete with Boston. He was at least the equal of any other horse in America of his day ; and not long afterwards a distinguished writer was found in the columns of the ' Spirit of the Times ' to maintain, that up to this period, the great son of Timoleus had displayed no manifest superiority over him.

" He had been in training continually since his third year;

in 1838 he had won three races of four-mile heats, and two of two-mile heats, beating *Extio* at New Orleans in 7.44—7.57—considered in those days all but the very best time.

"He was a beautiful chestnut horse of fifteen and a half hands, with a white blaze on his face, and two white hind feet. He was got by Sir Charles—he by Sir Archy, dam by imp. Citizen, gd. by Commutation, g. gd. by imp. Daredevil—g. g. gd. by imp. Shark—g. g. g. gd. by imp. Fearnought—out of Maria West by Marion, her dam Ella Cramp, by imp. Citizen—gd. by Huntsman, g. gd. by Wildair, g. g. gd. by Fearnought, g. g. g. gd. by Janus, &c.

"Marion was by Sir Archy, dam by Citizen, gd. by Alderman, g. gd. by Robuck out of a Herod Mare.

"*Grey Eagle* was in his fourth year, a magnificent horse nearly sixteen hands in height, said to be of almost perfect symmetry, although scarcely equal in his quarters to his forehand, which is described as sumptuous. His color, as his name indicates, was a fine silvery gray.

In his three-year-old form he had won two races of two-mile heats, in 3.41—3.43—3.48—and 3.44, respectively, and was honestly believed by his owner, and by Kentuckian Sportsmen in general, to be equal to any thing in America, both for speed and bottom; although, in truth, this opinion must be regarded rather as surmise than as judgment, since his powers had not yet been sufficiently tested to justify such boundless confidence. It is but fair to add, in the wonderful races which are to be described, his performance was such as to prove that this confidence was not misplaced—was such, indeed, as to render it probable that, had he been ridden by a jockey competent to make the most of his powers, he might have been the winner in the first match—in which case he probably would not have been lost to the Turf, by the rash, and as I must consider it, cruel trial, of running a second four-mile race of scarcely paralleled severity within five days.

"Grey Eagle was got by Woodpecker, he by imp. Dragon—dam, Irby's Daredevil mare, grandam by Old Wildair, g. gr. dam by Fearnought, etc., out of Ophelia by Wild Medley, gd.

Ophelia by Grey Diomed, g. gd. Primrose by Apollo, g. g. gd. by imp. Grandby, g. g. g. gd. by imp. Figure, &c.

" Wild Medley was got by Old Medley, dam by Wildair, g. d. by Tristram Shandy, g. gd. Sportley by imp. Janus, g. g. gd. Gen. Nelson's imp. Spanish Mare. There are no less than four Grey Diomeds and seven Apollos in Edgar's Stud Book, and it is not stated which of these horses are intended. They are all, however, of good blood.

" The description which here ensues," continues Mr. Herbert, " has been considered by competent judges, to be the finest specimen of turf-writing in the English language, and if the *laudari a laudato* be fame in literary matters, we know no one who has derived more from a single essay than the writer of the narrative annexed."

WAGNER AND GREY EAGLE'S RACES.

The editor of this Magazine had the pleasure of attending the last meeting of the Louisville Jockey Club, and witnessing the two splendid races between Wagner and Grey Eagle. Those who have noticed the spirit with which every thing connected with breeding and racing is carried on at present in Kentucky, will hardly be surprised to hear that the late meeting has never been equalled in the excellence of the sport, or in the number and character of the visitors. Turfmen and other distinguished strangers from the neighboring States mustered in great force; while the Kentuckians themselves turned out in such numbers that the hotels and lodging-houses literally overflowed. A week of more delightful weather we have rarely known. The fields were large every day; the horses ran well, " all the world and his wife " were on the course; the pressure was forgotten, and all

appeared to enjoy themselves without stint or measure.

In addition to the brilliant report of " *N. of Arkansas*," in the Spirit of the Times, the editor, since
his return, has given his impressions of the meeting
in the columns of that paper. Many readers of this
magazine have expressed a desire that we should also
give them a report of the two great races. * * *

In compliance with the general desire of these,
we proceed to give our own impressions of the two
races, which have contributed in an eminent degree
to give Wagner and Grey Eagle the high and enduring reputation they now enjoy. The races during the
week were characterized by good fields, strong running, fine weather, and an attendance unparalleled in
numbers and respectability. The Oakland Course
was in the finest possible order, the Stewards were in
uniform and well mounted, and the arrangements of
the proprietor, Col. Oliver, and of the Club, for the
gratification and convenience of their guests, were not
only in good taste but complete in all respects.

We have not room to speak in this place of a
variety of interesting circumstances connected with
the meeting, but shall be pardoned for alluding to the
unusual number of distinguished individuals present,
and the blaze of beauty reflected from the Ladies'
"Pavilion," on the occasion of the first race between
the champions of Louisiana and Kentucky. The
number of ladies in attendance was estimated at eight
hundred, while nearly two thousand horsemen were
assembled on the field. The stands, the fences, the

trees, the tops of carriages, and every eminence over-
looking the course, were crowded ; probably not less
than ten thousand persons composed the assemblage,
comprising not only several distinguished Senators,
and nearly the entire Kentucky delegation in Congress, with their families, but all the élite of the
beauty and fashion of the State.

Among the earliest on the ground were the Hon.
Judge Porter, of Louisiana, the distinguished Ex-Sen-
ator, and Mr. Clay. His colleague in the Senate, Mr.
Crittenden, soon followed, with Gen. Atkinson, Major
Stewart, and Capt. Alexander, of the army ; Judge
Woolley, Gov. Poindexter, Judge Rowan, the Hon.
Messrs. Menifee, Allan, Letcher, Hardin, Graves,
Hawes, etc. Among the guests of the Club, well
known to the sporting world, we noticed J. S. Skin-
ner, Esq., of Baltimore ; W. M. Anderson, Esq., of
Ohio ; C. F. M. Noland, of Arkansas ; the Messrs.
Kenner, Mr. Slidell, Mr. Parker, and Mr. Beasley, of
Louisiana ; Mr. McCargo, Mr. Beasley, and Capt.
Bacon, of Virginia ; Mr. Geo. Cheatham, of Tenn. ;
Maj. Fleming, of Alabama, and a great number more
whose names have escaped us.

Good breeding forbids an enumeration of the distinguished throng of belles. The young Miss just
from the trammels of school, flush with joy and fears,
the budding, blooming girl of sweet sixteen, the more
stately and elegant full-blown woman, the dark-eyed
Southerner, with her brown complexion and match-
less form, the blue-eyed Northerner, with her dimpled
cheek and fair and spotless beauty, were gathered

5*

here in one lustrous galaxy. The gentlemen were unmatched for variety; the Bar, the Bench, the Senate, and the Press, the Army and the Navy, and all the *et ceteras* that pleasure or curiosity attracted, were here represented.

We are very much tempted to essay to describe a few of these radiant belles—had kind heaven made us a poet, like Prentice, we would immortalize them; as we are only a proser, we can merely detail them. If any demand by what right we allude so pointedly to them, surely we may ask what right they have to be so beautiful? There was one with a form of perfect symmetry, and a countenance not only beautiful but entirely intellectual; like Halleck's Fanny, she may have been " younger once than she is now," but she is, and will ever be, " a thing to bless—all full of life and loveliness." With a purely Grecian bust and classic head, and with an eye as dark as the absence of all light, beaming with a lustre that eclipses all, her figure varied itself into every grace that can belong either to rest or motion. And there was a reigning belle, in the spring-time of her youth and beauty, with a face beaming with perfect happiness; it was like a " star-lit lake curling its lips into ripples in some stream of delight, as the west-wind salutes them with its balmy breath, and disturbs their placid slumber." It was the realization of Byron's idea of "music breathing o'er the face." There comes a bride—and from the East, too. A peep at her face, almost hid by clustering braids of raven hair, displays a belle of an Atlantic city, and ere we have time to ask her name, a lovely blonde sweeps by in a gay mantilla, changeable as the hues of evening, with a hat whiter than the wing of a dove, and as faultless as Neæra. It would puzzle a sphinx to divine the cause of her radiant smile. Walks she fancy free? Has Cupid's bolt passed her innocuous? In the centre of the pavilion stand two rival belles, of a style of beauty so varied as to attract marked attention. The face and figure of one is rounded to the complete fulness of the mould of a Juno; while the other, with the form of a sylph, and the eyes of an angel, is the impersonation of delicacy and loveliness. And there is a lady from the northernmost extremity of the Republic, nearly allied to the Patrick Henry of the south-west, with eyes of the sweetest and most tranquil blue "that ever reflected the serene heaven of a happy hearth—eyes to love, not wonder at—to adore and rely upon, not admire and tremble for." And then there was that beautiful belle from Scott County, and that brilliant wit from Lexington; here, the pearl wreath strove to rival the fairer brow—the ruby, a rubier lip—the diamond, a brighter eye; there the cornelian borrowed from the damask cheek a deeper hue; the gossamer floated round a lighter form—the light plume nodded over a lighter heart.

But what grace can flowers or sweeping plumes confer when the rich smile of beauty is parting her vermilion lips, and the breath of the morning, added to the excitement of the occasion, have given ripeness to her cheeks, and a fire to her eye, which, to our bachelor taste, would be worth a pilgrimage to Mecca to enjoy, as we did at that moment. Who can fail to detect the graceful being on our left, in a Parisian hat, lined with violets, whose soft liquid eye and raven braids render her the fairest gem in the brilliant cluster of Western beauties ? The flashing eyes of a dark-browed matron from Missouri are roving restlessly over the nodding sea of heads beneath ; and the pensive smile of a fair lily, just home from school, has become absolutely radiant as she shakes back, from her open brow, a flood of glistering ringlets, and gazes down upon the multitude with the innocent gaze of a young-eyed seraph. But how shall our pen do homage to the daughters of Old Kentuck, whose striking Di Vernon beauty, with their dark, lustrous eyes and sable tresses, is only rivalled by the high culture bestowed upon their minds, and the attraction of those feminine accomplishments which " gild refined gold," and render them among the loveliest and most fascinating women within the circuit of the sun ? The waters of Lethe must flow deep over our souls to banish the memory of the bouquets and gloves we lost and won upon that day ! The evening festivities that followed—the brilliant dance, the plaintive song that " lapt us in elysium," and she, too, the fairy masquerader, in the Suliote cap and bodice, lives she not last, as well as first, in our remembrance ?

But our pages forbid a longer retrospection. The hospitalities and courtesies of the West, joined to the smile of her beauteous women, are indelibly impressed upon our hearts, and shall be freshly remembered when we pledge our warmest friends in the generous wine-cup.

The occasion of this brilliant assembly was the stake for all ages, four-mile heats, which closed on the 1st of January, 1839, with ten subscribers at $2,000 each, half forfeit, as follows:

1. Y. N. Oliver and Miles W. Dickey, of Kentucky, named gr. c., *Grey Eagle*, by Woodpecker, out of Ophelia, by Wild Medley, 4 yrs.—Dress, Red, Blue and Orange.
2. Wm. T. Ward, of Kentucky, named b. m. *Mary Vaughan*, by Waxy, out of Betty Blusten, by imp. Blusten, 5 yrs.—Dress, Blue and White.
3. Willa Viley, of Kentucky, named ch. f. *Queen Mary*, by Bertrand, dam by Brimmer, 4 yrs.—Dress, White and Green.
4. Geo. N. Sanders and Lewis Sanders, Jr., of Kentucky, named b. c. *Occident*, by Bertrand, out of Diamond, by Turpin's Florizel, 4 yrs.—Dress, White.
5. Sidney Burbridge, of Kentucky, named b. c. *Tarlton*, by Woodpecker, dam by Robin Gray, 5 yrs.—Dress, not declared.
6. Jas. C. Bradley and H. B. Steel, of Kentucky, named ch. c. *Hawk-Eye*, by Sir Lovell, out of Pressure's dam, by Jenkins' Sir William, 4 yrs.—Dress, Orange and Black.
7. Archie Cheatham, of Virginia, named ch. h. *Billy Townes*, by imp. Fylde, dam by Virginian, 5 yrs.—Dress, Purple and Red.
8. James S. Garrison, of Louisiana, named ch. h. *Wagner*, by Sir Charles, out of Maria West, by Marion, 5 yrs.—Dress, Red and Red.
9. Wm. Wynn, of Virginia, named b. c. *Picton*, by imp. Luzborough, out of Isabella, by Sir Archy, 5 yrs.—Dress, not declared.
10. Wm. Buford, Jr., of Kentucky, named ch. f. *Musidora*, by Medoc, dam by Kosciusko, 4 yrs.—Dress, not declared.

The race came off on Monday, the 30th of September. Of the ten nominations, four only came to the post—Wagner, Grey Eagle, Queen Mary, and Hawk-Eye; of the other six, Tarlton and Musidora had given way in training; Picton was in Tennessee, and complaining; Occident's trials would not justify his starting; Billy Townes and Mary Vaughan were on the ground, but not up to the mark in condition. From the day the stake closed, the betting had been going on with spirit in different sections of the country, increasing daily in amount as the race drew nigh. From the first, Wagner was decidedly the favorite; and when it became reduced almost to a certainty that not above six would start, the betting was about 50 to 75 on him *vs.* the field. For many months previous to the race, and before it was known how many would start, odds were offered, from New York to New Orleans, on Wagner and Billy Townes against the field. Immense sums were laid out at odds, in Kentucky, on Grey Eagle's winning the first heat, and in many instances he was backed against Wagner for the race. In consequence of the un-limited confidence felt by the Kentuckians in the "foot" of Grey Eagle, it was resolved by the Wagner party not to run for the first heat, unless circum-stances should occur which might render it an easy thing for their horse. But the day before the race a commission from New Orleans was received, offering a large sum on Wagner's beating the gray the first heat, which induced them to change this determina-tion; indeed, the inducement to run for it was a pretty substantial one, for they could lose nothing, and might win several thousands—we do not feel at liberty to say how many, or who were the parties; it is enough that they were keen, and also successful. Two days before the race, Mr. McCargo gave Billy Townes a trial with Missouri and Texana, and though the result was entirely satisfactory, so far as his action was concerned, he soon after cramped to such a degree, that it was at once declared that he could not be started. Mary Vaughan, we believe, was plated for the race, but not being quite up to the mark, she also paid forfeit. On the morning of the race, it being understood pretty thoroughly that Wagner, Grey Eagle, Queen Mary, and Hawk-Eye only would start out of the ten nominations, "business" commenced in earnest, Wagner being freely offered against the field, and as freely taken, while Grey Eagle was backed at small odds for the first heat. The "call" for the horses was sounded at a quarter to one o'clock, and soon after all eyes were directed toward a motley group approaching from Mr. Garrison's stable; "with stately step and slow," the proud champion of Louisiana made his appearance. He was directly stripped, and a finer exhibition of the perfection to which the trainer's art can be carried we have rarely seen. His coat and eye were alike brilliant— *Wagner* is a light gold chestnut, with a roan stripe on the right side of his face, and white hind feet—about fifteen hands and a half high. His head is singularly small, clean and bony, set on a light but rather long neck; forehanded, he resembles

tho pictures of his sire, and in his carriage is said to
resemble him.   His shoulder is immensely strong,
running very well back into a good middle-piece,
which is well ribbed home.   One of the finest points
about him is his great depth of chest; few horses can
measure with him from the point of his shoulder to
the brisket.   His arms are heavily muscled, like
Mingo's, with the tendons standing out in bold relief.   He has uncommonly strong and wide hips, a
good loin, remarkably fine stifles and thighs, with as
fine hocks and legs as ever stood under a horse.
Wagner has been in training ever since his Three-year
old, and has travelled over three thousand miles, without three weeks' rest this season !   Mr. Garrison commenced galloping him just four weeks previous to
this race; he had not even been turned loose in a
paddock.

A murmur, which was soon lost in a suppressed
cheer at the head of the quarter stretch, announced
to the multitude about the stand the approach of
Grey Eagle; as he came up in front of the stand, his
lofty carriage and flashing eye elicited a burst of applause, which told better than words can express the
intense and ardent aspirations felt in his success,
by every son and daughter of Kentucky.   Clinton,
his trainer, immediately stripped off his sheet and
hood, and a finer specimen of the high-mettled racer
was never exhibited.   He was in condition to run for
a man's life—a magnificent gray, nearly sixteen
hands high, with the step of a gazelle and the strength
of a Bucephalus.   Mr. Burbridge had told us that of

one thing he was confident—his horse might want
foot, but of his game he was certain ; the correctness
of his judgment the sequel will show. In the hands
of Clinton, who, by the by, is a Kentuckian, not above
seven and twenty years of age, Grey Eagle had never
lost a heat; the previous October, he won a two-mile
sweepstakes, over this course, in 3.41—3.43¾; and a
week afterwards repeated the race in 3.48—3.44.
His form indicates more power of endurance than
any horse we ever saw in Kentucky ; from the girth
forward, his shape and make could hardly be improved, if he merely had the delicate, finely tapered
ears of a Sir Charles or a Wild Bill. Standing behind him, his quarters display a fine development of
muscle, but many would call them light in proportion
to his size and forehead ; in this respect he closely
resembles Priam. His coupling, thigh and stifle are
unexceptionably good, and his hocks come well down
to the ground, giving him great length from this
point to that of the whirlbone. His legs are clean,
broad and flat, with the ham-strings and leaders
beautifully developed—no son of Whip ever had a
finer set of limbs under him.

Two chestnuts next challenged the public's attention ; the first was Queen Mary, a very blood-like
looking filly, with white hind feet, that a single glance
would have shown to be a daughter of Bertrand.
She measures about 15½ hands, is well put up, and
when running in good form, must be a dangerous
lady to trifle with. Hawk-Eye, as we remember him,
is a heavy moulded colt, of nearly 15½ hands, with a

star and white fore feet; without the foot or the endurance of his half-brother, Pressure, he presents to the eye no such game appearance. We trust he was not himself on this occasion, or we should wish "ne'er to look upon his like again," for he cut a very sorry figure in this party. Both himself and the Bertrand filly have been winners, and the latter has ever been looked upon as a performer of great promise.

At half-past one o'clock, the jockeys having received their orders from the judges, the order was given to "clear the course." *Cato*, called Kate, in a richly-embroidered scarlet dress, was put upon Wagner; he is a capital jockey, and rode nearly up to his weight, 110 pounds. The rider engaged for Grey Eagle lost the confidence of his owners just before the race, and at the eleventh hour they were obliged to hunt up another. *Stephen Welch*, a three-year-old rider, was selected, though obliged to carry thirteen pounds dead weight in shot-pouches on his saddle! The friends of Grey Eagle, however, had entire confidence in his honesty; and it is clear that he did his best, though, weighing, as he did, but eighty-two pounds, he had neither the strength nor stamina to hold and control a powerful, fiery horse like Grey Eagle. He rode superbly for a lad of his years, while Cato's exhibition of skill and judgment would have done credit to Gil. Patrick. The horses took their places in accordance with the precedence of their nomination for the stake, Grey Eagle having the inside track, Queen Mary second, Hawk-Eye third, and Wagner the outside. Just at this moment Mr. Ward, the President of the Club, dislodged the band from their seats over the judges' stand, and Mr. Clay, Judge Porter, Judge Rowan, our friend Col. Whetstone, of the Devil's Fork of the Little Red, and the writer of this article, with two or three other gentlemen, were invited to occupy them, by which we all obtained a fine view, not only of the race, but—of the ladies in the stands opposite.

THE RACE.

All being in motion and nearly in line, the President gave the word "Go!" and tapped the drum. Grey Eagle was the last off, while Wagner went away like a quarter-horse, with Queen Mary well up second; they were taken in hand at once, which allowed Hawk-Eye to take the place of the Queen on the back stretch, and at the three-quarter mile-post, Wagner allowed him to take the track. Hawk-Eye led home to the stand at a moderate place, Wagner second, and Queen Mary third; both of them were pulling to Grey Eagle, at whose head Stephen was tugging with might and main. Hawk-Eye carried on the running for about half a mile further, until Gooding bid Cato "Go along." The pace mended at once; Wagner went up to Hawk-Eye, and might have cut him down in half a dozen strides, but the Queen was still lying back, and Grey Eagle had not yet made a stroke. Wagner came first to stand, and at the turn, Cato having held up his whip as a signal to the crowd of rubbers and boys on Garrison's stable, that "the old sorrel stud" was going just right, they gave him a slight cheer, at which Wagner broke loose, and made a spread-eagle of the field in "no time." The other jocks were not a little startled at this demonstration of Wagner's speed, and each called upon his nag, so that, opposite the Oakland House, near the three-quarter mile post, the field closed. Stephen here let out the phenomenon he so gracefully bestrode, and, like twin bullets, the gallant gray and Wagner came out of the melée. At the head of the quarter-stretch, Stephen was told to "pull him steady," so that, before Wagner reached the stand, Queen Mary had changed places with Grey Eagle, notwithstanding her saddle had slipped on her withers. Hawk-Eye was already in difficulty, and for him the pace was getting "no better very fast." Grey Eagle set to work in earnest on entering the back stretch, first out-footing the Queen and then challenging Wagner. From the Oakland House to the head of the quarter-stretch, the ground is descending, and from thence up the straight run to the stand, a distance of perhaps six hundred yards, it is ascending. At the half-mile post Cato called upon Wagner, and the critical moment having arrived, Stephen collared him with the gray, on the outside. For three hundred yards the pace was tremendous ; Grey Eagle once got his head and neck in front, and a tremendous shout was sent up ; but Wagner threw him off so far in going round the last turn, that, half-way up the stretch, Mr. Burbridge ordered him to be pulled up, and Wagner won cleverly, Queen Mary dropping just within her distance, 150 yards. Hawk-Eye was nowhere. Time, 7.48.

The disappointment and mortification were so great, that for the first twenty minutes after the heat, Queen Mary was freely backed against Grey Eagle, while so far as Wagner was concerned, it was considered "a dead open and shut." Before the forty-five had elapsed, however, a re-action took place in favor of Grey Eagle. *Not a Kentuckian on the ground laid out a dollar on Wagner!* From the first, the very few individuals who were disposed to back him on account of his blood, his form, his performances, and his condition, had not staked a dollar; their judgment prompted them to back the Southern Champion, but they *would not* bet against *Kentucky!* Talk of State pride in South Carolina! Why, the Kentuckians have more of it than the citizens of all the States in the Confederacy added together. They not only believe Kentucky to be the Eden of the world and the garden of the Union, but their own favorite county to be the asparagus-bed of the State! And they have good reason; Kentucky *is* a glorious State. The talent and chivalry of her sons are in keeping with the intelligence and peerless beauty of her daughters, and well may they be proud of her and of each other. But to the horses.

All cooled off well, but more especially Grey Eagle, who appeared not to mind the run a jot. They got, as Clinton remarked, "a capital scrape out of him," and he was "as fine as silk"—in good order for a bruising heat. He extended himself with a

degree of ease in the second heat, and changed his
action in a manner that convinced us that the sweat
had relieved him.   Wagner, who resembles Boston in
many other respects, showed all that placidity and
calmness of look and motion which characterizes " the
old White-nose."   Great odds were offered on him
for the race, but small amounts only were staked.
Grey Eagle's noble bearing and game-cock look, as
he came up to the contest in a second heat for the
meed of honor and applause, was the theme of universal admiration ; so much so, indeed, that a cargo of
laces, gloves, bijouterie, etc., must have been required
to pay the wagers made in the Ladies' Pavilion.

Second Heat.—The tap of the drum sent them
away with a beautiful start, Wagner leading off with .
a steady, business-like stride, while Grey Eagle, as
full of game as of beauty, waited upon him close up.
It was instantly evident that Mr. Burbridge had
changed his tactics ; the moment Stephen got Grey
Eagle into straight work on the back side, he made
play for the track, and after a terrific burst of speed
for one hundred and fifty yards, he came in front ;
keeping up his stroke, he soon after made a gap of four
lengths, and though Wagner drew upon him a little
in coming up the rising ground towards the stand,
yet he passed it far enough in advance to warrant the
warm and hearty plaudits of his friends.   As if inspirited by the cheers of the crowd, and the tokens
of unalloyed gratification exhibited by the galaxy of
radiant beauty in the stands, Grey Eagle kept up
his murderous rate throughout the entire second mile ;

Wagner lay up close, and there was no faltering, no flinching, no giving back, on the part of either. The stride was over twenty-two feet, perfectly steady, strong and regular, with no dwelling, no floundering, no laboring. Grey Eagle made the running to beyond the half-mile post on the third mile, and the pace seemed too good to last, but there were " links " yet to be " let out." From this point the two cracks made a match of it, in which Queen Mary had as little apparent concern as if out of the race. Near the Oakland House, Wagner set to work to do or die. "*Rowel him up !*" shouted his owner to Cato ; while Garrison, at the head of the quarter-stretch, was waving his hat to him to come on ! The rally that ensued down the descent to the turn was desperate, but Wagner could not gain an inch ; as they swung round into the quarter-stretch, they were lapped ; " spur your proud coursers hard, and ride in blood ! " were the orders on this, as they are described to have been on Bosworth " field." Both horses got a taste of steel and catgut as they came up the ascent, and on casting our eye along the cord extending across the course from the judges' to the Club stands, Grey Eagle was the first under it by a head and shoulders ; at the turn Stephen manœuvred so as to press Wagner on the outside, and soon after drew out clear in front, looking so much like a winner, that the crowd, unable to repress an irresistible impulse, sent up a cheer that made the welkin ring for miles around. The group on Wagner's stable again bid him " *go on !* " but Cato, " calm as a summer's morning," was quietly biding

his time; he seemed to feel that Patience has won
more dollars than Haste has coppers, and that there
was but a solitary chance of winning the race out of
the fire.   Fully aware of the indomitable game of the
nonpareil under him, he thought if he could bottle
him up for a few hundred yards, there was still another
run to be got out of him.   He accordingly took a
bracing pull on his horse, and though it was " go
along " every inch, Wagner recovered his wind so as
to come again at the head of the quarter-stretch.
Stephen long ere this had become so exhausted as
to be unable to give Grey Eagle the support he
required ; he rode wide, swerving considerably from
a straight line, and was frequently all abroad in his
seat.   From the Oakland House home, it was a terrible race !   By the most extraordinary exertions Wagner got up neck and neck with " the gallant gray,"
as they swung round the turn into the quarter-stretch.
The feelings of the assembled thousands were wrought
up to a pitch absolutely painful—silence the most
profound reigned over that vast assembly, as these
noble animals sped on as if life and death called forth
their utmost energies.   Both jockeys had their whip-
hands at work, and at every stroke, each spur, with a
desperate stab, was buried to the rowel-head.   Grey
Eagle, for the first hundred yards, was clearly gain-
ing ; but in another instant Wagner was even with
him.   Both were out and doing their best.   It was
anybody's race yet !   Now Wagner, now Grey
Eagle, has the advantage.   It will be a dead heat !
" See !   Grey Eagle's got him ! "   " No, Wagner's

ahead!" A moment ensues—the people shout—
hearts throb—ladies faint—a thrill of emotion, and
the race is over! Wagner wins by a neck, in 7.44,
the best race ever ran south of the Potomac; while
Kentucky's gallant champion demonstrates his claim
to that proud title, by a performance which throws
into the shade the most brilliant ever made in his
native State.

Summary :

Monday, Sept. 30, 1839.—Sweepstakes for all ages, 3 yr. olds,
carrying 86 lbs.—4, 100—5, 110—6, 118—7 and upwards,
124 lbs.; mares and geldings allowed 3 lbs. Ten subscribers
at $2,000 each, h. ft., to which the proprietors added the
receipts of the stands. Four mile heats.

James S. Garrison's and John Campbell's ch. h. *Wagner,* by Sir
Charles, out of Maria West, by Marion, 5 yrs. Cato, 1—1
Oliver & Dickey's and A. L. Shotwell's gr. c. *Grey Eagle,* by
Woodpecker, out of Ophelia, by Wild Medley,
4 yrs. . . . . . . Stephen Welch, 2—2
Capt. Willa Viley's ch. f. *Queen Mary,* by Bertrand, dam by
Brimmer, 4 yrs. . . . . 3—3
Bradley & Steel's ch. c. *Hawk-Eye,* by Sir Lovell, out of Press-
ure's dam, by Jenkin's Sir William, 4 yrs. . . dist.
Time, 7.48—7.44.

To say that Wagner was better managed and better jockeyed in this race than Grey Eagle, is to express
the opinion of every unprejudiced individual who
had the pleasure of witnessing it. What might have
been the result of *the race,* we cannot pretend to say,
but we assert with perfect confidence our belief, that
with Gil. Patrick on his back, Grey Eagle would have

6

won the *second* heat. People differ in opinion, luckily, and were it not so, we should be in a mass. Had the managers of Grey Eagle been content to bide their time, another tale might have been told. "Wait and win" carries off more purses than "Take the track and keep it." Grey Eagle could out-foot Wagner in a brush of one hundred and fifty yards—he clearly demonstrated that fact half a dozen times in the course of the week; but in a run of five or six hundred yards, Wagner could beat him about the same distance. The two horses were so nearly matched, that good generalship and good riding did the business. Instead of allowing him to go forward and cut out the work, Grey Eagle should have been laid quietly behind, with a steady, bracing pull, until within the distance stand, and then pulled out, and made to win if he could. That was his only chance; tiring down Wagner is like tiring down a locomotive.

We must here break off, but not without remarking, that after being weighed, Cato was put again on Wagner, and with the stakes in his hand—$14,000!—he promenaded in front of the stand, preceded by a band of music, playing "Old Virginny never tire." In bringing our report of this memorable race to a conclusion, we must not neglect to record the gratifying fact, that notwithstanding the immense throng of spectators on the ground, and the peculiar excitement of the occasion, not a solitary circumstance occurred calculated for a moment to interrupt the harmony and general good feeling which prevailed on all hands.

We have not room to give the details of the running on the intermediate days of the meeting. Suffice it to say, that the fine Medoc filly Cub won the Post stake for 3 years olds, in 3.45½—3.44; that the woodpecker colt Ralph won the three-mile purse cleverly, in 5.50 each heat; that the Eclipse mare Missouri won the Oakland plate, two-mile heats, in 3.50—3.44 —3.50; and that several other exhibitions of beauty, game and speed were given during the week. The first race between Wagner and Grey Eagle came off on Monday; on Saturday they again came out for the Jockey Club purse of $1,500, four-mile heats. Throughout the week the weather had been delightful, and the attendance good enough to realize $15,000 to the spirited proprietor; but on this day there was an immense gathering from far and near, and the sun never shone out on a more lovely morning. The attraction, it must be confessed, could not have been surpassed — *Wagner and Grey Eagle were again to come together!* After their race on Monday, both parties immediately interested, were willing to draw off their forces, and enjoy an honorable armistice until next spring; but the interference and misrepresentation of sanguine friends ultimately broke off the truce existing between them, and the high contracting parties set about prosecuting the war with greater zeal and energy than ever. Some one wrote from Louisville, directly after the race, to the effect that Wagner had declined to meet Grey Eagle in a match for $10,000, four-mile heats; which letter made its appearance in the columns of a Lexington journal. This statement the friends of Grey Eagle did not deny, though it was made without their authority ; and in consequence Wagner was forced to notice it.   In an article " by authority," from the pen of a distinguished correspondent of the " Spirit of the Times," published in the " Louisville Journal " on the 5th October, the writer remarked to the following effect :

" *Wagner and Grey Eagle.*—The *reputation* of his horse is dear to a turf-man, and it is his duty to shield and defend it as he would his own honor. The contest between Wagner and Grey Eagle will long be remembered by those who witnessed it. Wagner's honors were nobly won ; he earned them in a field where every inch of ground was closely contested ; and any one who would attempt to pluck a laurel from his brow, by falsehood or misrepresentation, deserves the scorn of every honorable man.

" The writer of this has been induced to make these remarks, from the fact that a letter has been published in a Lexington paper, written from Louisville, containing a statement that Grey Eagle had challenged Wagner for $10,000, and the latter had declined the contest. This statement is positively *false*, and the owners of Grey Eagle will cheerfully bear testimony to the truth of the assertion. The facts of the case are these : Wagner had gained a victory over Grey Eagle—a victory in which even the defeated party gained the brightest laurels, and won for himself imperishable fame. Hence Wagner's friends prized his victory the more highly ; and, with that courtesy towards the friends of Grey Eagle which is ever due from the victor to the vanquished, they would have been willing to leave Kentucky, perfectly satis-fied with his performance. He is willing to run him against Grey Eagle, or any other horse in the United States, four-mile heats, for $10,000, or any amount above that sum. This offer is made with no disposition to detract from the reputation of the game and gallant Grey Eagle, but solely on account of justice to Wagner, who has been placed in a situation by *some of the friends* of Grey Eagle that leaves no alternative." .

The article just quoted made its appearance in the
" Journal " on the morning of the second race, which
we are about to describe ; but the friends of Grey Eagle
were prepared to see it. If we are not very much
mistaken, it was read to its owner, as it was to several
of his friends, two days before its publication, but
was delayed in the hope that Grey Eagle's friends
would contradict the statement alluded to. In the
mean time both horses were got in order, to make
another race. We saw both immediately after their
first race, and on the following morning ; both recovered well, and Grey Eagle especially so, exhibiting
very little stiffness or soreness. They improved from
that time up to Saturday morning, and we never saw
two high-mettled racers in finer condition than they
were when stripped to run their second race.

In anticipation of a race, which, for severity and interest, would throw the first into the shade, both parties
were wide awake to secure every honorable advantage
within their reach. Wagner's rider, Cato, had become
free about the time of the first race ; if he rode the
second as well as he did the first, many are the odd
twenties and fifties he was promised. Stephen Welch,
Grey Eagle's jockey in his first race, weighing but 82
pounds, the managers of the horse endeavored to find
a rider nearer up to his proper weight, 100 pounds.
The only one on the ground preferable to their own, was
Mr. McCargo's Archer, a very capital rider, with a
good seat, a steady hand and a cool head. Mr.
McCargo having no interest whatever in the race, at
once placed Archer's services at the disposal of Grey

Eagle's friends; but as his doing so might possibly place him in a position of great delicacy and embarrassment, at his own request they relieved him from it, and concluded to put up Stephen Welch again, whose only fault was that there was not enough of him!

After the race on Monday, the topic of conversation in every circle was the prospect of a second one between the rival champions. The Wagner party were not anxious for a race, but they would not avoid one; their horse had not only realized their expectations, but had exceeded their most sanguine hopes, and they were prepared to back him to "the size of their pile." And well did that noble son of a worthy sire justify the high opinion of his friends—a small circle, it is true, but they were staunch and firm; and when it came to "putting up the mopasses," there were enough of them to "suit customers," and no mistake! The friends of Grey Eagle had every reason to be proud of the first performance of their horse, and they were so. He was the first discoverer of "the Forties" in a four-mile race, ever bred in Kentucky, and he had explored the degrees of pace to the latitude of 44 below the equator! All this he had done as an untried four-year old, and if his friends backed him with less confidence now, it was on account of the severe race he had made five days previous. He was in fine health, and his look and action indicated all the spirit and courage of a game-cock, but it was thought physically impossible for him to make such another race as his first in the same week.

The betting consequently settled down at two and three
to one on Wagner.

It will naturally be supposed that the rumor of a
second four-mile race between these two cracks,
attracted an immense crowd of spectators. Many
persons came down from Cincinnati, while the citizens
of Lexington, Frankfort, Georgetown and the circle
of towns for fifty miles about Louisville, turned out
in great numbers. Again the city was crowded, and
on the morning of the race every carriage and horse in
town was in requisition. Many were glad to get out
to the course and call it " riding," when jolting along
in a bone-setter, compared with which riding on a
white-oak rail would be fun! Again the ladies turned
out *en masse*, to grace the scene with their radiant
beauty, and " lend enchantment to the view " of the
race—and of themselves.

The jockeys having received their instructions .
from the judges, " mounted in hot haste," Cato on
Wagner, and Stephen Welch on Grey Eagle. The
third entry was Messrs. Viley & Ward's Emily Johnson—own sister to Singleton, and half-sister to Mistle-
toe—a four-year old bay filly by Bertrand, out of
Black-eyed Susan. She was not in prime fit, and
could not, therefore, live in such a crowd.

THE RACE.

At the word " Go," Wagner went off with the
lead at about three parts speed, Emily lying second,
and all three under a strong pull. Grey Eagle's long,

steady stride, after getting into straight work going down the back stretch, soon brought him up with the field; and opposite the Oakland House—about 300 yards beyond the half-mile post—the three were lapped. The pace now improved; Grey Eagle drew out at the last turn, but Wagner having the inside, and beginning to get warm, made sharp running up the stretch to the stand, and on the next turn came out clear in front. Down the back stretch they each kept up a good racing stroke, but at the Oakland House, Grey Eagle increased his stride and locked Wagner; as neither was yet called upon, a very fair view was had of their relative rate of going; Grey Eagle led down to the head of the stretch and up to the stand by half a length, and immediately after came in front. He carried on the running two lengths in advance to near the termination of the mile, when Wagner got a hint to extend himself; without lapping him, Wagner waited upon him to close up, and opposite the Oakland House made his run; the rally that ensued was a very brilliant affair, but Grey Eagle out-footed him in one hundred yards, and drew out clear amidst tremendous cheers from all parts of the course. The instant Wagner declined, Emily took his place, lapping the Grey as they swung round the turn. But Wagner had yet another run left, and they had no sooner got into the quarter-stretch than Cato set to work with him. Grey Eagle had been able to pull to Emily, and accordingly, when Wagner by an extraordinary effort reached him half-way up the stretch, he was able to outfoot him a second time, and came

away home a gallant winner by nearly a length,
Emily having the second place, amidst the waving
of hats and handkerchiefs, and tumultuous cheers,
that would well-nigh have drowned the roar of Nia-
gara! The first mile was run in 2.05—the second in
1.55—the third in 1.56—the fourth in 1.55; making
the time of the heat 7.51.

The heartfelt gratification and rapture exhibited
at the close of the heat by the assembled thousands,
know no bounds. Kentucky's most distinguished
sons, and her loveliest daughters, felt alike interested,
and Grey Eagle's success was enjoyed as if each was
personally concerned. The odds, from being two and
three to one in favor of Wagner, now changed, and
Grey Eagle had the call at four to three. Considerable sums were staked, as Garrison declared "the old
sorrel stud" had sulked, but would show his hand
the next heat. The fact was, Grey Eagle for the
first time had been properly managed; instead of
running the whole last half-mile, he had taken advantage of the ground, and made his first run down
the descent from the Oakland House to the head of
the stretch, and then being braced up for three hundred yards, which allowed him time to recover his
wind, he was able to come again and make a second
rally, as brilliant as the first. As we before remarked, we think Wagner could beat Grey Eagle by
a desperate rush for six hundred yards at the heel of
a very fast heat, but not over a head and shoulders at
that; while Grey Eagle had so much more speed,
that in a brush of one hundred and fifty yards he

6*

could let in the daylight between them. With so light and feeble a rider as Stephen on his back, it was impossible to place Grey Eagle exactly as his managers would have liked, though he is a fine-tempered horse, and runs kindly; the result of the race, we trust, will be a caution to them hereafter, how they venture in a race of so much importance without providing that most indispensable of requisites to success —a suitable jockey. Both horses perspired freely, and in much less time than could have been expected they cooled out finely; neither hung out a signal of distress, but came up for the second heat with distended nostrils and eyes of fire, betokening the most unflinching courage. At the tap of the drum the horses were hardly in motion, and Cato drew his whip on Wagner the very first jump. The pace was little better than a hand-gallop for the first half-mile, but as Wagner led past the entrance-gate, Gooding bid him "go along," and he increased his rate. Stephen seeing this, let the gray out a link, and in going down the descending ground below the Oakland House, went up on the inside so suddenly, that he had locked Wagner before Cato was aware of his close proximity. The run up the quarter-stretch was a pretty fast thing, though neither was doing his best; the time of the mile was 2.08. The crowd cheered them as they ran lapped past the stand, at which Grey Eagle pricked up his ears and set to work in earnest, shaking off Wagner at the next turn. The race had now commenced; Stephen braced his horse as well as he was able, and kept him up to his rate down the entire length of the back stretch. At the Oakland House Cato again called on Wagner, and steel and catgut came into play. The gallant gray led clear to the turn, and half-way up the stretch, Stephen beginning to use his whip-hand, and to give the nonpareil under him an occasional eye-opener with the spur. This mile was run in 1.52. They passed the stand neck and neck, Emily being already nearly out of her distance. From the stand to the first turn the ground is descending, and here almost invariably Grey Eagle gained upon Wagner, who kept up one steady stride from end to end, without flinching or faltering, and able always to do *a little more* when persuaded by the cold steel with which Cato plied him ever and anon throughout the heat. We said they passed the stand on the second mile neck and neck ; when they reached the turn Grey Eagle had got in front, but no sooner had they come into straight work on the back side, than Wagner made a most determined challenge and locked him ; the contest was splendid, and was maintained with unflinching game and spirit ; at the end of 700 yards, however, Grey Eagle had the best of it, for in spite of Cato's most desperate efforts Wagner could only reach Stephen's knee ; Grey Eagle seemed able, after a brush of one hundred yards, to come again with renewed vigor ; if well braced, for a dozen strides. Down the descent, on the last half-mile, Grey Eagle maintained his advantage, but on descending towards the stand Wagner's strength told, and they came through under whip and spur, Wagner having his head and neck in front, running this mile in 1.55. Stephen was here instructed to take a strong pull on his horse, and to "*keep him moving*," while "*ram the spurs into him*," were the orders to Cato. The result was that Wagner came in front, and the pace down the entire back stretch was tremendous, both being kept up to their rate by the most terrible punishment. Unfortunately, Stephen was directed to "*take the track*" about opposite the Oakland House, instead of putting the issue on a brush up the last 200 yards of the heat. Too soon the gallant Grey was called upon, but true as steel the noble animal responded to it. With the most dauntless courage he made his run down the descending ground, and though Wagner, like the bravest of the brave, as he is, made the most desperate efforts, Grey Eagle came round the last turn on the outside, with his head and shoulders in front, at a flight of speed we never saw equalled. Both jockeys were nearly faint with their exertions, and Stephen, poor fellow, lost his presence of mind. Up to the distance stand it was impossible to say which was ahead; whips and spurs had been in constant requisition the entire mile, but at this moment Stephen gave up his pull, and unconsciously yawed the horse across the track, which broke him off his stride, while Cato, holding Wagner well together, and mercilessly dashing in his spurs, at length brought him through, a gallant winner by a neck, having run the last mile in 1.48, and the heat in 7.43!

This was, without exception, the most game and spirited race we ever witnessed. The heat was Wagner's, and while we accord to him all the reputation so brilliantly won after a bloody struggle of nearly three miles, we feel bound to express the belief, that for an untried four-year-old, Grey Eagle's performance is without a parallel in the annals of the American Turf! The last three miles of a second heat, in a second four-mile race the same week, were run in 5.35, and the eighth mile in 1.48!

The enthusiasm of the spectators was now excited to the highest pitch. There was not on the ground, probably, an individual who would not have been pleased to see the horses withdrawn, and the purses divided between them, rather than farther task the indomitable game and courage of these noble animals; but no such proposition was made, and after the usual respite they were brought to the post a third time, and it would have been difficult to decide which had recovered best. So much feeling was manifested in reference to the horses, that the baser impulses to bet on the result of the concluding heat were almost entirely disregarded; odds, however, were in a few instances offered on Wagner. In detailing the contest for the third heat, we are compelled to record

"A few of the unpleasantest words
That e'er man writ on paper!"

At the word "*go*," they broke off with a racing stride, Wagner taking the lead by about two lengths; the pace was moderate, for Stephen on Grey Eagle was expressly charged to pull him steady, and wait for orders. Wagner accordingly led with an easy

stroke through the first mile, and being cheered as
he passed the stand, he widened the gap soon after to
four or five lengths. At the half-mile post Grey
Eagle made play, and had nearly closed the gap as
they came opposite the Oakland House, when he suddenly faltered as if shot, and after limping a step or
two, abruptly stopped! "*Grey Eagle has let down!*"
was the cry on all hands, and when the spectators
became aware of the truth of the painful announcement, the tearful eyes of a radiant host of Kentucky's
daughters, and the heartfelt sorrow depicted in the
countenance of her sons, indicated the sincerity of
the sympathy with which they regarded the untimely
accident to their game and gallant champion! It was
supposed, on a hasty examination, that Grey Eagle
had given way in the back sinews of his left fore
leg, but it has since been ascertained that the injury was in the coffin joint. Mr. Burbridge on the
instant tightly bandaged the leg with a stout strip of
dry canvas, which being kept wet, would have prevented the horse from coming down on his pastern
joints, even had his leaders given way. A fortnight
after the race the horse promised to recover perfectly;
Mr. Shotwell informed us that the ankle and joint
were a little swollen, but neither the horse's pastern
nor cannon bones were affected, and his leaders were
as stout as ever. We need not add, that, while his
owners and managers have the cordial sympathy
of their friends, and the Sporting World generally,
there is no one "with soul so dead" as to with-
hold the expression of their admiration of the gal-

lant gray, and their heartiest wishes for his speedy recovery.

Soon after Grey Eagle was stopped, Cato pulled Wagner out of his stride, and galloped him slowly round. The intelligence of the high-mettled racer was clearly indicated by Wagner's subsequent action; from the head of the stretch home he invariably went at a racing pace, and appeared as if he did not know what was required of him, frequently bursting off in spite of his rider. On the fourth mile, as he passed his own stable, the rubbers and riders standing on its roof gave him a hearty cheer, and the gallant horse broke off, and in spite of Cato's utmost exertions, ran at the very top of his speed for nearly 500 yards, as if plied with steel and whalebone the whole way! We never saw a more magnificent exhibition of unflinching game; even the friends of Grey Eagle forgot their distress for a moment, in doing justice by a cheer to the gallant and victorious champion of Louisiana!

RECAPITULATION:

Saturday, Oct. 5.—Jockey Club purse, $1,500, conditions as before, four-mile heats. James S. Garrison's and John Campbell's ch. h. *Wagner*, by Sir Charles, out of Maria West, by Marion, 5 yrs. . . . . . . Cato, 3—1—1
A. L. Shotwell's gr. c. *Grey Eagle*, by Woodpecker, out of Ophelia, by Wild Medley, 4 yrs. Stephen Welch, 1—2 *
Willa Viley's b. f. *Emily Johnson*, own sister to Singleton, by Bertrand, out of Black-eyed Susan, by Tiger, 4 yrs. 2 dist.
Time, 7.51—7.43—third heat, no time kept.

* Grey Eagle gave way in second mile.

For more convenient reference, we repeat the time of each mile in tabular form :

First Heat.		Second Heat.		Third Heat.
1st mile . . . 2.05		1st mile . . . 2.08		No time kept, as Grey
2d " . . . 1.55		2d " . . . 1.52		Eagle gave way in run-
3d " . . . 1.56		3d " . . . 1.55		ning the second mile.
4th " . . . 1.55		4th " . . . 1.48		
7.51		7.43		

American Turf Register, vol ii., p. 119.

CHAPTER VI.

In the month of October, 1840, the editor writes :

"During the whole of the last three years, the high rate of exchange, and the deranged condition of commercial affairs throughout the country, have rendered a continual struggle against the evils that followed in their train absolutely essential to the maintenance of our position, and have forced us to the most disagreeable and ruinous expedients. Like others, we flattered ourselves, from month to month, and from year to year, that a transition to better times could not be far distant, and we determined to defer yet a little longer the earnest appeal which we must now make to the sense of justice of every subscriber to either of our publications. The prompt payment of whatever sums which may be due to us, is the only means by which we can hope to sustain ourselves as proprietors of periodicals not entirely unworthy the countenance and support of the sporting world, as the sole accredited organs and official records of whatever pertains to the American Turf."

Another, and a vexatious annoyance, induced the editor to appeal to the "felons" who had deprived him, at one fell swoop, of new and valuable music, and an opera-glass :

" We live," said he, " in a musical age and in a musical country ; but that is not a good reason (though perhaps a rational one as times go) that there should be a community in musical property. Yet such a phase of agrarianism has certainly presented itself within these few days before our lamenting eyes. And now *experientia docet* what we had been before taught theoretically to believe—videlicet : Abstracting opera-glasses is a custom, which, as ' *Soft Recorders* ' have said or sung, ' is practised to a great extent in this country ! ' "

While Mr. Porter was at the South, the sad intelligence reached him of the death of his brother Benjamin, on the 11th of December, 1840, by pulmonary consumption.   He was designed for college, but preferred the stirring activity of mercantile pursuits, and while preparing for his chosen walk in life, was a member of the family of Hon. George Blake, of Boston, then United States Attorney for the District of Massachusetts.   Not long after commencing business, in Mobile, Ala., he married Rebecca Seton Maitland, of New York, a ward of the Rt. Rev. Bishop Hobart. He had clear perceptions, cool judgment, remarkable shrewdness, and was stamped with more than ordinary mental vigor.   In the words of Horace Greeley to the writer, " he was a strong character," but wanting that stimulus to exertion which the pursuit of a competency keeps alive and effective ; his really remarkable capabilities were never fully developed. Happy are they whose circumstances are the spur to

useful and generous toil, be it mental or bodily; so
that " the Spring and Summer of life may be preparatory to the harvest of Autumn, and the repose of
winter."

On his return to New York in 1841, from the
South and West, Mr. Porter thus playfully alludes to
the overwhelming load of commissions for Southern
and Western friends that required his first attention
upon getting home:

" Every nook and corner of the office we find filled with
letters and communications, and we have commissions enough to
employ seven men and a boy for a fortnight. All sorts of 'fixins'
are wanted from blood horses to copper coal scuttles—from long-
tailed sows and short-legged pigs, to jockey spurs and patent
lightning-rods. One gentleman alone wants a 3-year-old Bare-
foot colt, a gardener, a trotting stallion, a 3-year-old jockey, a
Durham bull, a trainer and a mousetrap! Nothing, however,
gives us more pleasure than to have it in our power to oblige our
friends; and as we are in want of all sorts of truck, persons would
do well to make known at this office if they have ' on sale or to
let ' either setters or saddles, chestnut horses or horse chestnuts,
rifles or radish-seed, fighting cocks or patent axle-trees, frogs
for frying or tragedians for dying, wet nurses or salmon flies,
Muscovy hens or pointers, pullets, Chifney bits, or Smith's Lay
Sermons, indelible ink or Ely's wire cartridges, camp meeting
hymn books or Conroy's best trout rods, three-year-old fillies or
presents for New Year's, Bowie knives or Nicholas Nickleby, the
last ladies' fashions or songs of Jim Crow, old files of the ' Spirit '
or the latest new caricatures, tandem whips or country-house
almanacs, racing plates or French mustard, patent side-saddles or
ivory toddy-sticks, timing watches or Troy-built coaches. We
cannot begin to think of half the things that are marked down in
our memorandum-book, under the general head of ' *wants*,'
though several leaves might be filled up with *our own* under the
head of ' New Subscribers,' and ' Available funds.'"

In the number for March 27, 1841, may be found that most admirable sketch of backwoods life, the "*Big Bear of Arkansas*," which was expressly written for the paper, by the author of "Tom Owen the Bee Hunter," Col. T. B. Thorpe, who, now in the mutation of all sublunary things, is no longer a resident of Louisiana, but of New York, and a successor to his old friend and patron, as one of the editors and proprietors of the very paper which, nearly a score of years ago, was enriched by his graphic delineations and quiet humor.

While in New Orleans, Mr. Porter witnessed the race between Sarah Bladen and Luda, which was won by the former in 7.45—7.40 ; and which he pronounced at the time to be the best race ever run south of the Potomac ; a few weeks afterwards he wrote to the ' Spirit ' :

"I have now to write that on this, the 20th day of March, I have seen a race which throws the one referred to, comparatively in the shade. Rely upon it *Grey Medoc's* race to-day, is *the best race ever run in America !* I have witnessed nearly all the great performances on the Turf for several years past, but I have never seen a race more desperately contested, or more gallantly won. Even the beaten horses have acquired a reputation which a succession of bloodless victories would not have won for them. I doubt if it will ever be my good fortune to see such another performance, and much do I regret that want of ability not less than leisure, prevents my doing justice to a race that will occupy the most distinguished place in the racing calendar, and go down through all time as one of the most magnificent exhibitions on record of the surpassing speed and game of the High Mettled Racer of America. It was a four-mile race over the Louisiana

Course, (*over a mile in length*,) won by *Grey Medoc*. Beating *Altorf* and *Denizen*. Time: 7.35—8.19—7.42—8.17."

The paper of June 5 contains several columns of interesting matter, written by the editor while in Kentucky; we can spare room but for a single paragraph:

"Since my arrival in Kentucky, I think I must have seen from one to two thousand thorough-bred colts! I have tramped miles upon miles through the magnificent woodland pastures, admiring the different varieties of the ' long' and ' short' horned cattle, and the cattle with no horns at all, and have come to think no small beer of myself as a judge of long-tailed pigs and flat-tailed sheep. I do not ' cotton' to mules, though I saw four driven up to the door of the Galt House this morning, (May 27th,) hitched to the mail stage between this city (Louisville) and Nashville; they run out and into town daily, making sixteen miles, and trot eight miles an hour, the driver tells me. But as for the ' splendid Jacks' you hear so much of, they can give odds to any thing wearing hair for ugliness; if Balaam's ass was such a fright as some I've seen here, it is not so surprising that he spoke; each particular bone and hair in his skin must have ached!"

In the ' Spirit" of Nov. 13, the editor thus chronicles the return of his friend Robert L. Stevens, from Europe, after an absence of a few months:

" ' Stephens' Travels in South America' is the most popular book of the season, but it would be so no longer if our neighbor Mr. Stevens, of Barclay Street, would ' witch the world' with an account of the thousand and one rare things he has seen and heard, men and women, too, inclusive, during his tour of some ten thousand miles or more. He heard Rubini and Lablache,

and saw *Coronation* win the Derby. He has seen Glaucus and
Louis Philippe, the Royal Yacht Club, and the Alps. He saw
much of Hamburg, but a good deal more of humbug. He visited
the most celebrated breeding studs in England, and the veritable
Maria Farina at Cologne. He saw Taglione in the Beyadere,
and the National Column at the Place Vendome. He visited
Tattersall's at ——, and the Emperor at Vienna ; raised his hat
to the Pope in Rome, and to the Queen of Beauty in Buckingham
Palace. He has ridden in the diligence at Calais, and the pony
phæton at Windsor. Has talked horse with Prince Albert, and
soft nonsense with Rachel. The doors of science, genius and
fashion were thrown open to him, and the Marquis of Waterford
wrenched off the knocker of his lodgings. He visited the 'Curiosity Shop' with the *Boss*, ('Boz,') and thought of 'Old Nap' and
Boston on the field of Waterloo. He achieved the dinners at
Milan while he abominated the *chops* of the Channel. He saw
Deaf Burke set-to in London, and set to Isabey himself in Paris.
Brougham he thought had a very queer handle, (who *nose?*) and he
saw all the world in Hyde Park. He found Compte d'Orsay's tiger
quite tame, and thought Mrs. Norton very like an 'undying one;'
He heard her new comedy, and Soult rehearse his old campaigns.
He saw Byron's Chateau near Genoa, and Harkaway's stables at
the ——. He walked through the Tunnel and the Louvre, over
the Vatican and Epsom Downs. He saw the sausage makers at
Boulogne, and the sausage eaters at Berlin. He 'took a private
drink' with Metternich at Johannisberg, and 'pot luck' with
the Duke at Apsley House. He saw Jem Ward and Mme. Laf-
farge ; the Duc d'Orleans and Mrs. Trollope ; the Tower and the
guillotine ; Crockford's Club and the Palais Royal ; the house
that Jack built and Westminster Abbey. He—but we must
stop short."

In 1842 a change took place in the proprietorship
of the paper, which resulted from a variety of circumstances. The management of all its departments,
fiscal and literary, in the hard times then weighing

down the community, was too great a tax on the
energies of any one person; while the ruinous dis-
count upon Western and Southern bank notes, added
to the depressed state of the country, and the back-
wardness of subscribers to liquidate their accounts,
(the amount then due to the office being more than
forty thousand dollars,) rendered it impossible longer
to carry on the war under such adverse circumstances.
To perfect some proposed improvements in the paper,
and to relieve the editor of a portion of the arduous
and responsible duties which had hitherto devolved
upon him, the *business* of the office was placed in the
hands of Mr. John Richards, a printer by profession,
and who, up to the last week of his life in February,
1859, gave strict attention to its various details. The
writer was acquainted with Mr. Richards for years
before the sale of the paper to him, and met him at
the " Spirit " office only a few days before his unexpected death; during all that time, he ever found
" The Governor " an honest, reliable and independent
man.

In April, Mr. Porter published a very thorough
and well-considered article called " Profit and Loss
Account " of the " Spirit," a part of which we insert.
After alluding to the perplexities of some of the previous years, he pertinently asks:

" What has been effected by all this labor of years, followed
up under such discouragement and annoyances; what has the
' Spirit of the Times ' done for the Turf or the Sporting World?
To this we proceed to answer:

" IT HAS ADDED THIRTY PER CENT. TO THE VALUE OF BLOOD

STOCK *throughout the United States!* In this we are borne out
not alone by our own observation, but by the testimony of the
most sagacious Turfmen in the country, and the most extensive
Breeders. Nor in the universal decline of prices consequent
upon the disordered currency of the last few years, has the price
of Blood Stock fallen so rapidly or so low as other descriptions
of property. This paper was the first that ever paid Travelling
Correspondents, by which the earliest and most important Sporting Intelligence was procured and disseminated, and by which a
system of Correspondence was established through which events
of interest transpiring hundreds of miles distant have been communicated and published in its columns at a date as early in
many cases as in the local newspapers. The utmost efforts were
requisite and immense expense was involved for several years
before it was possible to effect this consummation. In its early
career, too, the 'Spirit' had to contend with many formidable
rivals, which one by one either broke down or were withdrawn.

"The salutary effects of reporting *every race in the Union and
in Canada,* and the principal ones in Great Britain, are manifest
in the increased degree of good feeling and intimacy existing
between the Turfmen and Breeders of the different States—in the
promotion of the sales of horses, in the Importation of choice
Blood from abroad, and in the encouragement of the best of our
Native Bred Stock. And no sensible person can doubt that
hundreds of individuals have been induced, by reading of the
success of others, to invest large sums in Stock, and enter exten-
sively both upon Breeding and Racing—than which no investment can be more honorable, or more advantageous to the
Agricultural Interests of the country. Thousands have borne
testimony, and will yet do so, with what zeal this department of
the paper has been conducted, and how beneficial an influence it
has exerted upon their individual revenues. How many young
Trainers have we brought into notice, and inspirited to become
useful and respectable members of society; and how many
jockeys have been convinced that 'honesty is the best policy,'
from seeing their names in print, accompanied by a gratifying
remark! How many gentlemen about to decline the Turf have

been induced to persevere from reading of brilliant stakes and high prices paid for horses ; and how many sales of stock have been effected by making breeders and turfmen better acquainted with each other ! Of our friends and acquaintances, not a few are indebted to us, possibly unknowingly, for interposing a shield between them and detraction. Many have we served, and in their time of need. And how many have we rendered prominent and popular, whose modest, sterling worth, would otherwise have been unknown beyond their own neighborhoods? Others there are whose interests are watched over with as keen an eye as our own ; and there are many whom we have disenthralled from deep-rooted prejudices and absurd misapprehensions ; and many whom we have cheered on and supported in *the good cause* by a timely suggestion, a favorable notice, and an appeal to their pride, or by prudential advice. Nor may we altogether omit to mention that we have been in the constant habit for years, of executing commissions of all descriptions for our sporting subscribers, whether acquaintances or not, without any charge whatever, though frequently thereby subjected to serious inconvenience and expense. The person obliged being a SUBSCRIBER, we have performed whatever labor of love was required with the most cheerful readiness.

" Nor do our claims on the Sportsmen of the United States stop here. We claim to have elevated the character of the pursuits of the Turf to a pitch they had never before reached in public estimation on this side the Atlantic. When this journal was commenced, the strongest prejudice existed, especially at the North, towards Racing and Racing men. This prejudice had been lineally transmitted from the Puritans of New England, who, carrying to an extreme their hatred of the civil and religious principles of the Cavaliers, involved in a sweeping and indiscriminate censure the excessive loyalty, the haughty assumption, and the religious intolerance which distinguished the aristocratic party, with the gallantry, the courtesy, and love of manly amusements, which rendered the exercise of their power at least graceful and elegant. We have cautiously eschewed sympathy with such English amusements as are deemed brutal and gross in either

7

country, and as sedulously exhibited the fairer side of the picture, recording the proceedings on the Turf and in the Field of the legitimate ' Old English Sportsmen '—a class of gentlemen composed of the proudest, most enlightened, and most refined of the nobility and gentry of Great Britain. Holding up so constantly the example of the best blood of the old country, we have likewise made the public at large more intimately acquainted with the high character and social position of our Turfmen, till the prejudice which once universally here prevailed towards a ' horse-racer,' has become extinct, save in the breasts of those who equally condemn the most tasteful and delightful recreations of society.

"To effect our purpose, unwearied pains have been employed to give the ' Spirit of the Times ' some portion of Literary reputation, and we have great satisfaction in recording that we have upon our list many subscribers utterly indifferent to the sporting department of the paper, but who have taken it from first to last because they have approved the spirit in which we have culled for them from the Periodical Literature of England. And again, we have aimed still further to advance our primary design, by associating with Field Sports and Pastimes the pleasures of the Stage. A due share of room has ever been devoted to the subject, the most disinterested support has been given to managers and actors worthy of support ; a complete record has been kept of the current productions of the day, whether in Music, the Drama, or the Ballet, and we have faithfully chronicled the movements of the ' professionals ' in each art, their triumphs, and their reverses. This we have done with no expectation or hope of emolument from this class—their patronage, all told, never has repaid a tithe of the expense and trouble it has cost— but with the double intent of making the contents of the ' Spirit ' more various, and upholding in an accredited organ the pleasures of the Turf and the Stage, as these pleasures are *in fact* found associated in the minds of all true American Sportsmen.

"To the Agriculturists of the West, too, we have endeavored to make our journal acceptable by seasonable extracts from the Agricultural writers of Great Britain, where the science has reached nearest perfection. Considerable space has been given to original and selected hints upon the improvement of the Domestic Stock of the country ; and the enterprising, and in a national point of view, most deserving, importer and breeder of Cattle, and Sheep, and Swine, has been encouraged and assisted in the profitable disposition of his stock, by editorial comment, and private individual exertion.

"In fine, while we have made ours most emphatically a SPORTING PAPER, and as such, a paper accredited for accuracy, for fulness and impartiality, it has been our constant aim to elevate its character by associating with this peculiar feature the charms of Polite Letters, and the delights of Music and the Theatre ; to elevate in popular estimation the *true* position of our Turfmen, to commend their elegant hospitality and tastes, their devotion not alone to the Manly Diversions of the Field, but their warm sympathy with the Arts, by which Social Life is adorned.

"Measurably, we have succeeded in our purpose ; the character of the Turf has been redeemed at the North, and the standing of its devotees made familiar among gentlemen, not alone here, but in England. 'Tis but a short time since that in England the impression was universal that the only American sport was Trotting—our best thorough-bred but a three-minute roadster, and our proudest sportsman but a wily jockey of some ' fast crab.' Those days are gone. Our Turfmen are now known at ' the Corner,' to those best worth knowing ; our great races are reported in English newspapers; the merits of our ' cracks ' are understood, and the pages of their elegant magazines are adorned with portraits of Boston and Fashion, and costly illustrations of many capital articles contributed originally to these columns. Henceforth the United States will be regarded as the only nation that can compete with them in bringing to perfection the Blood Horse, and in carrying out a thorough and business-like system of Racing, by which alone all improvements must be tested. Throughout Great Britain, indeed wherever the English language is spoken, the ' Spirit of the Times ' is known as the ' Bell's Life ' of the New World—the organ of the American Sporting World. Through this medium the fame of our Horses and the spirit of our Turfmen are known not only throughout Europe, but in the Indies, West and East. The breeders of France and Germany, the best continental customers of England, are already turning their eyes to the United States, as likely to become at no distant day, the 'Race Horse Region' from whence their importations are to be made. Our system of racing—'long distances and heats to boot'—is eminently popular out of England, while even there many of the most sensible writers and speakers [*vide* Sir Francis Burdett's Speech upon the sale of His late Majesty's Stud] view with concern and regret the present British system of racing, which is calculated to deteriorate the old-fashioned, hard-bottomed stock of the English Race Horse—to produce speed at the expense of game and stoutness—to beget a breed of quarter horses instead of four milers,—the King's Platers of a former era. The 'Spirit,' too, has made the Turfmen of Europe familiar with the names of the Corinthian columns of the American Turf. Our HAMPTONS, our STEVENSES, our KENNERS, and our STOCKTONS, are known throughout the world like the PORTLANDS, the CLEVELANDS, and the BENTINCKS of England. The LIVINGSTONS and JOHNSONS of the New World are as eminently conspicuous as the CHESTERFIELDS and GROSVENORS of the Old.

"We approach now the last and most miserable topic in this long article. After having thus devoted ten of the best years of our life, with all the means, the influence, the industry, and the ability we could command, we have realized—what? Why *on paper*, quite a snug little property, but, in truth, not the first red cent! With nearly Fifty Thousand Dollars due it, this journal passed from ours into other hands, for an amount which would not command a moderate race-horse! What have we gained, then, beyond the ephemeral reputation of a newspaper writer? This, to be sure, is flattering enough to our vanity, but will it make the 'pot boil'? With the same reputation, enterprise, means, and perseverance, ought we not to have insured

—' that which should accompany old age,
As honor, love, obedience, troops of friends?'

We are not prepared to estimate the value of editorial popularity, nor the worth of the good opinion of the Sporting World, but we are almost tempted to say from *present indications upon which we shall shortly dwell*, that had we the past ten years of our life to live over again, and were offered the wages of a journeyman wood-sawyer, we should certainly *hesitate* before giving up the ' wages ' for the ' popularity '—the *saw* horse for the *race* horse.

" It is true that we have acquired a fund of knowledge and great experience, but that we can ever make them available is yet to be seen. We have won in high places the consideration of those whose mere passing acquaintance is a passport to general favor. ' Praise from Sir Hubert Stanley is praise indeed ! ' and we have received it spontaneously at the hands of thousands. Many, very many stanch friends have we made, and thousands of most desirable acquaintances. Of the former, several ' whose evil stars have linked them with us,' have a claim upon our never-ceasing gratitude and regard, which is inscribed in our heart of hearts. The consideration which most embitters our regret for past misfortunes, is, that we have involved some of them in our own losses, and those friends the most disinterested and generous.

" But we do by no means yet ' give up the ship.' With our habits of application, experience in the profession we have chosen, and claims upon the good wishes of the racing community, joined to good health, economy, and the energy of one determined to succeed, and not too old to grapple with the great world, it will be singular indeed if we are not able at no very distant day to stand upon our legs again, free from obligations of every description."

CHAPTER VII.

THE great sectional match for $20,000 a side, four-mile heats, between the North and the South, came off on Tuesday last, the 10th inst. Since the memorable contest between *Eclipse* and *Henry*, on the 27th of May, 1823, no race has excited so much interest and enthusiasm. It attracted hundreds of individuals from the remotest sections of the Union, and for months has been the theme of remark and speculation, not only in the sporting circles of this country, but in England, where the success of the northern champion was predicted. It was a most thrilling and exciting race—one which throws in the shade the most celebrated of those wonderful achievements which have conferred so much distinction upon the high-mettled racers of America !

In the early part of the year 1842, the *annus mirabilis* of Turfmen, came off the great race between *Boston* and *Fashion*. It was a match between the North and the South. Col. William R. Johnson, of Virginia, challenged in the newspapers the whole world to run against his horse *Boston*, and gave a special challenge to William Gibbons, Esq., of New Jersey, to run for $20,000 a side. The latter was not in the habit of betting, and gave the use of his mare *Fashion* to some of his friends, who made up the money and accepted the challenge. The subjoined article by Mr. Porter, in regard to the challenge and the pedigrees and performances of the two horses, will be a fit and valuable introduction to his subsequent and spirited report of the race itself:

The following letter containing the acceptance of Boston's challenge to Fashion has been communicated exclusively to the " Spirit of the Times," by the gentleman who made the match on behalf of the friends of Fashion:

NEW YORK, *November* 30, 1841.

WILLIAM R. JOHNSON, Esq. : *Dear Sir,*—The challenge from yourself and Mr. JAMES LONG, to run *Boston* against *Fashion,* Four-mile heats, over the Union Course, L. I., agreeable to the rules of the Course, in Spring 1842, or any day during the month of May, for $20,000 a side, (New York money,) one-half, or one-fourth forfeit, as may be agreeable to the friends of Fashion—is accepted by me on their behalf. I name the second Tuesday in May, (the 10th,) 1842, as the day of the race; and $5,000 (or one-fourth) as the amount of forfeit, which sum has been placed in the hands of J. PRESCOTT HALL, Esq., President of the New York Jockey Club. The same amount being received by him from you, the whole forfeit ($10,000) will be deposited by him in one of the city banks. Yours most respectfully, T.

The acceptance above was mailed on Tuesday last, the 30th ult., being the last day of November, according to the terms of the challenge, and the forfeit on each side has since been deposited in one of the city banks. As the match will be a general topic of discussion during the winter throughout the country, we have thought the sporting world would be obliged to us for an authentic statement of the several performances of the two horses, with a brief account of their characteristics, etc. With this view we have compiled with the utmost care the following brief memoirs :

BOSTON'S PEDIGREE, CHARACTERISTICS, AND PERFORMANCES.

Boston was bred by the late John Wickham, Esq., of Richmond, Va., the eminent jurisconsult, and was foaled in Henrico County, in 1833. He was got by the celebrated *Timoleon* out of Robin Brown's dam (an own sister to *Tuckahoe*, also bred by Mr. W.) by Ball's *Florizel*, her dam by Imp. Alderman, out of a mare by Imp. *Clockfast*—her grandam by Symmes' *Wildair*, etc. [For a detailed memoir, and a portrait of *Boston*, see the "Spirit of the Times," of March 7th, 1840.] *Boston* was sold by Mr. Wickham, in his two-year-old form to Mr. Nathaniel Rives, of Richmond, Va., for $800, and was trained in 1836–'7 by Capt. John Belcher, who had charge of one "cavalry corps" from Col. Johnson's stable, while Arthur Taylor had another. Cornelius, a colored lad, was *Boston's* jockey up to 27th April, 1839. Ever since the spring campaign of 1838, *Boston* has been trained by Arthur Taylor and ridden by Gil Patrick, until this spring when Craig took Gil's place, the latter having gone to Kentucky to ride several important races, all of which he won. In May, 1839, after the first heat of his race against *Decatur* and *Vashti*, *Boston* was sold to Mr. James Long, of Washington City, for $12,000 and half of the purse, and he is still owned by Mr. L. and Col. Wm. R. Johnson, of Petersburg, Va.

Boston is a chestnut, with white stockings on both hind feet, and a white stripe down the face. In other respects than color and marks, *Boston* closely resembles the British phenomenon, *Harkaway*. They have alike prodigious depth of chest, and immensely powerful loins, thighs, and hocks. *Boston* is a trifle only above 15½ hands high, under the standard, but to the eye seems taller, owing to his immense substance; he is a short-limbed horse, with a barrel rather flat, or " slab-sided " than round, and well-ribbed home, while his back is a prodigy of strength ; ten pounds extra weight would hardly " set him back any." Though he has occasionally sulked, *Boston* runs on his courage, and is never ridden with spurs. He is no beauty, his neck and head being unsightly, while his hips are ragged, rendering him " a rum 'un to look at ;" that he is " a good 'un to go," however, we imagine will be *generally* conceded after reading the annexed recapitulation of

HIS PERFORMANCES.

1836.

April 20, Broad Rock, Va...Sweepstakes...Mile heats....lost $
Boston 8 years old, bolted in the 1st heat, when running ahead.

7*

Oct. 12, Petersburg, Va.....Purse........2 mile heats..won $300
  Beating N. Biddle, Mary Archie, Juliana, John Floyd, and ch. f.
  by Henry.

Nov. 3, Hanover C. H., Va..Purse........3 mile heats..won 400
  Beating Betsey Minge, Upton Heath, Nick Biddle, Alp. Bayard,
  and a Gohanna filly.

1837.

May 4, Washington City....Purse........3 mile heats..won 500
  Beating Norwood, Mary Selden, Meteor, Lydia, bro. to Virginia
  Graves.

Oct. 5, Washington City....Purse........3 mile heats..won 500
  Beating Prince George, Stockton, Mary Selden, Virginia Graves,
  Caroline Snowden, and Leesburg, in 5.50—5.52.

Oct. 19, Baltimore, Md......Purse........3 mile heats..won 500
  Beating Camsidel, Cippus, and Red Rat, in 5.51—6.08.

Oct. 25, Camden, N. J......Purse........3 mile heats..won 500
  Beating Betsey Andrew and Tipton, in 5.51—6.02.

1838.

May 3, Union Course, L. I..Purse........3 mile heats..won 500
  Boston, now 5 years old, walked over.

May 18, Beacon Course, N. J.Purse........4 mile heats..won 1,000
  Beating Dosoris, without extending himself.

May 25, Camden, N. J......Purse.........4 mile heats..won 1,000
  Beating Decatur, who had just distanced Fanny Wyatt, in a
  match for $10,000, in 7.45, at Washington.

June 1, Union Course, L. I..Purse....... 4 mile heats..won 1,000
  Beating Charles Carter, who broke down, in 7.40—the first three
  miles run in 5:36½ !!!

June 8, Beacon Course, N. J.Purse........4 mile heats..won 1,000
  Beating Duane, who won the 1st heat in 7.52—7.54—8.30. B.
  Sulked.

Oct. 4, Petersburg, Va......Purse.... ...4 mile heats..won 700
  Beating Polly Green in a canter.

Oct. 13, Baltimore, Md.....Purse........4 mile heats..won 700
  Beating Balie Peyton, who had won a heat from Duane in 7.42.

Oct. 19, Baltimore, Md......Purse........4 mile heats..rec. 500
  Boston was paid $500 out of the purse not to start.

Oct. 27, Camden, N. J......Purse........4 mile heats..rec. $500
Boston was paid $500 out of the purse not to start.

Nov. 2, Union Course, L. I..Purse........4 mile heats..won   1,000
Beating Decatur with ease in 8.00—7.57½.

Nov. 9, Beacon Course, N. J.Purse........4 mile heats..won   1,000
Beating Decatur. This year B. won nine Jockey Club Purses,
and received $1,000 more for not starting.

1839.

April 16, Petersburg, Va....Match........2 mile heats..lost
Beaten by Portsmouth in 3.50—3.48, B. being off his foot.

April 27, Broad Rock, Va...Purse........3 mile heats..won   500
Beating Lady Clifden and Brocklesby in 5.46 with ease—the
best time ever made on this course.

May 9, Washington City....Purse........4 mile heats..won   800
Beating Tom Walker, Black Knight, Reliance, and Sam Brown,
7.53—8.06.

May 24, Camden, N. J......Purse........4 mile heats..won   1,000
Boston, now six years, walked over, though several "cracks"
were on the ground.

May 31, Trenton, N. J......Purse........4 mile heats..won   1,000
Beating Decatur and Vashti with ease. V. had just won a 2d
heat in 7.46.

June 7, Union Course, L. I..Purse........4 mile heats..won   1,000
Beating Decatur and Balie Peyton cleverly in 7.47—8.02.

Sept. 26, Petersburg, Va....P. and Stake..4 mile heats..won   7,000
Beating the Queen and Omega in 8.02—7.52—best time made on
the course, to this date.

Oct. 17, Camden, N. J......P. and Stake..4 mile heats..won   7,000
Beating Omega in 7.49. O. had won a heat at Washington in 7.40!

Oct. 23, Trenton, N. J......Purse........4 mile heats..won   1,000
Beating Decatur and Master Henry in 7.57—7.56.

1840.

May 1, Petersburg, Va.....Purse........4 mile heats..won   700
Beating Andrewetta, who won the 1st heat in 7.50—8.04—the
best time ever made on the course.

May 8, Washington City....Purse........4 mile heats..won   1,000
Beating Reliance and Cippus without a struggle.

Oct. 2, Petersburg, Va......Purse........4 mile heats..won $700
  Beating Brandt, who was drawn after 1st heat in 7.57.

Oct. 8, Broad Rock, Va.....Purse........3 mile heats..won   500
  Beating Texas, Balie Peyton, and Laneville in 5.56—5.49.

Dec. 7, Augusta, Ga........Match........4 mile heats..won 10,000
  Beating Gano in a gallop in 7.57, after which G. was drawn.

Dec. 17, Augusta, Ga......Purse........4 mile heats..won   800
  Beating Santa Anna and Omega in 7:52—7:49.

1841.

In the Spring, Boston stood at Chesterfield, Va., and covered 42 mares at $100 each.

Sept. 30, Petersburg, Va...Purse........4 mile heats..won   700
  Beating Texas without an effort.

Oct. 8, Alexandria, D. C....Purse........4 mile heats..won   800
  Boston walked over, though several cracks were present.

Oct. 15, Washington City...Purse........4 mile heats..won   800
  Beating Accident, Ned Hazard, and Greenhill with ease.

Oct. 21, Baltimore, Md.....Purse........4 mile heats..won   600
  Beating Mariner, who won the 1st heat in 8.00½—8.05—8.10—
  course very heavy.

Oct. 28, Camden, N. J......Purse........4 mile heats..lost
  Distanced by John Blount and Fashion in 7.42—Blount broke
  down in 2d heat, which was won by Fashion, in 7.48. Boston dead amiss, and unable to run a mile under 2:10.

Starting thirty-eight times, and winning thirty-five races—
 twenty-six of them at four mile heats, and seven at
 three mile heats—winning...................... $49,500
Add for his earnings in the breeding stud, Spring of 1841, 4,200

Boston's winnings and earnings amount to the enormous
 sum of.. **$53,700**

It is due to *Boston* to state that in his four-year-
old form he was prevented from starting for the large
purses offered for four mile heats, by being in the
same stable with *Atalanta, Lady Clifden, Argyle,*

and *Mary Blunt*. And it is no less due to him than to his liberal and high-spirited owners to add that from a regard to the best interests of the Turf, they have frequently allowed him to remain in his stable, when by starting him they could have taken the purses without an effort. *Boston*, after his match with *Gano*, at Augusta, could have won a Jockey Club purse there, and at Savannah and Charleston. In the spring of 1840, he started but twice, though he could have easily won every four-mile purse given between Petersburg and Long Island. His owners, in the latter instance, were personally appealed to and consented to send him home from Washington, while one of the Northern proprietors proposed to exclude him from running. Several other occasions might be named on which *Boston* has been withdrawn from the contest, at the request of the proprietors of courses, upon a representation that his entrance would destroy the sport and disappoint the public.

Boston, now at the advanced age of *eight years*, after a racing career of unparalleled severity, is still as sound as a dollar, with legs as free from blemish as a three-year old. The field of his brilliant, never-fading victories extends from New York to Georgia, and he has not only beaten, one after another, every horse within his reach, but he has challenged all others, offering to meet them on their own ground. Napoleon found a Waterloo and so has *Boston*, but the latter is beaten, not defeated; like the former it will be found that "he is never more to be feared than in his reverses." When dead amiss he was beaten, it is true; the race was a splendid one—one of the best ever run in America—but *Boston* had no part in it; he could not have beaten a cocktail on that occasion, and instead of being backed as usual at "1,000 to 300, nineteen times over," his owners did not lay out a dollar on him! Since he was taken up this fall his owners determined to give him a trial to see whether his speed or game had been affected by his services in the breeding stud. An eye-witness of this trial, who went over two hundred miles to see it, has assured us that it was not only the best trial *Boston* ever made, but it was the best trial ever made over a course which has been trained on for half a century! Since that event *Boston* has offered to run four-mile heats "*against any two horses in the world,*" for $45,000, which was not accepted, and since his defeat at Camden, by *Fashion*, he has challenged her to run him next spring for $20,000. The winner of this match will richly merit and most assuredly receive the proud title of CHAMPION OF THE AMERICAN TURF; let us hope, therefore, that each will come to the post in tip-top condition, and we may confidently anticipate witnessing the best race, without exception, ever run in America.

FASHION'S PEDIGREE, CHARACTERISTICS, AND PERFORMANCES.

Fashion was bred by William Gibbons, Esq., of Madison, Morris County, N. J., where she was foaled on the 26th April, 1837. It would be difficult to sit

down over the stud book and compile a richer pedigree than her's, and the same remark will apply to
Boston. Each is descended from the most eminently
distinguished racing families on the side of both sire
and dam, that have figured on the Turf for a hundred
years. *Fashion* was got by Mr. Livingston's imp.
Trustee, out of the celebrated *Bonnets-o'-Blue* by *Sir
Charles,* and she out of *Reality*—"the very best race
horse," says Col. Johnson, "I ever saw." *Reality*
was got by *Sir Archy,* and her pedigree extends
back through the imported horses *Medley, Centinel,
Janus, Monkey, Silver-Eye,* and *Spanker,* to an imported Spanish mare. *Trustee,* the sire of *Fashion,*
was a distinguished race-horse in England, and sold
at three years old for 2,000 guineas, to the Duke of
Cleveland, after running 3d in the race for the Derby
of 101 subscribers. He was subsequently imported
by Messrs. Ogden, Corbin, and Stockton. *Trustee*
was foaled in 1829, and was got by *Catton* out of *Em-
ma* by *Whisker,* and combines the blood of *Hermes,
Pipator,* and *Sir Peter,* on his dam's side, with that
of *Penelope* by *Trumpator,* and *Prunella* by *High-
flyer,* on the side of his sire. *Trustee* is not a chance
horse ; in addition to other winners of his family, in
1835, his own brother, *Mundig,* won the Derby of
128 subscribers.

Fashion is a rich, satin-coated chestnut, with a
star, and a ring of white above the coronet of her left
hind foot; on her right quarter she is marked
with three dark spots, like *Plenipo,* and other "ter-
ribly high-bred cattle." She is about 15½ hands high

under the standard, rising high on the withers, with a light head and neck, faultless legs, an oblique, well-shaped shoulder, and a roomy, deep, and capacious chest. She has good length of barrel, which is well ribbed out, and her loins are well arched and supported by strong fillets. Though finely put up forehanded, her great excellence consists in the muscular developments of her quarters, thighs, and gaskins. As in the greyhound and the hare, the seat of the propelling power in the horse, which enables him to move with a great degree of velocity, is centred in his hind-quarters; necessarily in proportion to their strength there, will be the impulse which impels the whole mass forward.

Fashion has been trained for all her engagements by Mr. Samuel Laird, of Colt's Neck, N. J., and ridden by his son Joseph, the best jockey at the north. Mr. Gibbons, her owner, having been unfortunate with his former trainer (who nearly ruined *Mariner* in breaking him), and who is opposed to the general plan of training colts at two years old, resolved that *Fashion* should not be taken up until her form had attained a greater degree of maturity; consequently she was not brought out until the fall of her three-year-old year. *Fashion* goes with a long rating stroke, gathers well, and moves with the utmost ease to herself; what is rather singular, she runs with a loose rein; she is true as steel, has a remarkable turn of speed, can be placed anywhere, and nothing can be finer than her disposition; a more bloodlike, honest mare was never brought to the post. Being in a public training stable, with *Clarion* and *Mariner*, her half brother, both of them winners at three and four-mile heats, *Fashion* has been compelled to " take her turn " in running for " the big things," else the amount of her winnings might have been increased as well as the number of

HER PERFORMANCES.

1840.

Oct. 21, Camden, N. J......Sweepstake...2 mile heats..won $800
Beating Amelia Priestman in the mud ; two paid forfeit.

Oct. 27, Trenton, N. J......Sweepstake...2 mile heats..won   1,100
Beating Fleetwood and Nannie ; two paid forfeit.

1841.

May 5, Union Course, L. I..Purse........3 mile heats..won   500
Beating Sylphide, Prospect, Fleetfoot, and Meridian.

May 19, Camden, N. J......Purse........2 mile heats..lost
Beaten by Tyler, after winning 2d heat. Trenton won the 1st, and Tyler the 3d and 4th. Fashion second in 4th heat, Telemachus being ruled out—time, 4.06—3.52—3.51½—3.56.

Oct. 7, Union Course, L. I...Purse........2 mile heats..won   200
Beating Trenton in 3.51—3.46½, on a heavy course.

Oct. 20, Baltimore, Md.....Purse........3 mile heats..won   400
Beating John Blount, Lady Canton, and Stockton ; course slippery.

Oct. 28, Camden, N. J......Purse........4 mile heats..won   800
Beating John Blount, who broke down in 2d heat, after winning the 1st and distancing Boston in 1st heat; time, 7.42—7.43.

Starting, in three trainings, seven times, and winning six races, one at four, and two at three-mile heats, winning....................................   **$3,800**

We have noticed the fact of her not having been trained in the spring of her three-year-old year ; last spring, too, unfortunately, after her race at Camden she went amiss and was prudently turned out until the fall, when she came out again and won not only at two and at three-mile heats, but at four. Her last race is one of the best, at four-mile heats, ever run in the United States. In the only race she ever lost it will be seen that she was beaten by *Tyler* after winning the 2d heat; *Tyler* won the 3d and 4th heats, in the last of which she was 2d, having beaten *Trenton* (who won the 1st heat) and *Telemachus*. From the fact of being turned out after this race and of her having since twice beaten *John Blount*, who easily defeated *Tyler* in a match for $5,000, it is fair to conclude that on the occasion alluded to she was out of condition. The brilliant reputation she acquired by her last great performance, added to the confident impression everywhere entertained of her surpassing speed and extraordinary powers of endurance, are such, however, as to render quite gratuitous any explanation as to the cause of her having once been defeated.

As *Fashion's* friends have accepted the match offered by *Boston*, it is to be hoped that each will come to the post in condition to run for a man's life. *Fashion* will be trained as usual by Mr. Laird, and *Boston* by Arthur Taylor; Joe, no doubt, will throw his leg across the pig skin on the mare, while Gil Patrick, who has more strength, though not more science or coolness than Craig, will probably be put up again on *Boston*. The latter being an aged horse (9 years old) will have to carry 126 lbs., while the mare's appropriate weight being then 5 years old, will be 111 lbs. No match, the South against the North, has been made up at all comparable with this in interest, since that between *Eclipse* and *Henry*, which came off over the Union Course on the 27th of May, 1823. Each champion has, and is worthy of troops of confident friends, and each is in good hands. Let them come together in good condition—give them a fair field and no favor, and—who can name the winner ?

At an early hour on Tuesday morning our streets were filled with carriages of all descriptions, wending their way to the ferries, while thousands upon thousands crossed over to the cars of the Long Island Railroad Company. But after eleven o'clock the Company found it impossible to convey to the course the immense crowd which filled and surrounded the cars.

    *   *   *   *   *   *

The race commenced about two o'clock. For more than a quarter of a mile in front of the stands, the spectators ranged on the side of the course and of the field, presented one dense mass of thousands, through which the horses run the gauntlet. The course itself, owing to the rain of Sunday night, was not deemed quite so well adapted for speed as upon some other occasions ; still it was in fine order. The prospect of the weather, in the morning, was unfavorable, but though at ten o'clock there was a slight sprinkling of rain, it soon cleared off. The day was warm and pleasant, but with scarce a glimpse of the sun.

The betting was a shade in Boston's favor. Before the race came off, however, his friends were obliged, in order to get on their money, to lay 100 to 60, and in some cases 2 to 1. We never saw so little money bet on a race here of any importance; of *heavy* betting we did not hear of a solitary transaction, though the backers of each were sanguine.

Having previously given in the preceding pages complete memoirs of the rival champions, with their pedigrees, characteristics, and performances, in detail, we have only to speak of their fine condition. Both stripped well. Boston was drawn unusually to our eye, but his coat looked and felt like satin. Fashion's curb, though quite prominent, did not seem to affect her a jot; otherwise she was in condition to run for a man's life. We need hardly say that she was admirably trained by Mr. Laird, nor that she was splendidly jockeyed by his son *Joseph*—a chip of the old block— Mr. Laird having formerly been a conspicuous jockey. Boston, of course, was managed by Col. Johnson, and ridden by Gil Patrick, in his usual superb style; Arthur Taylor brought him to the post in unusually fine order. Gil Patrick rode the first heat without a spur. The jockeys having received their orders, mounted, and had their girths taken up another hole, brought their horses up in fine style without any assistance whatever from their trainers, and were off with a running start for the race.

First Heat.—Boston on the inside went away with the lead at a rattling pace, the mare laying up within two lengths of him down the straight run on the back stretch ; the half mile was run in 55 seconds. The same position was maintained to the end of the mile, (run in 1.53,) but soon after Fashion made play and the pace improved. Both made strong running down the back-stretch over the hill (opposite the half-mile post) and down the slight descent which succeeds, and though this seemed favorable ground for Boston, the mare gained on him, at this place, in this mile, and placed herself well up. Boston threw her off on the turn, and led through clear, running this mile in 1.50½. The pace seemed too good to last, and Boston's friends, as he led closely down the back-stretch, were "snatching and eager" to take any thing offered. Again Boston led through, this mile—(the 3d) being run in 1.54, Fashion keeping him up to the top of his rate. The contest was beautiful and exciting beyond description ; there was no clambering, no faltering, no dwelling on the part of either ; each ran with a long rating stroke, and a pace that kills. Soon after commencing the 4th mile Joe Laird shook his whip over her head and gave Fashion an eye-opener or two, with the spur, and not 100 yards from the ground where Boston took the track from Charles Carter, *she collared and passed him in half a dozen strokes* at a flight of speed we never saw equalled, except in the desperate brush at the stand between Grey Medoc and Altorf, in their dead heat ! When Fashion responded to the call upon her, and took the track in such splendid style, the cheers sent up from the "rude throats" of thousands might have been heard for miles ! Fashion made her challenge after getting through the drawgate and took the lead opposite the quarter mile post. Boston, however, like a trump, as he is, did not give back an inch, and though it was manifest the Northern Phenomenon had the foot of him, he gave her no respite. He lapped her down the back-stretch for 300 yards, when Gil Patrick very sensibly took a strong bracing pull on him, and bottled him up for a desperate brush up the hill, where Eclipse passed Henry. Here Gil again let him out, but unfortunately he pulled him inside so near the fence that Boston struck his hip against a post, and hitting a sharp knot or a nail cut through the skin on his quarter for seven or eight inches! He struck hard enough to jar himself very much, and we observed him to falter; but he soon recovered, and though at this moment Fashion led him nearly three lengths, he gradually closed the gap round the turn to within a few feet. At this moment the excited multitude broke through all restraint in their anxiety to witness the termination of the heat, and the course was nearly blocked up! On coming out through a narrow gauntlet of thousands of spectators excited to the highest pitch, both horses very naturally faltered at the tremendous shouts, which made the welkin ring. Up the quarter stretch Gil made another desperate effort to win the race out of the fire. He applied his thong freely, while Joe Laird drew his whip on the mare more than once, and tapped her claret at the same time. Inside of the gate it was a " hollow thing " though Boston nearly closed the gap at the distance stand. Gil fairly caught Joe by surprise, but the latter, shaking his whip over her head, gave Fashion the spur, and she instantly recovered her stride, coming through about a length ahead with apparently something in hand to spare, closing the heat in 7.32½—the fastest, by all odds, ever run in America. The time was kept on the Jockey Club stand by Messrs. Robert L. and James Stevens, and in the Judges' stand by Senator Barrow of Louisiana, Hon. Mr. Botts of Virginia, J. Hamilton Wilkes, Esq., and the official Timers. We took the time of each mile from the Messrs. S., between whom we stood. Mr. Neill, Major Ringgold, and other gentlemen of acknowledged accuracy as timers, stood in the same circle, and there was but a fraction of difference in the time each declared " by watches, too, not made in Kentucky! " Messrs. S. made the time 7.33, but as they kept the time of the half, and in some cases of the quarter miles, their difference of that half a second from the Timers in the Judges' stand demonstrates the remarkable accuracy of the parties.

The result of the heat was the more astonishing to a few of Boston's friends as no one ever supposed Fashion could make *this* time, though she might *beat* him. We were prepared to expect the best time on record, not only from the fact that we had been informed of the result of Fashion's *private trial* on the 25th ult., but from a circumstance which we shall be excused, we trust, for alluding to here. After retiring to our room at the Astor House on Monday night, at a late hour, we had the pleasure of a " domiciliary visit " from Mr. Long, the owner of Boston, and several mutual friends. The "party" were attired in costumes that would be esteemed somewhat unique out of the circle of the Marquis of Waterford's friends, who ride steeple chases in their shirts and drawers! Nevertheless, there was no lack of fun or spirit: in the course of an interesting "horse talk," Mr. Long gave us several "items," one of which was, that Boston would run the first heat, "sure," in 7.34! Said Mr. Long, "He will run the first mile in about 1.53; the second in 1.52; the third in 1.54; and the fourth in 1.55."

After he retired we made a memorandum of the time, as a curiosity after the race. And we refer to it now, to show that though beaten by the Northern Phenomenon, the gallant Boston amply sustained all the expectations formed of him from his trials and previous performances. He not only made vastly better time than *he* ever did before, but better time than ever *had* been made—time that quite eclipses the most wonderful achievements on the American Turf! The vaunted performances of the Southern "cracks" at New Orleans are almost thrown in the shade, wonderful as they are! Had any one offered to beat the time of Eclipse and Henry on the Union Course, three to one would have been laid against it; or had the friends of Boston been assured that he could run, as Mr. Long told us he could, in 7.34, his friends would have staked a million of dollars upon his winning the match! For the first two miles, Boston, in the opinion of many shrewd judges, had the foot of the mare, and it is thought that had he trailed her as he did Charles Carter, the result of the first heat might have been different. But what shall be said of the incomparable daughter of Trustee and Bonnets o' Blue. Too much *cannot* be said of her, or of her jockey. She ran as true as steel, as game and honest a race as was ever recorded of a high-mettled racer!

Both horses cooled out well. Boston always blows tremendously, even after a gallop; but he seemed little distressed. Neither was Fashion; her action is superb, and as she came through on the fourth mile, it was remarked that she was playing her ears as if taking her exercise. She recovered sooner than Boston, and though her friends now offered large odds on her, Boston's were no less confident; the seventh mile they thought would "fetch her." We should not have been surprised to have seen both swell over the loins, nor to have found them greatly distressed. We examined them carefully after the heat, and state with great pleasure, that though they "blowed strong," they recovered in a few minutes, and came to the post again comparatively fresh. After the heat was over, the crowd rushed into the enclosed space *en masse;* an endeavor was made to clear a portion of the track of the multitude who had now taken possession of it, and after great exertions a line was formed, through which the horses came up for the

Second Heat.—Fashion led off with a moderate stroke, and carried on the running down the back stretch with a lead of about three lengths. After

8

making the ascent of the hill, Boston challenged, closed the gap, and lapped her. A tremendous shout arose on all hands at this rally, but as it subsided on the part of Boston's friends, it was again more tumultuously caught up by the friends of the mare, as she outfooted him before reaching the head of the quarter stretch. She came through—in 1.59—three or four lengths ahead, and kept up her rate down the entire straight stretch on the rear of the course. After getting over the hill, Boston, as before, made a rush, and succeeded in collaring the mare, while she, as before, again threw him off, and led through by two or three lengths, in 1.57. Gil relieved his horse for the next 600 yards, but instead of waiting for Fashion to ascend the hill at the half-mile post alone, he called on Boston just before reaching it, and the two went over it nearly together ; no sooner had they commenced the descending ground, than, gathering all his energies for a final and desperate effort, Boston made a dash, and this time he succeeded in taking the track ! The scene which ensued we have no words to describe. Such cheering, such betting, and so many long faces, were never seen nor heard before. After being compelled to give up the track, Joe Laird, with the utmost prudence and good sense, took his mare in hand, and gave her time to recover her wind. This run *took the shine out of* Boston ! Instead of pulling him steadily, and refreshing him with a slight respite, Gil Patrick kept him at work after he took the track, and run this mile—the third—in 1.51½ ! The pace was tremendous ! Nothing short of limbs of steel and sinews of

catgut could stand up under such a press! On the
first turn after passing the stand, Fashion, now fresh
again, made a dash, and as Boston had not another
run left in him, she cut him down in her stride, opposite the quarter-mile post, and *the thing was out.*
The race, so far as Boston was concerned, was past
praying for! If any thing can parallel Fashion's turn
of speed, it is her invincible game. She now gradually dropped him, and without another effort on his
part to retrieve the fortunes of the day, she came
home a gallant and easy winner in 7.45! Boston
pulled up inside of the distance stand, and walked
over the score! As she came under the judges'
cord extended across the course, Boston was exactly
sixty yards behind, though he could have placed himself in a better position had Gil called upon him.

As Joe Laird rode Fashion back to the stand,
the shouts were so deafening, that had not the President of the Club and another gentleman held on to
her bridle, she would not only have " enlarged the
circle of her acquaintance " very speedily, but " made
a mash " of some dozen of " the rank and file," then
and there assembled. She looked as if another heat
would not " set her back any."

And thus did *the North* settle its account with *the
South*, for the victory achieved by Bascombe over
Post Boy. It was a magnificent race—one which
will be remembered by every one who witnessed it
" while Memory holds her seat." Though beaten, it is
conceded on all hands that Boston has acquired a
more " vast renown " by this wonderful race than by

his thirty-five previous victories combined. He is worth more since than he was before the match. " All that can be said is, that Boston has beaten himself, and Fashion has beaten Boston ! " The spirit of his owners on this, as upon a like memorable occasion, in May, 1823, is worthy of them, and of the Old Dominion. Of one of them it has been well said, that, " like another Napoleon, he is never more to be feared than in his reverses ! "

In congratulating each other upon the brilliant triumph achieved by the Northern Champion—now *the* Champion of the American Turf, let no one forget to do honor to those to whose admirable skill and judgment the North is mainly indebted for its victory. To Mr. Samuel Laird, the trainer and jockey of Fashion, and to his fine-spirited son, who jockeyed her in a style that would have conferred credit upon Jem Robinson, too much credit cannot be given. Nor let us forget that to the gallant Boston we are indebted for ascertaining the indomitable game and surpassing speed of our Champion. What *else* could have displayed it in such bold and beautiful relief? Arthur Taylor brought him to the post in the very finest possible condition, and Gil Patrick, his jockey, rarely distinguished himself more than upon this occasion. Most of our contemporaries state that he rode with spurs. He wore one only, and that only in the second heat.

It is peculiarly gratifying to ourselves, though we have the pleasure of numbering all the parties among our personal friends, that Mr. Gibbons, the owner of

Fashion, is among the oldest, most stanch, and most generous of the number. Unfortunately he was prevented from witnessing the race, in consequence of an accident which for some time has confined him at home. In his absence, another tried friend, Walter Livingston, Esq., the owner of Trustee—the sire of Fashion—was congratulated on all hands; he has never doubted Fashion's success from the first. Col. W. Larkin White, of Virginia, who was also in attendance, came in for a liberal portion of the good feeling displayed. Nor should it go unrecorded that Col. Johnson was by no means forgotten in the general outburst of congratulation. He " sold the stick which broke his own head," and no mistake, for after breeding Bonnets o' Blue from his own Sir Charles, and running her with great success, he parted with her to Mr. Gibbons, who bred from her a filly, which has beaten the best horse Col. Johnson has ever had in his stable, since the days of his favorite Reality, the renowned grand-dam of Fashion herself.

RECAPITULATION :

Tuesday, May 10, 1842.—Match, the North vs. the South, $20,000 aside, $5,000 ft., four-mile heats. Henry H. Toler's and William Gibbons' ch. m. *Fashion*, by Imp. Trustee, out of Bonnets o' Blue, Mariner's dam, by Sir Charles, 5 years, 111 lbs. . . . . . . Joseph Laird, 1—1

Col. Wm. R. Johnson's and James Long's ch. h. *Boston*, by Timoleon, out of Robin Brown's dam by Ball's Florizel, 9 years, 126 lbs. . . . . . . Gil Patrick, 2—2

First Heat.					*Second Heat.*				
Time of 1st mile	.	.	.	1.53	Time of 1st mile	.	.	.	1.59
" " 2d "	.	.	.	1.50¼	" " 2d "	.	.	.	1.57
" " 3d "	.	.	.	1.54	" " 3d "	.	.	.	1.51¼
" " 4th "	.	.	.	1.55	" " 4th "	.	.	.	1.57¼
Time of First Heat	.	.	7.32¼		Time of Second Heat	.	.	7.45	

At the Jockey Club dinner, after the match, Mr. Long offered to run Boston *against* Fashion, for $20,-000, $5,000 forfeit, four-mile heats, at any time to be agreed upon by the parties between the 25th of September and the 25th of October next. He also authorized us to state in our *Extra*, that he would bet $1,000 he wins the regular Jockey Club purse, four-mile heats, on Friday, on the Union Course; $1,000 that Boston wins the Jockey Club purse at Trenton, and $1,000 that Boston wins the Jockey Club at Camden, the week following.

Last Day.—The attraction of three races, in one of which Boston was to contend with a son of Bonnets o' Blue, drew a large assemblage to the Course, and they were amply entertained by a race, if not so brilliant as that of Fashion on Tuesday, at least as critical, and apparently more doubtful. The sport commenced with a trial of speed at mile heats between Tempest and Prima Donna, the colt winning in two heats, the latter of which was particularly interesting. Time: 1.55—1.55. Joe Laird jockeyed the winner, who, we regret to say, was sold at auction after the race, and was knocked down for the paltry sum of $180, to Capt. Shirley of the 7th Hussars, B. A., who has been in attendance upon our races. Other stock was offered, but we learn was bid in.

Now came off the great race of the day—the struggle between Boston and Mariner. The former was backed in the morning at 100 to 30, and before the start at 100 to 20, which were not taken with alacrity. Boston had the pole, but retained it for a few yards only, Mariner going to the front on the first turn, and leading by several lengths. The pace for the first mile was so slow as 2.13, Mariner cutting out the work; he increased his rate in the second mile, which was run in about 2.05, opening the gap on the back side between Boston and himself, while Boston lessened it a little in the straight, running in front. In the third mile, the pace was still further improved, both horses tasting the persuaders freely; the fourth mile was yet more desperately contested, though without much change in the position of the horses. Boston, who was ridden by Gil, without spurs, was most severely scored in coming home; but as it was all in vain, he pulled him up inside the distance stand. Mariner came in amidst the most tremendous shouts, in 8.13.

The friends of *Old Whitenose* were undismayed by the loss of the heat, and he still retained the call in the betting at about 100 to 80. As in the former heat, Joe Laird went away with the lead, and driving his horse at a much better pace than before. At the south turn in the commencement of the second mile, the old horse showed a taste of his old style of going, challenged for the lead, and gained it in a twinkling. No respite, however, was given by Joe to Mariner, who ran well up throughout that and the following mile, though the running was strongly forced by Gil Patrick. In the first quarter of the fourth mile, in very nearly the place where Fashion made her run, Joe went up with a rush, took the track with apparent ease, continued to urge his horse with whip and spur, widening the gap with every stride. · Before they came into straight running, he was leading by six or eight lengths, and the race was apparently safe. But here Gil Patrick brought up his nag in a style quite incomparable; such a rush we do not remember ever to have seen made; the old horse appeared to sympathize with his eager rider, and showed all of that speed which has won for him his great renown. Joe did not appear to be aware of his close proximity till he came within the gates, when he too found his whip, and plied it lustily. The thing was out, however, for nothing but a locomotive could have held its way with Boston, who in his turn came home, amid the enthusiastic cries of the populace, in 7.46. Many watches made the time a half-second quicker. The heat, which was won by a length, was the most interesting we recollect ever to have seen. We have heard the riding of Joe in the last mile criticized; it is said he took too much out of his horse after he had passed Boston, by forcing the run as he did. Our impression is that he pursued the safer course, and that he lost the heat only in consequence of the tremendous speed which his antagonist exhibited in the quarter stretch. There is no difference of opinion as to the masterly style in which Gil took the heat; it would compare favorably with any performance of Chifney or Robinson.

The third heat was scarcely less interesting than the previous one. Boston took up the running early, but was followed by Mariner at the best pace steel and catgut could get out of him. This severe chase continued throughout three miles and a half, when Mariner closed up a little. In coming into the quarter stretch home, Gil gave the pole a wide berth, and Joe immediately took advantage of it, and made a rush to take the lead *on the inside*. The struggle was now most exciting, as Mariner was evidently drawing rapidly upon his antagonist. At about the distance stand he lapped on to him, when Gil appeared to pull his horse towards the pole again, and thus crossed the path of Mariner and interrupted his stride. The pace was terrific, however, till the finish, Boston taking the heat, with his tail flirting directly in the face of his competitor. Time, 7.58¼. A complaint was then made of foul riding against the winner, but it was not deemed by the judges to be substantiated, and the race and purse were accordingly awarded to Boston. All know how critical and hazardous is the attempt to pass a leading horse on the inside. Many believe that Joe Laird was authorized by the position of Boston to make the effort he did, and that for being crossed and crowded, he would have won the race by it. The rightful authorities decided otherwise, however, and we acquiesce in their decision without hesitation.

The race will be long remembered as one of the most interesting that ever came off on Long Island. The performance of Mariner surprised all his friends by the unwonted *speed* which he displayed, while he

8*

ran as *game* a race as any horse that ever made a track. After the wonderful performance of Boston on Tuesday last, his race of yesterday will, we have no doubt, be esteemed one of the most remarkable in the annals of the Turf.

The profound disappointment which was experienced by the Southern friends of Boston is plainly and honestly acknowledged in the columns of the Richmond "Whig" three days after the race. "Boston is beaten! We did not announce the defeat of the Whigs with a profounder sorrow. We feel a melancholy on the occasion, akin to that inspired by the death of some great public benefactor. A noble steed—the boast and glory of his native State—the victor of a hundred fields—has been arrested in his illustrious career, and in one brief day been stripped of all his glories; and that too by a *parvenue*—a thing of to-day —unknown yesterday, and destined, but for this unfortunate occurrence, to be forgotten to-morrow. *We wish we had lost money upon him!* That would have been an earnest of our sympathy for the noble sorrows which rend his generous bosom—and might, by the compliment implied, have tended to assuage the bitterness of his grief. But it is idle to indulge in lamentations. The times are sadly out of joint, and no longer is the race to the swift or the battle to the strong. Boston is outstripped, and the Whigs overthrown! No event has excited so much commotion in the city, since the news of the Revolution of the Palisades in Paris."

It has already been stated that the bold and honorable course taken by the editor of the "Spirit" in regard to matters connected with this exciting race, had drawn upon him unmerited and low abuse; in his paper of May 21st (which by the way is a proud specimen of Mr. Porter's industry, as nearly ten of its wide columns consist of solid editorial matter) he notices the ungenerous comments upon his course in a spirit exceedingly creditable to his courage and truthfulness, and which was pronounced a triumphant vindication of these qualities which with him were inborn and ineffaceable. He closes with these words:

"We have little left us in this world besides an humble reputation, and a character hitherto untarnished. We are in a position, however undeserved, of great responsibility, and oftentimes requiring the exercise of great judgment and the most delicate and adroit modes of expression—occasions where silence would be the worst possible course, and the obligation to say something can neither be shunned nor fulfilled by a hollow counterfeit. When we are so circumstanced and are *compelled* by a sense of duty to express our sentiments, we do not intend to look calmly on and see our 'good name filched from us' because they may have conflicted with *the interests* of any man. And we now take leave to say, once for all, that when any reader of our sheet finds in its columns an editorial article that unfortunately clashes with his interests, he may be sure, and we beg of him to believe, that it was written under a sense of the highest obligations to waive all personal predilections, and disregard individual interests, for the general good. But if his charity cannot extend so far, let him not go so far as to *calumniate us* for telling *the bare truth*—let him not preach homilies on honesty to us because we do not suppress important facts that he may realize extravagant anticipations—and let him not hope to muzzle the expression of our candid convictions or to forestall swift coming rumors by confiding to us as a secret what he well knows we must learn in a few short hours from a hundred sources. But if charity and confidence cannot go so far, and if any one still chooses to pursue a different course with us, he may rely upon it we shall ever be found ready and prompt to vindicate our conduct to the world, and by such means as lie in our power will we show our determination of not tamely submitting to abusive charges and vindictive imputations, gross as they are groundless."

About this time George Porter concluded an arrangement to become an associate editor of the New Orleans "Picayune." He still retained a lingering affection for his original profession, which he hoped he should ultimately be able to resume in that city. The first intelligence we had of all this was communicated in a letter from George, dated at New York, October 20th, 1842, in which he stated his purposes, and that he was on the eve of sailing for New Orleans; he added: "My desire is to return exclusively to the law." In compliance with his request, we furnished him with a letter of introduction to the Hon. Balie Peyton, then U. S. Attorney for the Southern District of Louisiana, soliciting his aid and countenance in furthering the cherished object of Mr. Porter.

On his arrival at New Orleans, he entered at once on his duties in the office of the " Picayune." In a letter of the 23d of March, 1843, he writes :

"No dray horse on the levee works more steadily than I. I have the hang of the office at last, and have little difficulty; but I pull most decidedly the laboring oar, if I except Kendall, who works like an engine of a hundred horse power, though much of his labor is given to revisals of what others may have written. * * * I shall hold fast, always being ready, how-

ever, to embrace any thing like a living in the law. As it is, I
have not missed a day's work since I have been here. * * *
So you see I am likely to live here as long as *Yellow Jack* will
allow."

" Here I am," said he in a letter of the previous November,
" perched up in the St. Charles, some ten feet nearer heaven than
any other spot of land, I believe, in the whole State of Louisiana. * * * I am grinding out inanities for the " *Picayune*,'
which is a paper too neutral in its character—as well in religion,
literature and criticism as in politics—to allow a Northerner to
express therein such poor thoughts as may enter his dull
brain. * * * Mr. Peyton has not yet reached New Orleans,
nor is he expected much before the 1st proximo. Judge Porter
resides in the Attakapas, a goodly distance hence, where he is
now awaiting Mr. Clay's arrival, who will spend some days at
Oak Lawn, and then both the ex-Senators will come to New
Orleans.

" Nothing definite in regard to my legal pursuits will be determined till such time as I can see both Mr. Peyton and the
Judge."

It so chanced that a year or two before he started
for the South, Francis T. Porter the youngest of the
brothers, had returned to New York, after a protracted residence in Mississippi, to the great delight
and advantage of his brothers. Of more delicate organization than either of his family, Frank, as his
friends loved to call him, was of abundant spirit and
talents—of irresistible will, precise habits, and the
very soul of honor. In resolution and fixedness of
purpose, he was superior to either of his elder brothers. A comparatively fragile frame seemed to require
the hardening process of an active life, and he was
accordingly educated in reference to becoming a mer-

chant. In 1835, when about seventeen years of age, he entered a counting-house in New York. Thus all the brothers, one by one, had migrated from the quiet scenes of childhood, and settled in the wilderness of a vast city.

On reaching his majority, Frank became one of the firm of Davidson, Porter & Co.; the partners being then well established at Amsterdam, Hind's County, Mississippi, to which place he at once removed. He writes on the 7th of February, 1837: " Although the youngest of the family, I have wandered farther from the spot where our parents sleep than any. * * * My health is passable ; as well, perhaps, as I could expect after having the bilious fever five times this year ! "

In subsequent letters he gives animating accounts of his business prospects, and facetiously alludes to his election as one of the "*Selectmen*," and to the offer that he should be *Postmaster*. He devoted himself to business, until his impaired health warned him to leave the pestilential climate of Mississippi, and he again became a resident of New York in 1839. It was then that the natural taste for writing, so characteristic of the family, became confirmed, and the " Spirit of the Times " shared the benefit of his judicious theatrical criticisms, and other productions of his pen.

In the autumn of 1842 he received an appointment in the Custom House from Hon. Edward Curtis, the Collector of New York. The duties were agreeable, and he performed them with fidelity, until he was removed by the successor of Mr. Curtis, on account of his Whig principles. In the month of December, 1846, he sailed for New Orleans with the purpose of again embarking in mercantile pursuits. His brother George was delighted at his unexpected arrival, which seemed almost providential; for he had just written to him, urging his acceptance of a post in the office of the "Picayune." Frank wrote to William in reference to this proposition: "If I do not get a mercantile offer this week, I shall accept it, until I can get one." He adds: "George is well, but looks very thin and pale —works very hard. He lives in good style, and has every thing about his house comfortable and elegant."

In 1843 the "Picayune" reported the Fall races on the Louisiana course in New Orleans, and pronounced the race between *Miss Foote, George Martin* and *George W. Kendall*, which came off on the fourth day, as "the best three four-mile heats ever made in the world,"—time 7.36½—7.39—7.51½—Miss Foote being the winner.

On this statement the "Spirit" thus comments:

"'*Nine cheers for Miss Foote!*' were duly proposed and responded to in the 'Spirit' office, on Wednesday morning last. Throughout the day the 'front office' was crammed, while in the sanctum sanctorum of the editor there was not room for a man as thin as Calvin Edson. Three several times the report above, written by 'THAT OTHER GENTLEMAN' for the 'Picayune,' was read aloud. The original report was surmounted by the caption of 'THE BEST RACE EVER RUN IN THE WORLD!' which it is— *in a cornucopia!* We have taken the liberty of altering that same caption. We concede the point, however, that Miss Foote and George Martin have run 'the best three heats' of four miles 'ever run' in this world or any other, though there are many

sticklers for *proper weight for age* who will not. The races of
Lady Clifden and Picton, of Grey Medoc and Altorf, and especially that of Henry against Eclipse, when, though not quite *four*
years old, he carried *one hundred and eight pounds*, have been
discussed over and over again, in connection with this performance of Miss Foote and George Martin. Assuming the English
axiom that ' seven pounds is equal to a distance ' (or 240 yards
in four miles), the difference in weight in Miss Foote's favor gave
her an advantage over Henry of about *Five Hundred and Sixty-
five yards!*—nearly one-third of a mile in each heat. Miss
Foote's three heats were run in $17\frac{1}{2}$ seconds less time than the
three heats of Lady Clifden. She, as a 4 yr. old, carried 101 lbs. ;
Miss Foote, two months later in the season, carried, as a 4 yr.
old, 97 lbs. We do not, however, subscribe to the opinion that
' seven pounds is equal to a distance,' as a general rule, though
it has obtained in England for more than half a century. In the
races between Muley Moloch and Glaucus, 3 lbs. given to the
latter enabled him to beat Muley Moloch, who had beaten him
two days previous, and this in a race of two miles, when both
were 5 yrs. old. Indeed, horses are now handicapped there with
such consummate judgment [*vide* case of Charles XIIth and Hyl-
lus] that JEM ROBINSON, the famous jockey, wittily remarked not
long since, in accounting for losing a closely contested race, that
he lost it from having carried the key of the stable in his pocket !

" ' The only horse,' remarks the ' Picayune,' ' which has any
title to assume an equality with Miss Foote is *Fashion,*' and then
it goes on to state that ' the *aggregate* time of Fashion's two heats
with Boston was two seconds slower than the two first heats of
the race there.' The ' aggregate ! ' Stuff !—as if the ' aggregate ' had any thing to do with the matter. Why, they ciphered
the heats of a *three*-mile race in Kentucky not long since, in such
an extraordinary way as to beat Eclipse and Henry's time at *four*-
mile heats into fits ! Inasmuch as Miss Foote did not happen to
win the first heat of ' her ' race, [won by George Martin ' in $7.36\frac{1}{2}$,
by three or four open lengths,'] we are surprised the ' Picayune '
does not give George Martin, instead of Fashion, a ' title to as-

same an equality with Miss Foote.' What a compliment to the Northern Champion! This grant to Fashion of a 'title to ASSUME an *equality*' with any horse on the American Turf is 'piling up the agony' a 'leetle too mountainous!'

"In another paragraph the 'Picayune' states that 'the eight miles in Fashion's race with Boston were run in 15 minutes 17½ seconds, while the two heats in this race [George Martin's and Miss Foote's] were run in 15 minutes and 15½ seconds.' Here is the monstrous discrepancy of *two seconds* in a race, won by Fashion in two heats in the one case, while *two horses* were required to make the time in the other. Moreover, Fashion as a 5 yr. old, carried on the 10th of May 111 lbs., (though foaled so late as the 26th of April.) Miss Foote runs as a 4 yr. old on the 24th of Dec., carrying 97 lbs., when seven days later she would have been rated at *five* years old, and been obliged to take up *ten pounds more*, or 107 lbs. Fashion, less than five months later than Miss Foote, and at the same age, carried FOURTEEN POUNDS MORE WEIGHT. She *won* her two heats in 7.32½—7.45, while Miss Foote *lost* the 1st heat of 'her' race in 7.36½, and won the 2d in 7.39. If she or George Martin *could* have run the 1st heat in 7.32½, does any one in his senses suppose either could have repeated it 'low down in the forties'? Fashion won her 2d heat with ease, 'by exactly sixty yards,' while Miss Foote, after 'a desperate contest, *under the spur*, from end to end,' won by only 'two lengths' from George Martin, who having been passed 'inside of the distance stand' was 'taken in hand and galloped past the stand.' And notwithstanding all this, the 'Picayune' gravely informs the friends of Fashion that she is 'the only horse which has now any title to *assume an equality* with Miss Foote!' This is really outrageous; as Dogberry said, 'It is most tolerable and not to be endured.'"

This criticism drew from William's especial friend, the Hon. Alexander Porter, of Louisiana, the following admirable letter:

"OAK LAWN, *January* 23, 1848.

"MY DEAR SIR:—I ought long since to have answered yours of the 30th November. But I have had a busy winter; Mr. Clay's visit to me, the crowds which thronged Oak Lawn during his stay, my trip with him to New Orleans, &c., &c., have interfered a good deal with my quiet and punctual habits. I saw George in the city, and had a good long talk with him about his prospects and intentions. He is doing better in the 'Picayune' establishment at present, than he could if he had a license to practise law in his pocket. But whether greater success in the department which now exercises his talents (and they are very good) is an equivalent to the greater rewards which would follow distinction at the bar, is perhaps a question not unworthy of consideration.

"He has written some very good accounts of the races here, for the paper to which he is attached, and I don't think you have done *the exactly clear thing* towards him. Your criticisms on his remarks about the comparative excellence of *Miss Foote's* and *Fashion's* races are very ingenious, but, my dear sir, *they are the arguments of a counsel in a cause, and not the judge who decides it.* You call his taking the aggregate of the two heats *stuff.* Why you so name it, unless you mean *good stuff,* I cannot see. If *Miss Foote* made eight miles in less time than *Fashion,* is not that an evidence of her superiority, *ceteris paribus?* And is that in any way affected by another horse having beaten Miss Foote in one of the heats? The *Little Lady* could have won the first heat, in the opinion of *every one* who saw it, had it not been for the great gap she most unadvisedly suffered the horse to make between them. As it was, she was only two lengths behind. And then this idea, now for the first time (I think) put forward, that her race is not of the value it appears at first blush to have, because she will have to carry more weight next year—I do not think there is any thing in that. Have you ever met with that as a reason given elsewhere why a race should be considered better or worse? If it is a good one, it ought to have been mentioned this fall when Fashion won her two races. But to leave controversy, will you permit an old man, and one who loves

you well, to make a few remarks to you of quite another character? Your position at present in this country is in many
respects an enviable one—it embraces high duties and it involves
great responsibilities. You are in some respects the arbiter of
horse reputation. Men look up to your opinions with deference,
and they yield to them, because they believe them to be the
result of intelligence and calm reflection. Nothing could shake
you so soon in your high position, as an idea going abroad that
your feelings were enlisted on one side or other of any matter of
controversy. Hence language that would be perfectly appropriate
in one of your correspondents will not do for you. Your reason-
ing and your remarks must, if you expect to give satisfaction, *take
a judicial tone.* That in a conflict of pride and opinion between
the North and the South you should, *unconsciously to yourself,*
feel enlisted in favor of the former, is inevitable. You live
there, you hear those around you continually dwelling on the
perfections of a noble animal; you see her—you witness her
generous exertions, and you end *by being in love with her.* All
this is as it should be. If you were otherwise, you would want
those ingredients in your composition without which no man rises
above the dull level of the ' *sons of earth !* ' But then, my good
namesake, *true wisdom consists in watching our strong qualities,
and preventing them running into excess.* And there is this additional reason for your standing sentinel on your thoughts, that
your paper is national, that it is meant by you for the whole
country, and the topics of which it treats belong more to the
South than to the North.

"I think I see you smile at reading this sermon—perhaps ex-
claim, Well, this is quite droll, an Irishman preaching prudence to
a Yankee. I plead guilty myself to all the errors I dare to find
in you. I know if I lived in Jersey, I should think *Fashion* the
best race-horse in the world, and if you lived here, my life on it,
you would think Miss Foote a *nonpareil.* Just as if you had
been born and educated in Spain, you would have proved a good
Catholic, and I a good Mahometan if I had been reared in Tur-
key. But then, I am not now a judge—you are. I can indulge
my feelings—you must restrain yours.

"I saw the great race in New Orleans so well described by your brother. It is very faithfully reported. The race since, between Reel and Miss Foote, I did not witness. It terminated as I expected. Under the circumstances, nothing else could be looked for. I rather think Reel can beat her any time two four-mile heats. But if they should be broken and a third one comes, then I do not believe there is an animal in America can prove to be a better nag. I crave your pardon for the heresy. But if Fashion should be able to do so, she must *repeat* in a very different style from what she has hitherto done.

"If I did not know the character of your mind, I would apologize to you for venturing any counsel to one of your experience. But my heart tells me my motives are pure and kind, and I know you have intelligence and feeling to appreciate them.

"With constant regard, yours,

"A. Porter."

The great foot-races, in which Gildersleeve and Greenhalgh were the respective victors, came off in 1844—the former making over ten and a half miles within the hour, and the latter accomplishing twelve miles in 68.48—and were reported at great length by the editor of the "Spirit." "The interest of these races was not attracted to see the running. It arose from the accidental contact of several of the circumstances of the races with strong under-currents of national interest. It was a trial of the Indian against the white man on the point in which the red man most boasts his superiority. It was the trial of the purely American physique against the long-held supremacy of English muscular endurance. * * * The white man beat the Indian, the American beat the English." These are the words of Willis, who in the same connection, alluding to the editor of the "Spirit," calls him "the admired turf-chronicler, secretary (of the Jockey Club) and prophet, Porter the tall."

On the 1st of March, 1845, the paper entered upon a new volume, with an unsurpassed number of correspondents in addition to hundreds of old ones ; yet in consideration " of the low price of stock and agricultural products generally " the subscription was reduced from ten to five dollars, its original price—a change, it may be added, that very materially increased its circulation among the farmers and stock breeders of the country. Perhaps no more appropriate place than the present will occur for the introduction of the Editor's matured opinions on the importance of horses of pure blood to the farmer, and on kindred topics.

In reply to a letter from Mr. Botts' " Southern Planter," urging the necessity of sustaining that spirited, talented and unrivalled sporting paper, " The Spirit of the Times," as the means of regenerating the Sports of the Turf, and achieving the reform and sustaining the character of the thorough-bred in America, Mr. Porter prepared an admirable argument in support of those great interests, which to this day remains unanswerable :

" There is no room for doubt that ' over and above the policy of sustaining the popular sports of the country, every lover of the horse—every individual who has occasion for the services of this useful animal (as who has not ?) is deeply interested in the regeneration of the sports of the Turf.' We shall endeavor to demonstrate that *for daily service and common use*, the most enduring, active, vigorous and handsome horses are those who have a generous strain of *pure blood* coursing through their

veins. We shall prove that the surpassing speed and game of
the *American Trotter*, whose fame extends throughout the world,
dates no farther back than the introduction of thorough-bred
stock into the New England States and remote sections of New
York and Pennsylvania.   This stock went from Long Island and
New Jersey ; it consisted mainly of young thorough-bred colts,
which being unsuited for the race-course, were disposed of at
low rates to country breeders; occasionally, too, a thorough or
three-quarter bred mare found its way into the country, the
result of all which was that every year or two a Dutchman, a
Ripton or a Confidence made his appearance.

   " Fifteen years since thousands of dollars would have been
wagered that no horse in the world could trot a mile within
three minutes ; now, in this city alone, there are dozens of roadsters in daily use which can do it before a wagon, while there
are twenty in the Union which can trot a mile in 2.30 ! Twelve
years ago to drive a horse seventy miles between sun and sun
would have been deemed a remarkable performance, but since
strains of the blood of Messenger, Mambrino and Eclipse have
been introduced into our road stock at the North, hundreds of
horses can be found which can travel from eighty to ninety miles
without distress.   There are several horses now in this city,
Philadelphia and Boston, which can travel one hundred miles
in a day without injury.   The use of thorough and half-bred
horses for domestic purposes has already become so common in
England that few others are employed for the road.   The half-
bred horse is not only much handsomer, but his speed and powers
of endurance are infinitely greater.   His head and neck are light
and graceful, his limbs fine, his coat glossy and soft as satin,
while his action is spirited, and his courage and stamina sufficient
to carry him through a long journey without his falling off in
condition, or to undergo an extraordinary trial of speed and
game without distress.   The ordinary cocktail is in most instances
a mere brute, that in travelling sinks daily in strength, losing his
appetite, and, of course, his flesh and action, so that at the termination of a ten days' journey he is nearly knocked up; he can

travel but about forty miles per day, and requires the whole day
to perform the distance.

"In the course of the year 1843, probably not less than *six
thousand thorough-bred mares*, and as many more of cold blood,
were bred to horses of pure pedigree in the United States. Out
of the vast produce of these mares, not above 1,500, if so many,
will ever come upon the Turf, probably, so that more than one-
half will eventually find their way into harness. The colts of
good form, that have plenty of bone and substance, will, of course,
oust the common tackies that infest country taverns, while the
others will be used for the saddle and the road. The result will be
that in a few years the stock now in use will be supplanted by
horses of superior action, wind and courage, whose greater beauty
will not be more apparent than their better style of going and
their unequalled powers of endurance.

"The breeders of New England and Western New York have
already became so sensible of the absolute necessity of an infu-
sion of 'blood' for the improvement of their common stock, that
they will only send their mares to thorough-bred stallions, or
those which claim to be so. Abdallah, Andrew Jackson and
other popular trotting stallions, though not quite thorough-bred,
command as high a price in the market, and for their services in
the stud, as fashionably bred and distinguished performers on the
Turf. A fine-looking gelding, a son of Abdallah, readily commands $500, while he has several sons and daughters in this
vicinity, which can be sold at auction for $2,500 each! At
the New York State Fair held at Albany in '42, there were
not less than fifteen thorough-bred stallions exhibited, some
of which were remarkably large, active and handsome. It
is from such horses as these, crossed upon the common mares
of the country, that the superb '*Northern Carriage Horses*'
are derived. We know of nearly one hundred mares of most
fashionable lineage which are owned in this and the Eastern
States, which for several years have been breeding stock for the
road. To these and such as these is the Sporting World indebted
for its Lady Suffolks, its Forrests, its Rattlers and its Pizarros.

"As a national benefit, it may be asserted by some—and the

'Planter' would seem to take this ground—that we do not require that breed in use for the Turf technically termed the 'blood horse.' To this a familiar intercourse with the most eminent breeders and turf-men of the Union, combined with no inconsiderable knowledge of horses and their relative powers, authorize us to dissent. Our extent of country and climate require horses of great action and durability, not encumbered with unnecessary masses of flesh or cumbrous bone, forming an over-weight of carcass. Our farmers in many situations have a great extent of road to pass over, in order to reach a market, and that too, upon ground often bound as hard as marble by the winter's frost, or parched dry, and rendered equally obdurate by the summer's sun : upon roads of this description, or such as are macadamized, (now coming into general use,) no heavy-moulded animal can for any length of time bear to be urged beyond a walk or slow trot, without encountering much bodily distress, and permanent injury of both feet and limbs. Nor are any, except such as possess a large share of 'blood,' equal in extreme warm weather to the task of a mail stage, or other duty where expedition and continuance are required. The coarse, heavy horse will not answer in a warm climate; the varying face of our country and the heat of our summer months are ill adapted to him, and his slow, tedious movement equally repugnant to the genius of our people.

" In regard to selection, we cannot but recommend adhering as closely as possible to such as come nearest in pedigree or purity of blood, symmetry, form, apparent strength and action, to those in use for the Turf, denominated 'blood horses,' as most adequate to long and severe exertion, under which horses of inferior description so frequently sink for want of that constitutional stamina and inherent fortitude, that those of high pedigree and pure 'blood' so eminently possess.

" In opposition to what we have here set forth as an established and incontrovertible fact, we shall no doubt be told by some, that the 'blood horse' has not sufficient *bone* and strength for the generality of business purposes. Upon this point we ask leave to introduce a few remarks. This *want of bone*, so fashionably and eternally echoed and transmitted from one affected connoisseur to another, without the least knowledge of the external conformation of the animal, or the most distant idea that any difference exists in the strength of bones of the same size, taken from horses of different breeds, or knowing that two bones exactly of the same dimensions, the one appertaining to the 'blood horse,' and the other one of the common breed, bear no comparison in point of either solidity, weight, fibre, or strength, or that the muscular and ligamentous appendages of the former, the very source of action and power, are much larger and stronger than those of the latter—that the use of bones are principally to extend the parts and support the frame—that, being in themselves inactive, the excess beyond what is thus required operates as dead weight to be carried along; thus an undue proportion, in place of being an acquisition, forms an encumbrance, and hence arises the folly which we daily witness of selecting for severe service horses over-loaded, like cart-horses, with this same *bony* structure, whose undue weight and inactivity of parts render them totally unfit for either rapidity of motion or continuance.

"There are some who in their selections affect a preference for such as are not of pure 'blood,' but a cross of the breed, between the thorough-bred and the common horse, in England technically termed 'cocktails,' and an indifference for the possession of those high-bred qualifications which are indispensably necessary to constitute a runner; while they decline purchasing, at any price, such as are incapable of great performance and continuance; nor will any other, at this day, bring a price in a city market that will defray the expense of rearing. We ask such connoisseurs, if every good racer does not possess these innate qualifications? And while we admit that there are many valuable horses of the '*cross-breed*,' we assert that they derive the very perfections which constitute their worth, not from the parent stock of the *common* horse, but solely from the species which we recommend; hence it follows, that before we can obtain even a 'cross-breed' with the necessary acquirements, we

9

must be in possession of parent stock having these same requisites, only to be obtained from the ' blood horse ' in his greatest purity.

" We do not hesitate to assert, that ' blood horses ' of proper size, formation, and symmetry, full fifteen hands (five feet) and upwards in height, of full and just proportions and muscular appearance, bred from such as are known to possess constitutional stamina and fortitude sufficient to enable them, when carrying the weight of 126 to 140 lbs., to continue their rate for four miles, and to repeat the same distance after a short interval of thirty or forty minutes, will exceed in speed, strength, or durability, whatever horses may be brought against them, on the road, in the field, the chase, or any service whatever; and when offered in market, either at home or abroad, command prices more than double that of any other class. How is this superiority to be tested, to enable us, with unerring certainty, to select the best for breed? for among the good there is always a preference. How has this test been made, for the last hundred years and more, in England, whose horses at this day excel all others on the globe? We answer with confidence, by *course racing*, and that only. Premiums for the production of the best and most elegant horses have of late years been given by our agricultural societies, but without any test of excellence or guidance, other than the whim and caprice of those from year to year nominated to decide as to the perfections or imperfections of a medley of horses, cattle, sheep, and swine, among which motley group this noble animal has been doomed to pass in review, and to be adjudged and criticized upon by those more conversant with the bristly tribe, and who value things by the weight and bulk only! We would ask if even this good intention on the part of agricultural societies produces any material improvement? We think not. We would next call attention to the high prices which have been paid to the State of New York by her sister States, and institute an inquiry as to the cause of such prices as $15,000 in one case, $10,000 each in two different instances, $5,000 each for several, $4,000, $3,000, and $2,000 each

for many, $1,500 and $1,000 for numbers—$500 is an every-day
offer for roadsters—and, at this time, $2,000 each has been
offered and refused for two. Let candor say whether such prices
could have been had, and such sums realized, by a few spirited
breeders, in the State of New York and New Jersey, but for
the partial exemption from the prohibition of horse racing, which
the legislative body of the former were prevailed upon to grant,
about the year 1821, to the favored county of Queens, Long
Island. If, again, an inquiry is instituted as to what particular
section of the State produced those valuable animals, it will be
found to be the identical district or immediate vicinity of that
exempted from the penalties imposed by the otherwise general
law enacted to prevent horse racing; and the adjacent State
of New Jersey, also benefited thereby, has, of late, totally re-
pealed her prohibitory statute. We would further ask, by what
test the superiority and extraordinary value of these particular
horses was discovered? The answer is obvious—the fact noto-
rious—*course racing!*

"That the excellence or superiority sought for can in no way
be tested except by actual trials, the most impartial and disinterested experiments, during a lapse of many years, have fully
demonstrated. For this purpose course racing was originally
instituted, and for more than a century and a half has been
adopted and pursued with unremitting zeal in Great Britain;
where the government, aware of its importance in a national
sense, promote it by giving a bounty in numerous cases, under
the appellation of Queen's Plates, yearly or semi-annually run for
upon all the principal courses in the kingdom, and in almost all
of the British Colonies. Thus encouraged and countenanced,
their horses, whether taken into view for the field, the road, or
the army, have, from judicious selections for breeding, afforded
by this same test, arrived at a state of pre-excellence hitherto
unheard of, and far surpassing the famed Arabian or Barbary
horse, from which they derive their origin. Witness the ever-
memorable battle of Waterloo, upon which hung the fate of
Europe, decided, in a great measure, by the vast superiority of
the British cavalry, which, while it roused the fears, drew forth

the admiration of the greatest captain of the age! '*Regardez ces beaux chevaux gris—quelles terrible chevaux!*' he exclaimed, as they swept through his ranks. On the other hand, take a retrospective view of the horses in the State of New York and the adjoining State of New Jersey, as they were twenty-five years back; view the scanty sample of improvement made, or permitted to be made, save in a certain favored district of New York, contemplate what the whole, or rather, those in distant parts of the State, in all probability, would have been at this date but for legislative interference, and picture to yourself what, in a comparative sense, they actually are. Compare the superb steeds that carried dismay through Napoleon's ranks, with the miserable louches our brave soldiers had to mount during either the Revolution or the late war, and what of necessity our army would be equipped with, were they even at this late day compelled to take the field! What a contrast! 'If I wished to ruin a province,' said the Great Frederick of Prussia, 'I would send a philosopher to govern it.'

"We may take occasion hereafter—though we should much prefer to leave the matter with our numerous corps of intelligent correspondents—to suggest some means for the general revival of the Sport of the Turf in the North as well as in the Old Dominion. RACING CANNOT GO DOWN! The immense amount of capital invested in Blood Stock in the United States—*not less than* FIVE MILLIONS OF DOLLARS!—*absolutely forbids it!* Every one acquainted with the Turf is aware that a three-year-old colt like Ruffin, The Colonel, and others, will command $5,000 at any moment—that a nonpareil like Fashion is worth $10,000 (though she would not be parted with under $12,000)—that a young brood mare like Delphine is worth $3,500 or more, and that a stallion of the pretensions of Priam, Eclipse, or Medoc, in their prime would readily fetch $15,000, notwithstanding 'the hard times.' Break up your breeding and training establishments and Blue Dick would not sell for $300!—Grey Medoc and Trustee would be worth each, about $600!—Bonnets o' Blue would command at auction $100, possibly!

"It behooves the friends of *the good cause* to give this matter their grave and earnest consideration. The sports of the Turf, like every thing else, have been seriously affected by the monetary reverses of the country. But we have now, we trust, seen the worst, so that 'things *must* mend.' Already business and confidence are reviving throughout the Union. With the steady advance in the price of real estate, and the great staples of the country, that of Blood Stock should keep pace. 'A long pull, a strong pull, and a pull altogether,' by the parties interested, will effect so desirable an object. Will they unite with us, and put their shoulders to the wheel ?"

The number of subscribers was never larger than in 1847, and the correspondents of the paper had increased forty-fold. Instead of the usual array of literary articles from the British magazines, which had so long enriched its columns, the editor substituted original sketches and letters written expressly for the "Spirit," giving a preference to those which were thoroughly American, and presenting the peculiar characteristics and illustrating scenes and incidents of the "Universal Yankee nation," from the St. Lawrence to the Rio Grande.

The officers of the army, and the same remark will apply to those of the navy, not only liberally contributed to the "Spirit," and gave it the material aid of a very general subscription, but also from their strong personal attachment to the Editor, forwarded to him all manner of curiosities, both natural and artificial, which were obtained by them in their expeditions, so that his "Curiosity Shop," as he called it, had a "charm," which would well compare with that in the Witches' Caldron, in Macbeth:

"Eye of newt, and toe of frog,
　Wool of bat, and tongue of dog,
　Adder's fork, and blind-worm's sting,
　Lizard's leg, and owlet's wing."

One of his gallant friends presented to him a pair of South American or Mexican stirrups; the editor writes of them:

"They were of wood, and weighed about five pounds each! elaborately carved on three sides; the foot cannot project through them, and no one could imagine for what possible purpose they were intended, unless informed. They no more resemble an American stirrup than does a chest of drawers a coal scuttle, a bet on the Presidential election, or any thing else in which a man has a chance 'to put his foot in it!'"

From the great variety of queer things which the thoughtfulness of familiar friends heaped upon him, he selects the names of a few, and thus acknowledges the receipt of Sherred India Rubber Pantaloons, that were warranted to stretch to the crack of doom; a pair of Saxon Wool Socks, knit expressly for him by the industrious wife of a Mississippi planter; colored maps of the battles in Mexico; a superb collection of artificial flies; Limerick hooks; a dozen " droppers; " an assortment of colored gut " leaders; " a harpoon and lance, used in the whale fishery; the head of a pike, which, when dressed, weighed twenty-two pounds; a dozen cane fishing-rods from South Carolina; the skin of an enormous bear; half a dozen skins of the White Fox and Hare of Newfoundland; the white partridge from Nova Scotia; a tandem whip; the skin of an immense Pelican, from C. D. Bunce, Esq., of N. O.; colored engravings of the Revolutionary scenes of Paris, from G. W. Kendall, Esq.; a sash worn by the late Capt. S. H. Walker, of the Texas Rangers, who was killed in Mexico, from Lt. Stonehall of the U. S. R. Service; and lastly, a snake from North Carolina with "thirty-one rattles besides the button;" "this pleasant musical box," says the Editor, "being seven inches in length."

In this connection, though not in chronological order, we insert his acknowledgment of a "service of plate" and other articles of value, which is in his own peculiar and quiet style of humor:

PRESENTATION OF PLATE TO THE EDITOR.

"The Editor of the 'Spirit of the Times' begs leave to offer his acknowledgments to his friends in Alabama, Louisiana, Mississippi, Kentucky, Virginia, and New Jersey, for their very acceptable present of a 'Service of Plate'—or rather of 'Plates,' which 'have done the State some service.' Connoisseurs in antique gold or silver Plate may call our taste in question, as may the admirers of fine Engravings, but we, notwithstanding, take occasion to express the belief that no specimen of the Fine Arts, nor of the Goldsmiths' art, will for an instant sustain a comparison with the pieces of Plate presented us as a mark of the distinguished consideration of the donors. Be it known, then, that the 'Plates' presented us are of neither gold nor silver —neither draughts nor drawings, but the 'Plates,' or 'pumps' worn by High-Mettled Racers in their exhibitions of game and speed, in place of shoes!

"We have received two of those worn by Mr. GIBBONS' *Fashion*, the Champion of the American Turf, in her great match with LONG and JOHNSON's *Boston*, and two also of those worn

by him on the same memorable occasion. One of each is intended for the editor of 'Bell's Life in London,' after they shall
have been properly set and lettered, with the number of races
run by the rival champions of the The North and The South.
The time of ' The best race ever run in America '—7.32½—7.45—
will not be omitted.

"We have also received one of the plates worn by Mr. Bos-
WELL's *Jim Bell* of Kentucky, and one of those worn by Col.
BINGAMAN's *Sarah Bladen* of Mississippi, when they ran four-
mile heats at New Orleans, in 7.37—7.40!

"We also have one of those worn by Mr. BAIRD's *Miss Foote*
of Alabama, when she beat Earl of Margrave, Hannah Harris,
and Luda, in 8.02—7.35!

"Also one of those worn by Mr. WELLS' *Reel* of Louisiana,
when she beat Luda and John R. Grymes, in 7.40—7.43!

"The above, added to one worn by Messrs. KENNER's *Grey
Medoc*, of Louisiana, in his race beating Altorf and Denizen, in
7.35—8.19—7.42—8.17, makes our 'Service of Plate' sufficiently
complete for the accommodation of ' a pleasant party,' which in
number should not be less than the Graces nor more than the
Muses! This ' plate ' of ours is of a description of ' ware ' that
will not readily *wear out!* Indeed, it has seen service already,
and has withstood a deal of '*wear and tear!*' Those of Boston
and Fashion especially, have received some hard knocks, and in
size, as compared with those worn by Miss Foote and Reel, they
are as ' fish dishes ' to ' dessert plates.' In weight one of Fashion's plates exceeds that of Jim Bell and Reel added together.
Sarah Bladen has the largest foot, and Miss Foote the smallest;
the latter's plate weighs exactly one ounce! The plates of
Fashion and Boston are of the same size; for a fore and hind
foot they weigh five ounces."

Again, he writes:

"We have to acknowledge this week the receipt of an addition to our collection of *Sporting Curiosities* of extraordinary
interest. We are indebted for it to Mr. GILBERT W. PATRICK

of this city, better known to the Sporting World as ' *Gil Patrick,*' one of the most distinguished jockeys that has figured on the American Turf. ' Gil ' has given us nothing less than one of his steel-plated *Spurs*, which he wore constantly from the time he rode Post Boy in his match with Bascombe in 1836, up to the day when he rode Boston in his match with Fashion! It will be recollected that on the last occasion Gil rode the gallant veteran with a single spur; that identical Spur is before us as we pen this paragraph; it has not been worn since, its mate having been lost. The rowel is still discolored with the blood and sweat of old Boston, and there are half a dozen short chestnut hairs attached to its point, each one as precious in our eyes as those Benedick offered to bring ' from the Great Kham's beard.' How much ' claret ' has Gil ' tapped ' with this little instrument, and how many glossy sides has he ' tickled ' with it, between '36 and '42! What shouts have been raised, what enthusiasm excited, what fortunes won and lost, what ' vast renown ' achieved, by ' the still small voice ' of this ' eloquent persuader '! Omega, Blue Dick, Santa Anna, and Argyle, have made some of their most brilliant races under the magic touch of Gil's heel when armed with this ounce of steel. Though he may never have felt its tickling, Monarch for two seasons was on intimate terms with it, while Atalanta and Emily, Rocker and Blacknose, Lord of Lorn and Treasurer, must have retained for some time a keen sense of Gil's use of it. Wonder and Fordham, with Charlotte Russe, Zenobia, and many more, were no little indebted to it for the character they maintained on the Turf. Armed with this little spur, Gil ' won golden opinions from all sorts of people,' and we regard it, as do many who have seen it, as one of the most interesting articles in our collection."

Mr. Porter was solicited to make a compilation of humorous articles from the " Spirit," and having consented, he published " The Big Bear in Arkansas " and other sketches, illustrative of characters and incidents in the South and West, illustrated by Darley.

9*

The volume contained twenty-one sketches or stories, not unworthy of Hood or Dickens, and met with a rapid sale, as a capital specimen of amusing narratives and vivid descriptions. Besides this addition to his ordinary labors, in 1846 he edited the English work, " Guns and Shooting," by Col. Hawker ; how faithfully he accomplished it may be inferred from the fact that out of four hundred and fifty-nine pages, two hundred were American and original. It was the first purely sporting work ever published in the United States, and was in every respect a well-executed manual for the sportsman ; by universal consent, it was considered as conferring infinite credit on the editor.

As Mr. Porter felt a deep sympathy for the friends of manly recreation, he watched with lively interest the organization of a Yacht Club in New York, chronicled its movements, and frequently acknowledged the great pleasure he had received from the civilities and consideration which it had extended to him. We well know that he loved to " wet a line," but doubt if he ever fancied a " wet jacket " on board any kind of craft. In one of his papers, he gave an animated picture of the Annual Regatta of the Club, which he closed with this playful remark : " It is all very well, this talk about Demosthenes and Cicero, but the ancients never heard Mr. Blunt when presenting a Cup to the winner of a New York Yacht Club Regatta, nor his response." At the next race, each yacht was to be manned exclusively by members of the Club : " A race with Gentlemen Riders," writes

Mr. Porter, "will be nothing to this in excitement. If we could not wade out or swim anywhere where it is moist, we should immediately order a life-preserver!"

Akin to this interest in sports connected with physical training was his prompt support of all rational amusement; and though not a constant or ardent playgoer, he was from the start a discriminating friend of the Drama; the following article is proof of his appreciation of the stage and solicitude for the comfort of those who gave it attractiveness and character:

"*A Theatrical Fund Association.*—Although for the last few years the genius of invention, that characteristic of the American nation, seems to have expended itself in the creation of charitable associations—in a popular display of individual sympathy, still it is remarkable that we have but few institutions of a definite and beneficial nature. While we have zealously organized philanthropic combinations of every imaginable species, we appear to have forgotten to provide for those of our fellow-beings, whose professions are of the more elevated order of life— more especially the followers of Literature and the Drama. With commendable exertions we act as guardians to the temporal welfare of every aspirant to mendicity, and, with a like zeal, we take charge of the spiritual concerns of every afflicted member in our community, and, while all these things are publicly applauded, we omit a consideration of the sufferings of another class of fellow-men. The very life of the actor, subject to the whims and oddities of the public taste, the foibles and follies of vulgar prejudices, renders him in a great degree dependent not only on his own exertions, but on the benevolence of the community. The stage may be, with justice, termed the charnel-house of intellect—the crypt wherein are annually buried many bright and aspiring minds, enticed from the walks of every-day life by the pomp and glitter of a scenic world. We gaze with rapture on the actions of the actor—the minister of our happiest pleasures, and little do we dream of the vicissitudes of the inward life of him, whose external aspect is so inviting. If we look at the biographies of any of those who have from time to time swayed the sceptre of the theatrical monarchy —Garrick, Kean, Molière or Talma—we always find them keenly alive to the afflictions and necessities of their comrades— the flickering and uncertain careers of their associates. Without doubt these considerations, based on the hardship of their early existence—their toil and labors to attain their subsequent reputation, induced Garrick and Molière to urge the establishment of the Drury Lane fund, and that of the *Comedie Francaise*. The self-same causes which led to the institution of these associations in England and France, exist, in a greater degree, in our country, and therefore we would deem the establishment of similar funds not only as an act of justice, but of absolute necessity. We have no doubt but that, in the furtherance of a national dramatic fund, the many eminent tragedians, comedians, and vocalists now in the Union would be happy to contribute their aid, and for the consummation of this wholesome charity, the public will never be remiss in seconding the efforts of a few leading men. The first movement must, as a matter of necessity, come from the actors themselves; to their listlessness can be alone attributed the non-success of prior schemes; it is for them to digest and arrange the mode of operation of the society, as being far better qualified to judge of the wants of a theatrical community, than those who have never entered within the precincts of the actor's world. When once firmly instituted on a liberal basis, one neither too diffuse nor too exclusive, we can assure them of a response on the part of the public. Of the success of such a fund we are sanguine, as benefiting not only the actor, but the drama in all its manifold branches."

Within something like a twelvemonth, death had deprived Mr. Porter of some of his most distinguished friends and safe counsellors. Among them was Judge Duval, of Maryland, whose familiarity with the Turf

for more than forty years was only equalled by his
accurate knowledge of Jurisprudence. His death
was followed by that of John Boardman, Esq., of
Alabama, whose valuable essays on breeding, training, and other kindred topics, contributed to the interest and usefulness of the "Spirit" and "Register,"
and were republished in England with signal commendation. The Hon. Alexander Porter was the
next honored friend whose loss he deplored most
acutely; then succeeded that of Henry Inman, one
of his best and choicest friends, on the 24th of January, 1846; they were very differently organized, yet
had many kindred tastes, and for years were united
by a strong brotherly attachment, which death only
could break asunder. Mr. Porter thus feelingly la-
ments the event:

"A great and good man has sunk to rest—one who has illustrated the genius of his country by the most imperishable monu-
ments. HENRY INMAN is no more! Rarely gifted as he was by
nature, his acquirements were of such a character, that he would
have ennobled any station to which he might have been called,
or graced any circle into which his enthusiastic and lofty impulses might have thrown him. This is not the time to write
his epitaph; eminently appreciated as he was by his countrymen generally, not to speak of the almost idolatrous regard entertained for him by all those who came within the range of his
personal acquaintance and intercourse, yet not until his memory
is hallowed by time, and we are made fully to realize the loss we
have sustained, can ample justice be done to his genius, his character, and undying fame.

"Eminent as was the position he enjoyed as an artist, and
proud as his friends were of the universal homage paid to his
surpassing merit on both sides of the Atlantic, by 'mouths of

wisest censure,' yet as a friend, a poet, and as a scholar, was he most endeared to those who enjoyed the unqualified pleasure of his companionship. His scholastic attainments were of the very highest order, and though he indulged in literary pursuits, rather as a relief to his mind than for any settled purpose, yet he has left behind him many fugitive sketches in prose and verse that will endure through all time. His intellect was not only highly cultivated, but his knowledge was vast, and his brilliant imagination so teemed with images of grandeur and beauty, that his conversational powers surpassed those of any man we ever met; yet was he as guileless and simple as a child. If he excelled supereminently in any thing beyond his art, we are not sure but we should give the palm to his epistolary correspondence; and when the time arrives—as it inevitably will—when '*I have a painting of* INMAN'S!' will be no common boast, how much more dearly cherished will be the mementos of his unalterable friendship and regard!

"Next to his devotion to his friends and his art, was Inman's fondness for Field Sports. In trout-fishing, especially, he excelled; as in the case of Prof. WILSON and other kindred spirits, this was emphatically his hobby. And a more ardent, accomplished or delightful disciple, good old Izaak Walton never had. In throwing a fly or spinning a minnow, he had few equals.

$$* \qquad * \qquad * \qquad * \qquad * \qquad *$$

"But alas! 'Where be your gibes now? your gambols? your songs? your flashes of merriment, that were wont to set the table in a roar?' On Tuesday last the grave closed over the remains of the illustrious dead. He yielded up his spirit to the God who gave it, on the previous Saturday at noon, in his forty-fifth year, after taking a final leave of his bereaved family and friends. He appeared to be perfectly aware for some time previous of his approaching dissolution. On giving the last touch to his 'October Afternoon'—a painting finished during the month of October past, and which was almost his last production—he remarked that he had painted his last picture! A mutual friend, in paying a feeble tribute to his memory, truthfully remarks that 'Rarely does there pass away from earth a man

whose life more endeared him to those who knew him, than
Inman. He had all the qualities which go to the making up of
a true man : and so genial was his character ; so full of every
thing which could qualify a companion and form a friend ; so
abounding was his eloquent conversation with the riches of a
cultivated and well-stored mind, with suggestive philosophy,
sparkling wit, genuine humor, and illustrative anecdote ; so
keenly did he enjoy life and life's blessings, and the many friends
that enjoyed it too, and the more for his companionship—and all
this, too, while Disease was weighing him down with her heavy,
crushing hand,—that we could hardly realize the fact of his being
destined to an early grave. Yet now we feel it, keenly feel it,
true. * * * * * He has gone in and out among the wide
circle of his friends and acquaintances, for many years laying up
stores of future association with his memory, and rearing all the
while a beautiful and enduring monument of his excelling
genius. To few in our country, in their own lifetime, has Fame
sounded a clearer and more assuring pæan than that which she
has breathed over the easel of Inman. He was one of the elect
of Genius, to whom was vouchsafed the glorious vision of his
own immortality.

"Henry Inman was born at Utica, in this State, (of which
his father was one of the earliest settlers,) but had long made this
city his place of residence ; he died of disease of the heart, an
event which, for months, we have trembled with the assured
apprehension of being called upon to record, and yet so appalling
to us is it that we can hardly do more than write the sad and
simple fact. His taste for art began to develop itself in boyhood, and we are informed by a contemporary that 'notwithstanding he received a commission to enter the Military Academy
at West Point, he evinced so unequivocal a bent for the profession in which he has since become so eminent, that his father
placed him in New York under the tuition of the elder JARVIS.
The young artist soon rose to that position due to his talents and
assiduity. Some of his first paintings were made in Albany,
and are in possession of her citizens.' About a year since, Mr.
Inman sailed for Europe, where he spent ten months. During

this time he painted portraits of Dr. Chalmers, Wordsworth, Macaulay, and Lord Cottenham—a sketch of Rydal Water, near Wordsworth's residence—one equally beautiful of a salmon-fishing scene in Scotland, and several others. His portraits, by which, perhaps, like Sir Thomas Lawrence, he will be longest known, comprise those of the highest dignitaries of the State and city governments, the most distinguished ornaments of the bench, the bar, the pulpit, etc. His portraits of Bishops Hobart, Moore, and Doane, of Mrs. Gen. Hampton, and others, are perfect gems, while those of several of the Mayors of this city, and the Governors of the State, and of a great number of distinguished citizens of this and other States, must now be regarded as almost priceless.

"Mr. Inman has left a wife and five children. His eldest son, JOHN INMAN, Jr.,—a youth of seventeen,—is rarely endowed. For some years he has practised drawing under the eye of his father, and has lately produced several pictures in oil that prove him not unworthy to sit at his father's easel. As upon the occasion of the demise of the late lamented WASHINGTON ALSTON, we beg to suggest that the Academy of Design, supported by the thousand friends of the deceased, his brother artists, and his fellow-citizens generally, open an *Inman Gallery* for the exhibition of his pictures, and the sale of such drawings, sketches, etc., as he has left behind him, for the benefit of his family. All are ready to move in the good work, and only await the suggestion of the most feasible and appropriate plan of accomplishing it."

Two years before Mr. Inman's death, just before sailing for Europe in 1844, he made a sketch of Mr. Porter, an engraved copy of which accompanies this volume. The likeness is admirably preserved, while the head is idealized in the true spirit of genius. All that gave individual mark to the outer man, or genial warmth to the inner dwelling of his loving spirit, is here faithfully portrayed. The more it is dwelt upon, the more it strengthens in living sweetness of expression, until we can scarcely believe that his " smile of perpetual sunshine " is among the joys of the past!

The next week Mr. Porter writes:

"It is with melancholy pleasure that we are enabled to announce the adoption of a plan in aid of the family of the departed Inman. The plan thought most feasible, and likely in its results to be productive of most benefit, is that suggested in our article of last week, and which was proposed and adopted at a meeting of the Academy of Design, held for the purpose of taking the matter into consideration. It embraces the formation of a gallery, to be composed of the different pictures painted by Inman, and collected from all attainable sources, and its exhibition at some appropriate place, the proceeds to be devoted to the ulterior object in view. The exhibition will be opened during the ensuing week."

A numerous committee took the matter in hand, and the Inman Gallery was opened. It contained one hundred and twenty-six paintings, sketches, and drawings of the artist—many portraits tendered by the owners being reluctantly declined for want of room in the " Art Union," where the collection was exhibited. It was a most successful enterprise, and made glad the heart of the beloved friend who suggested it.

During the year there was a large accession of subscribers to the " Spirit " in various parts of the country, including a valuable roll of the names of officers in the Army of the United States, many of whom were contributors to its columns ; indeed, there was scarcely a military post which had not its brilliant writer for a paper which was a universal and favored guest wherever the flag of the Union floated. G * * de L * *, whose letters to the "Spirit" were considered the most graphic and animating from the army during the war with Mexico, and which were republished in half the papers of the day, was Capt. W. Seton Henry, of the 3d U. S. Infantry. He was in the battles of Palo Alto, Resaca de la Palma, Monterey and Vera Cruz, in all of which his regiment was on the most perilous ridge of battle. It was said of this gallant officer, not now living, "He fights as well as any man, and writes as well as he fights."

CHAPTER VIII.

IT is but justice to Mr. Porter as an angler, that his hints and suggestions upon his favorite source of recreation should be kept alive; especially as they contain more unconscious displays of the man than can be found in any of his other writings.

He was esteemed master of the higher art of trout-fishing, and to his unrivalled dexterity and grace in throwing a line, he added a thorough theoretical knowledge of his favorite department, as well as a practical familiarity with all its details. So long as this exhilarating sport shall be enjoyed either as an occasional pastime or as a " grand and expansive passion " by the over-tasked statesman, the hard-worked scholar, the naturalist, the inbred sportsman, or a single faithful pupil of the Walton school, in the length and breadth of the sporting-grounds of America, so long will Mr. Porter's practical hints be read with advantage, and his name be breathed softly and affection-

ately by those lovers of the angle, who in coming
time will only know him as he is connected with this
chapter.

No book ever made him a practical angler. Old
Dame Nature, who is supposed by many to have been
born several years previous to the birth of Mascall, or
Taverner, or Markham, or old Izaak Walton, directed
him at a very tender age to the asylum of some of
her wriggling family in the vicinity of the kitchen
spout, and gave him a realizing sense of their value
in connection with a crooked pin, a tow string, and
willow rod. From the eventful moment which witnessed his first breathless but successful experiment
with these unsophisticated forces to land a gigantic
chub from one of the crystal brooks of Newbury, it
was " all go " with him for the remainder of his
mortal time up to within a few weeks of his death.
Though his duties pressed almost exclusively upon
his time during his laborious manhood, he generally
contrived to find leisure to steal away in the ripest
glow of the hot months with a party of brother anglers,
to some distant fishing-ground, or to stray off to Long
Island alone, for the enjoyment of his favorite sport.
In writing of Kendall's Santa Fé Expedition, he says :
" No man ever truly polished a book unless he were
something of an angler, or at least loved the occupation.
He who steals from the haunts of men into the green
solitudes of nature, by the banks of gliding, silvery
streams, under the checkering lights of sun, leaf and
cloud, may always hope to cast his lines, whether of
the rod or the ' record-book,' in pleasant places."

TROUT-FISHING ON LONG ISLAND.

" Of all sports ever sported, commend me to angling. It is the wisest, virtuousest, discreetest, best; the safest, cheapest, and in all likelihood, the oldest of pastimes. It is a one-handed game, that would have suited Adam himself; it was the only one by which Noah could have amused himelf in the ark. Hunting and shooting come in second and third. The common phrase, ' Fish, flesh, and fowl,' hints clearly at this order of precedence. * * * To refer to my own experience, I certainly became acquainted with the angling-rod next after the birchen one, and long before I had any practical knowledge of ' Nimrod ' or ' Ramrod.' * * * The truth is, Angling comes by nature. It is *in the system*, as the doctors say. Plenty of children are born with water in the head; but whoever heard of a boy coming into the world with gunpowder on the brain, or tops and leathers on his legs ? "

Thus discourses, in praise of Angling, that " klevver dogge and phunne poette," Tom Hood. And who shall gainsay him ? Does not every ardent disciple of honest old Izaak Walton feel its truth tingling to the tips of his fingers' ends ?

Fly-fishing has been designated the royal and aristocratic branch of the angler's craft, and unquestionably it is the most difficult, the most elegant, and to men of taste, by myriads of degrees the most exciting and pleasant mode of angling. To land a trout of three, four, or five pounds weight, and sometimes heavier, with a hook almost invisible, with a gut line as delicate and beautiful as a single hair from the raven tresses of a mountain sylph, and with a rod not heavier than a tandem whip, is an achievement requiring no little presence of mind, united to consummate skill. If it be not so, and if it do not give you some very pretty palpitations of the heart in the performance, may we never wet a line in Lake George, or raise a trout in the Susquehanna. Fly-fishing requires many natural attributes, among which must be chiefly enumerated, a light and flexible hand and arm, a quick eye, and one that can "squint straight," caution, coolness, and an extreme delicacy of touch. From the sources of the Delaware and the Susquehanna to those of the Kennebec, and in the thousand mountain streams flowing into the St. Lawrence, trout-fishing may now be enjoyed (May and June) in the utmost perfection. We have dreamed, or have somewhere heard, that it is not until the cowslip has shed its golden smiles over the meadows, and your ears are saluted with the vernal notes of the reed-sparrow; when the "ephemera" or May-fly is seen (courting its destruction) giddily to wanton over the surface of the stream which only a few hours before brought it into existence, that trout are "initiated into condition," and rise freely to the fly. You may now see them lurking in every direction in the ponds of New England; while on Long Island, he that cannot kill twenty brace at the close of a summer afternoon, or before the sun gets up, should not be allowed to wet a line. The gray and green drake,

which the nearest resemble the May-fly, succeed it
in their season, and are equally welcomed by "Johnny
Trout." The *palmer* family follow in order, and may
be used throughout the season with success. But
there is, during the still evening of midsummer, a
minute black gnat, which riots in myriads over every
stream, and we have seen trout in a continued state
of excitement for above an hour in carping at these
gnats. We confess our entire disbelief in a doctrine
considered orthodox by many, that each season and
stream has its peculiar and appropriate flies; and we
have arrived at this conclusion after as much practical
experience as many Waltonians who have attained the
age of fourscore. Since we were stout enough to
wield a rod, our "constant custom of an afternoon"
has been to put it to use, if, by hook or by crook, we
could; for the which propensity many is the birchen
one we have had applied to our shoulders, and we
are free to say, that our experience goes to prove, that
with three flies well matched, there is very little necessity of cumbering one's hook with an infinite variety.
Give us a red or brown hackle for the end of our
leader, with a black midge for the first dropper, and
a light salmon-colored butterfly not larger than your
thumb-nail for the second, and we can raise from his
cool retreat the craftiest trout that ever gorged a
grasshopper, or turned up his nose in scorn at the
bungling efforts of a greenhorn.

TROUT-FISHING, FISHING-TACKLE, &c.

In reply to one of William's correspondents, ask-

ing for minute information upon certain points connected with trout-fishing, the former rejoins:

"We have a shrewd suspicion that the identity of
our correspondent is not unknown to us; that we have
had the pleasure of seeing him *at home*, while enjoying
the hospitalities which his honored father dispenses
with such infinite grace at Lexington. In answer to
his inquiries: the best practical treatises on fishing
are Sir Humphrey Davy's '*Salmonia,* or Days of
Fly Fishing,' and 'The Rod and the Gun,' by Wilson
and the author of 'The Oakleigh Shooting Code.' *But
experience is the best teacher.* To become a first-rate
angler, one must be born to it, as one must be born a
poet, a painter, or a musician.

"Izaak Walton eloquently sustains us on this point:
  *   *   *   " 'Doubt not but that Angling is an art;
is it not an art to deceive a Trout with an artificial
fly? a Trout! that is more sharp-sighted than any
Hawk you have named, and more watchful and timor-
ous than your high-mettled Merlin is bold? and yet, I
doubt not to catch a brace or two to-morrow for a
friend's breakfast. Doubt not, therefore, sir, but that
Angling is an art, and an art worth your learning:
the question is rather, whether you be capable of
learning it? for Angling is something like Poetry,
men are to be born so; I mean with inclinations to
it, though both may be heightened by discourse and
practice: but he that hopes to be a good Angler, must
not only bring an inquiring, searching, observant wit,
but he must bring a large measure of hope and patience, and a love and propensity to the art itself; but

having once got and practised it, then doubt not but Angling will prove to be so pleasant, that it will prove to be like virtue, a reward to itself.'

"To justly appreciate the truth, the poetry, the honest purpose and the good feeling expressed in the above quotation, one must be an enthusiastic disciple of the good, the pious and the time-honored old Izaak. In a vast country like ours, where the different modes of fishing are almost as numerous as the varieties of the finny tribe themselves, it is manifestly impossible to lay down other than very general directions for the information of the neophyte. Wilson tells us, with equal candor and truth, that ' expert angling never was and never will be successfully taught by rule, but is almost entirely the result of assiduous and long-continued practice.' Of ordinary rod-fishing for *trout* with worms or live bait, we presume our correspondent understands the first principles, consequently he has in fact already commenced his primary lessons in Fly-fishing and Trolling. But in this section of the country, whether fishing for the common speckled trout or the salmon trout of the lakes, he cannot use a fly with advantage until the middle of May, nor can he troll successfully for salmon or salmon trout until about the first of June. Before the appropriate season commences, we will endeavor to enlighten our correspondent on both matters, though we beg him distinctly to understand that no one can do much more for him after informing him when he can find sport, than to recommend suitable tackle, and show him how it may be best adapted to his wants in his 'pursuit

10

of knowledge under difficulties.' The art of throwing a fly is readily attained by one who handles his rod well in bait-fishing, but nothing like perfection will be achieved until after careful and persevering practice.

*　　*　　*　　*　　*　　*　　*　　*

"Trolling and hand-line fishing is about as simple as set lines through the ice or otherwise: an apt scholar will learn to practise either in a few hours. In trolling with flies or live bait (and it is well enough to have both attached to your leader at the same time) you can pay out your line better, and it will play more freely, by having your largest fly or live bait at the extreme end of your leader; let your drop-flies or bait be diminished in size in proportion as they are looped on the leader from the end. In trolling (with a rod is much the surest and pleasantest method) your gut leader may be made within a few feet of its length; if longer, you will fray and soon ruin it in reeling in your fish. Until you get accustomed to it —until you begin to play, kill and land your fish like an artist, you should use a short leader, not above six feet long; its length you can increase as you get on. In rod-fishing, we would recommend, at first, the trial of a single hook; when you can use two, let the bait on the lowest be heaviest. It is not a bad plan in early spring fishing for trout, with worms or live bait, before they begin to rise freely to the fly, to attach a fly to your line several feet above your bait, (in proportion to the depth of water.) Every one using a float must have remarked an occasional 'rise'

to it by some very old trout, that would not be tempted with bait. Very early in the summer it is advisa-
ble to bait your lower hook with worms, and the other
with live bait; that is, if you can catch killies or
shiners with a scrap-net. We dislike using a float,
but in some streams that are overhung with low trees,
or have a light current, one is absolutely necessary, in
order to get your bait carried clear of roots and out
of eddies, into the dark, deep holes under banks,
rocks, stumps, etc. Next to fly-fishing, there is nothing so delightful nor so difficult as brook fishing; in
nothing is patience, skill and indomitable perseverance more required, and in the *successful* angler these
qualities stand out in bold and beautiful relief.

"In *pond* fishing, or in streams too deep for wad-
ing, (which is greatly to be preferred whenever prac-
ticable,) the utmost care must be exercised to *keep
your boat out of the channel*, where, with their heads
to the current, trout always lie. If once disturbed,
they become shy, and will rarely bite or rise to the
fly for some time. Paddle your boat quietly, and in
anchoring make as little noise as possible; go no
nearer a good 'hole' than will enable you barely, by
a good cast, to throw into it; by this means, instead
of frightening them all, you may take half a dozen of
the twenty fish in it. If you use a float and sinker,
let them be as slight as may be, and be careful to drop
them lightly into the water.

"As for *places where to find sport*, every reader of
the 'Spirit' in this vicinity well knows. There is not
a babbling brook or tide stream, nor a pond, public

or private, of any repute, within a hundred miles of
our sanctum, in which we have not at some time wet
a line. On the south side of Long Island one can
hardly go amiss, while at Smithtown there are three
fine ponds and two creeks, in all of which we have
had capital sport. Stump Pond was ever a favorite
resort for us. There are several in the immediate
vicinity of Babylon. Seven miles further on, at Islip,
will be found a good place, and one of the finest
creeks on the Island. It is worth ten times the drive
just to spend a day or two at Crandall's Hotel. An
hour's drive will take you to Snedicor's, and two
hours more will land you at Uncle Sam Carman's at
Fire-Place. To be sure, there is capital fishing to be
had within ten miles of town, but unless you know
something about the proper time of tide, the holes,
etc., you might as well fish in a tea-kettle as in Spring
Creek.

"Of the trout-fishing in Hamilton and Sullivan
Counties in this State we have repeatedly spoken, as
also of that in the Sacondaga and the Hudson, near
their junction at Hadley Falls. Out of Maine, the
best trout streams in New England are situated in
that district of Massachusetts known as Cape Cod.
The Marshpee Brook at Marshfield is beyond all dispute the best one over which we ever held a rod.
The nearest good salmon-fishing is the Kennebec
River, Maine, and the Jacques-Cartier in Canada;
but in Piseco, Lake Pleasant, and other lakes in
Hamilton County, salmon trout weighing from three
to forty-five pounds, are taken in great abundance.

Most of these lakes are within sixty miles of Saratoga Springs.

" Our correspondent desires us to mention what an angler's *complete* outfit would cost at Conroy's? Now, this is no easy matter; the prices of rods vary from one to twenty-eight dollars; reels from one to eight; lines from sixpence to five dollars. A ' complete outfit' for a Northern man comprises three times as many articles as is required for a gentleman residing in the South or West, with the exception perhaps of South Carolina. We do not deem it necessary to have a different rod for trout, bass and salmon fishing; we have had for years half a dozen excellent rods, but very rarely use but one for any kind of rod-fishing; indeed, the two largest bass we ever caught were taken at the same instant with an extremely light and fragile London fly-rod, not heavier than a tandem-whip. Conroy has recently got up a new *general rod*, from a pattern we furnished him eighteen months since, which answers every purpose, either for fly, salmon, bass, black or pickerel fishing. He has immortalized the writer of this article by giving it the name of ' Porter's General Rod.' The idea of the rod in question was suggested by circumstances occurring in the use of a very fine one, made expressly for us some years since, by our venerable old friend Leutner. It has four joints for bass or pickerel, and five for trout or salmon fishing, with three extra tips. It can be so put together as to make a rod either ten or sixteen feet in length; you may make out of it a light hand-rod for fly-fishing, or a heavy, powerful rod, sufficiently strong to play a thirty-pound salmon or bass, at the end of a hundred yards of line! Instead of rings on one side, 'Porter's General Rod' has fluted guides on both sides, through which the line can play; the sockets of the joints are double instead of single, that end of the joint fitting into the double sockets having double ferrules around it. There is no difficulty in taking this rod apart from the swelling of the wood from wet, while at the same time you may use it all day without tightening the joints; it can never get out of order with fair usage. Its weight is about three pounds only; the smaller joints are of lancewood, and the ferrules, guides, tips, rockets, etc., are of German silver. Conroy informed us a few days since that he had more orders for this rod than for all others added together. Conroy has lately got up a Patent Balance *Reel*—the most perfect thing ever invented. It is of German silver, which, by the way, is admirably adapted for all metal apparatus, save hooks, embraced in the paraphernalia of an angler, as it does not corrode. A reel that will multiply twice is preferable to any other; it is difficult to make a cast with one that multiplies more—or less, either, unless it be of very large size. On no account buy a *cheap* one, whatever rod you may select. A poor reel is of all mean things the meanest.

"Hooks of the best quality are to be found for two or three shillings per dozen, (always excepting Limericks of 'the O'Shaughnessy bend,' which are not to be had in this country for love or money, if you except, perhaps, a single one which *we* may give

you,) and these you must tie on yourself. Whether
the hooks of *Kirby & Co.* (vulgarly yclept ' curbed ')
or the Limerick are preferable, we shall not decide ;
for trout and salmon we prefer the latter, and the former for bass.   For trout you require hooks ranging
from No. 1 to 3—for salmon, from No. 1 to 5—for
bass, from No. 1 to 3.

" Instead of purchasing hooks on snells, buy a
hank of choice Spanish gut, and make your own snells
and leaders.   *Quill* floats are preferable for begin-
ners, as they are more quietly dropped into the water.
Duck-shot split make the best *sinker*, and let this be
as light as the current will admit.

" In the matter of *Lines* you must consult your
taste and purse.

" For *Flies*, a dollar expended with judgment will
' start you in business ;' before you use them up you
must learn to make your own.   Select of the Brown,
Red and Black Hackle two each ; then get two of
Martin Kelly's, (Dublin,) two March Browns, and two
Green Drakes.   If you fancy a Stone Fly, or any
other variety, get it, and Conroy will probably add a
Miller just for luck !

" A complete outfit for *Trout Fishing* may be obtained for about $40 ; that is, assuming that every
article is the very best of its kind.   Purchase nothing
that you do not actually require, and let every thing
be plain and substantial.   Remember, however, that
with five dollars more you may provide yourself with
every additional article that may be required in fishing for bass, bream, tautog, perch or pickerel.   The

$40 will provide you with a capital rod and reel, two lines and floats, two dozen assorted hooks, one dozen flies, one hank of gut, a hook for flies and snells, a bait-box, scrap-net, gaff, and a patent-leather drinking cup, (a capital French invention, that may be folded and carried in your vest-pocket.) If you *do* purchase a ' landing ' or ' scrap-net,' select one that has a brass frame which will fold up and also screw off; have your gaff made so as to screw on in its place, to the handle of the landing-net. If you propose visiting a sparsely inhabited region, where you may be obliged to camp out o' nights, buy an inch auger inserted as a handle in a light hatchet, the whole being secured in leather. With it you can erect a comfortable shanty in twenty minutes, or fasten together a raft strong enough to support ' half a horse and half an alligator.'

"There, that will do for the nonce. If our correspondent will do us the honor to pay us a visit during his next vacation, it will give us great pleasure to afford him the aid of our poor counsel in all matters pertaining to the subject of these crude paragraphs, penned in great haste, out of the affluence of a heart overflowing with charity and good will towards every disciple of honest old Izaak."

TROUT-FISHING IN HAMILTON COUNTY, N. Y.

(Which was accompanied with an illustration by Dick.)

How many scenes as romantic and wildly beautiful as that presented by Mr. Dick's engraving, are exhibited to the delighted gaze of the enthusiastic

angler among the lakes of Hamilton county, in this
State! The bold shores of these miniature seas, upon
which are piled, like "Pelion upon Ossa," ranges of
"everlasting hills," are covered with a luxuriant
growth of timber, presenting every brilliant hue and
variety of tint so characteristic of American forest
scenery; the pigmy promontories stretching far out
into the broad expanse of gently rippling waters, terminating in sand-bars glowing like molten silver in
the sun's rays; groups of islands, whose picturesque
beauty Calypso and her nymphs might envy, dotting
their placid surface like flocks of water-fowl, with here
and there a sail-boat moored in some quiet cove or
under a towering headland, from which the skilful
angler

"Lures from his cool retreat the crafty trout: "

how many charming scenes of this peculiar character
will be found in this wild and mountainous region!
Look again at our illustration. How well is depicted
a bright clear morning, at the moment when

"Jocund day stands tiptoe on the misty mountain-top."

The cool land-breeze has excited such a capital ripple
for fly-fishing, that one can almost fancy he sees
the trout "breaking" in all directions. Take the
figures in the foreground. How many hearts will instinctively yearn to enjoy "the royal and aristocratic
branch of the angler's craft," so felicitously indicated in the engraving! The fortunate individual
who is wielding his fly-rod with such palpable success,

10*

is evidently no greenhorn, though we should recommend him to allow Johnny Trout to keep his nose under water for a while longer, if he would assure himself of the pleasure of his company at dinner. How much like Alba Dunning or Tim Skidmore looks that tough young boatman resting on his oars, and watching with the keenest interest the fierce struggles of that five-pound trout, while with gaff in hand he is waiting his nearer approach to assist him safely on board! That rod fastened in the stern looks as if it might be useful; doubtless our friend has been trolling a minnow or two and half a dozen flies at the end of eighty feet of line, but astounded at the boldness of a sockdollager, in making a " rise " within twenty feet of the boat, he has evidently snatched up his single-handed fly-rod, and with a magnificent cast has dropped a most killing green-drake on the precise spot. Of course, a morsel so delicious and so temptingly displayed is not to be resisted by a salmon-trout suffering under " the keen demands of appetite," and results in a bold " break," a whir of the reel, a dash up fifty yards, consummate skill in making play on both sides, until the " tottle of the whole " matter is presented as in the scene illustrated by the engraving.

*   *   *   *   *   *

He writes in June, 1840, that the finest trout-fishing at this season of the year north of the Susquehanna, is to be had at Cape Cod; we are entreated not to be too definite, for a fortnight at least, when we shall be at liberty to flare up with the particular localities in

the towns of Sandwich, Barnstable, Warcham, &c.
A despatch from the head-quarters of the "Cape
Division," now at Marshpee, reached us last week.   It
was accompanied with two champagne baskets of fat,
rosy trout, of from one to three pounds weight.   The
run was splendid, nearly twenty weighing two pounds
each, while several came well up to three pounds.
One of his correspondents wrote from the Cape that
" we killed to-day eighty-eight trout—yesterday thirty-one, seven of which weighed twelve and a half
pounds ; * * * to-day we killed thirty, four of which
weighed ten and a half pounds, the largest weighing
three pounds."   "These trout," writes William, "were
caught in salt creeks ; were taken with minnows,
though after putting on a minnow, the Limerick was
tipped with a worm.   It is impossible to use a fly in
the Marshpee, owing to the foliage which completely
embowers the brook ; the best trout stream in which
it was our good fortune to wet a line.   In several
streams, however, the trout rise freely to the black
midge and brown hackle, and occasionally great execution may be done with a salmon-colored member
of the palmer family."

" Having returned last week (Sept. 1844) from
Hamilton Co., N. Y., we have no hesitation in express-
ing the opinion that more good fishing and hunting
may be found there than in any section of the country on this side of the Alleghanies.   It is now four
years since we first cast our line into these lakes, and
enthusiastic as our description of the trout-fishing
there was deemed at the time, we have been assured

by many gentlemen, who were induced to visit them
from our representations, that the reality far exceeded
their most sanguine expectations.   Although this is
not the best season of the year for killing trout, yet
it is far better there even now than it *ever* is on
Long Island ; while the shooting and hunting are
' immense.'   The fishing, as well as the hunting,
will be much better for the ensuing four weeks, than
it was during the period of our recent visit.

" Hamilton County is very sparsely settled, and still
less cultivated.   There are wood and water enough in
it for a pretty smart State, and the county is so
healthy, that ten men run away where one dies.   At
a majority of the best places for sport, one is five
miles from any house, and twenty from anywhere
else ; so you will be obliged to build a shanty and
camp out.   The salmon and lake trout are taken all
over the county, of prodigious size, occasionally weighing thirty-five pounds, while the speckled or brook-
trout run from one to four pounds, and are killed in
immense numbers.   The shooting is splendid ; there
are more moose and deer killed annually in Hamilton
County, than in any other half-dozen in the State.
Partridges, woodcock, etc., and a great variety of
water-fowl also, are found in untold abundance.   If
you would like a shy at a panther or bear, or a pack
of wolves, you can enjoy it ; but a moose, that is an
affair just a huckleberry over any American field
sport, short of buffalo-hunting.   A full-grown bull
moose is seventeen hands high, and his antlers sometimes measure eight feet from tip to tip.   A large

one weighs sixteen hundred pounds; the highest
fences would offer no obstruction to them, as they
can clear in their stride an immense log higher
than a man's head. They are gifted with extraordinary powers of speed and endurance, their gait
something between a trot and a rack; barring a buffalo chase, there is nothing so exciting or so dangerous
as moose-hunting on snow-shoes.

*"For 'things' required for Fishing, Shooting,
etc.*—Take your rifle with you, if you hope to knock
over a moose, but above all your double-barrelled
Westley Richards, and if you have one of Colt's or
Rolen's revolving pistols, take that along also. Take
your trout and your bass-rod, for in trolling you can
make use of each, and moreover an extra rod is not
a bad idea in case of accidents. Lay 'in a complete
supply of ammunition, including some wire cartridges.
For your fishing apparatus you must have at least one
braided silk line, not less than one hundred yards long
and on a good reel, for salmon-trout fishing. Let it be
stout. Recollect that half the *cheap* lines, after a few
days' fishing are not strong enough to pull a sitting-
hen off her nest! Killing a twenty-pounder at the end
of eighty yards of line is no child's play. Add two
or three nice elastic lines for ordinary trout-fishing.
If you are an artist, you will have a delicate fly-line,
to match your single-handed rod. Recollect that you
cannot splice a line so as to play a heavy fish well on a
jointed rod, and that one less than fifty yards long will
be of no account when you are about to use it. If

you can find a braided hair-line eighty-five feet long, nearly as large as a quill, and stout as a bed-cord, buy it, to use as a hand-line for lake trout. Take an extra reel or two : and 'Porter's General Rod.' We have used one for four years, and have not broken or strained so much as a tip ; it is in as fine order as when first turned out, and few rods have seen harder service. Brough caught a shark with it at Stonington nearly as long and heavy as himself, and we have killed with it three sockdollagers at a time repeatedly ; both trout, bass, and blue-fish. Get a hank of salmon-gut, and make your own leaders ; if you can't yet tie your flies, it is high time you set about acquiring the art. You want half a dozen sets of snap-hooks for trolling, we prefer the Kirby to the Limerick ; they should be quite small, not above half the size used for pike or pickerel. Have a couple of dozen of trout-hooks of assorted sizes, to provide for an emergency, and half a dozen of the smallest possible size for bait. Instead of a landing-net use a gaff ; the hook of the latter you can take in your pocket, while the former gives you as much trouble as a lady's bandbox. With regard to flies, use your own discretion as to colors, but be sure they are large. You will require a dozen salmon-flies tied on long Limerick hooks, and not less than two dozen trout-flies, that is, if you cannot make them. Fill your hook with the red and brown hackles ; green drakes, gray palmers and blue jays ; make their bodies gay and brilliant, and the longer their wings and tails the better. The most successful fly we ever used, we tied on during a furious

gale on Piseco Lake; it was a large, gaudy, coarsely
made thing, but a regular killer; body dark blue
hackle, with blue wings, and tail tipped with white
of the blue jay, head of golden red from a black-
bird's wing. A very little experience will enable
any person of moderate ingenuity to tie his own flies,
and a day's practice will teach him more about size
and color than he would acquire from books by a
month's study. 'Meadows' recommends a tyro to
take a well-made artificial fly to pieces, examining it
carefully as he proceeds; in a few trials he will succeed
in tying one to his mind. Do not embarrass yourself
with superfluous traps; the apparatus of a true disciple of the gentle art consists of a few plain, first-
rate articles. He looks upon the nicknacks of the
greenhorn, as if they were intended to catch trout
by dropping salt on their tails.

"Extra matters and things worth a consideration.—
If, perchance, you happen to be a modern 'Temperance
Society man,' you had better lay in your stores, for
you will find little or nothing better than ' old bold-
face' in Hamilton County, save at Van Derwarker's, at
Lake Pleasant. Having the fear of im-Providence
and bad dinners before us, we took the precaution to
lay in a few cold tongues, a delicious Virginia ham,
and some pressed corn-beef, an invention of mine
hosts of the Astor, on whom, and for which Danæ, or
some other pretty woman, should descend in a shower
of gold, if we could have a few minutes' conversation
with ' her man ' Jupiter. You also had best take

a small frying-pan and a griddle, both without handles, and an apparatus for striking a light. Lay in your cigars, if you smoke, and your tobacco, and provide yourself with a good pack. A light hatchet, with an inch auger for a handle, will be worth its weight in gold. If you have a large stout pair of India-rubber boots, put them in your carpet-bag : if. otherwise, get a pair of thick seal-skin ; have the heels made broad and flat, and be sure they are made a size or two larger than your foot. Don't carry a trunk large enough for a rhinoceros, and in packing it, make up your mind that every thing you wear will be torn into the size of bullet patches, before you return, provided you ' go in ' for the whole strength of the game ; such as walking for miles through a pathless forest, and camping out, though you may not be obliged to do any thing of the kind.

"*The Routes to Hamilton Co.*—If you start from New York, take the night-boat to Troy, and proceed to Saratoga Springs. Ask Maroni, of the United States Hotel, to get you a good pair of horses and a strong wagon, which you can always obtain, even in July and August, at a very moderate price. If you do not expect to be absent above a week, hire the horses for that time. Maroni will supply you with stores, and you can take a fair start. From the Springs to the handsome new hotel at Lake Pleasant, the distance is about sixty miles ; the route lies up through the Sacandaga Valley, a picturesque country, and the road is so good, that by an early start you can get through in a day.

"*Places for Sport about Lake Pleasant.*—The hotel here will be your head-quarters. It is within thirty rods of both Round Lake and Lake Pleasant, which are connected by a creek. The Sacandaga River is the outlet of these two lakes, and unites with West River (the outlet of Piseco Lake) at Wells. From your hotel you are within six miles of Piseco Lake, fourteen of Louis, eighteen of Indian, forty of Racket, and fifty of Long Lake. After fishing in the lakes in the immediate vicinity of the hotel, you must visit Louis Lake, taking ' Indian Clearing ' in your way. You can go a few miles in a wagon, and the remainder on horseback ; if there are four in the party, take two horses and ' ride and tie.' The distance is fourteen miles, but if you walk it you will think it forty. After Piseco, Louis Lake has afforded us the very best trout-fishing we ever enjoyed. And then the deer-shooting, as at Lake Pleasant, is capital. On the day of our last arrival there, they killed a fine bear, and one morning, of seven deer run into the lake, five were killed, including four bucks. Moose-hunting proper does not commence until after a heavy fall of snow. Some idea may be formed of the hunting to be had when we state that it is estimated that not less than one hundred moose and five hundred deer were killed last season within a range of thirty miles of Lake Pleasant.

" N. B.—On your way to Louis Lake, be sure to try a large and deep hole at the Indian Clearing. We once caught there forty odd trout, with a fly, in about an hour. There is good fishing, too, at the falls of

Jessup's River, which are not far from where you cross that stream on your way to the lake. There are a dozen small lakes near Lake Pleasant we have not mentioned. Indeed, there are not less than a hundred laid down in Mr. Hoffman's survey of Hamilton County, but we are assured the number falls little short of five hundred. A very inconsiderable portion of the county has been cleared, much less settled, so that, except in Lakes Pleasant and Piseco, visitors must expect hard fare at the best. A great number of the inhabitants secure a livelihood by hunting and trapping; otter, martin, etc., are caught in great numbers during the winter, and the beaver is far from extinct. Every week during the season a heavy load of game is sent from Lake Pleasant to Saratoga, so that you can communicate with the world, for you are essentially out of it in this region.

" *The First Thing to Do upon your Arrival.*—We will suppose you snugly quartered at the Lake Pleasant Hotel, where you will find every thing neat, plain and quiet about the place; and a man that can *almost* hold fire in his hand, ' by thinking of the frosty Caucasus' can get on quite comfortably. The first important step now to be taken is to hunt up Nat Morrill, Tim Skidmore, Randall or Cole, and you will find your hands full to match either, as woodsmen or sportsmen. Nat and Tim know every trout-hole, deer-stand or moose-yard, within twenty miles. Morrill is a trapper by profession, and Tim inherits all the knowledge of woodcraft which made his late uncle so celebrated in this region. Dunning you will find too a capital fellow in the woods; he can carry a pack, build a shanty, catch bait, work, and make himself generally useful; Cole, too, can do this, and beside, has several fine hounds. Van Derwarker will lend you a pointer or a setter, and oblige you in any way.

"*Something about Fishing.*—The best time to visit Hamilton County for the purpose of *fishing* is the last week of May or first of June, but trout in abundance may be taken from one year's end to another. From May until September they rise freely to the fly, but in June the *large* lake trout are to be seen breaking like speckled trout, and may be taken in the same manner. After this time they gradually return into deeper water, and in July, and subsequently, you fish for them —usually with a hand-line—in from fifty to one hundred feet of water. A Mr. Jewett, at Lake Pleasant, makes capital hooks for this kind of fishing. They resemble in shape the celebrated Limerick hooks, which have what is termed the 'O'Shaughnessy bend,' and are exceedingly well tempered. They are as large as the hooks used for cod, haddock, etc., and require to be. We have seen the largest of them snapped off, and lines broken that appeared strong enough to hold an alligator. The point of these hooks is not above half the ordinary height, and it has a barb on each side of it. We think, however, we have a better hook yet; the pattern sent to us by General Brooke of the U. S. army, one of the most

distinguished disciples of Izaak Walton, as he is one
of the most gallant and accomplished officers in the
service.   We have had several made for distribution
among our friends, and have induced Conroy to order
several thousands of various sizes from England.   General Brooke has used them with great success in Lake
Superior and Florida.

" Salmon or lake-trout fishing is practised here as at
Lake George.   It is not to our taste, by the by, but you
shall have the benefit of our experience.   In the first
place, select what seems to your eye a good location
. or two in a lake, and mark the spot by sinking a rock
attached to a strong cord, the upper end of which you
tie to a shingle as a buoy, which floats directly over
your 'anchor,' so that you can at any time hit upon
the precise spot ; the water where the anchor is sunk
should be over fifty feet deep.   Cut up half a bushel of
small fish, shiners, suckers, etc., and throw them over
it, and upon the following day you may safely calculate
upon taking as many salmon trout as you care to lug
home.   These same lakes you will also find to abound
with speckled trout, of large size and exquisite flavor.
The fly-fishing cannot be paralleled in our opinion,
and we have wet a line in nearly every stream or
pond of note beween the Susquehanna and the Kennebec.   You will find great sport in trolling.   For this
you require a leader of your strongest gut, nearly as
long as your rod ; put on a set of snap-hooks at the
end, and another set three feet above it, on each of
which spin a live minnow.   Above the snaps, at uniform distances, loop on three or four large salmon-

flies, and our word for it, in Piseco or Louis lakes you will take two or three at a time. Let out from forty to seventy feet of line, and use your heaviest rod ; bend a lighter line on your second rod, and use smaller flies; an hour's fishing will dictate to you the most successful sizes and colors of your flies. You can troll and throw your fly at the same time.

"The river and brook fishing, except that it is incomparably finer, is very like that found in other sections of the State, with this difference, that instead of fishing down a stream for a mile or two, you strike from one hole to another, and sometimes fish in the same place two or three days. These deep 'holes' are more properly eddies, not usually over six rods wide, but from a quarter to a half-mile in length ; they are full of trout, and you can take a hundred brace in a day sometimes, but this is sheer waste, and unless you have a packhorse, you can't carry above half the number away, especially if you have to wallow for half a dozen of miles through a thick growth of witch-hopple and shin-hemlock, the very thought of which makes our legs ache.

"To return to trolling. We plead guilty to having had recourse to an arrangement which we are con-fident our friends 'G.,' 'Piscator' and 'Meadows' will think any thing but orthodox. In trolling with flies, we found half the time that a 'rise' was but the weak invention of the enemy, and we proceeded to 'circumvent' him after the following fashion : we tied two flies together, selecting a large yellow salmon-fly, for instance, and an ordinary·

sized red or brown hackle trout-fly. You should have seen how it worked ; it was good for weak eyes. In casting in the ordinary way, with a single or double-handed rod, of course it was unnecessary to resort to any such heretical practice.

"*Sport at Lake Piseco.*—After spending a week in the vicinity of Lake Pleasant, get Van Derwarker to drive you behind his first man to Arietta, a little village located close by the inlet of Lake Piseco. The lake is very large, and the best one for trout we ever threw a fly in. At Arietta is a nice house, kept by Hiram Jones, a clever man in all respects. And here we must introduce you to Alba Dunning, as fine-spirited and gallant a young woodsman as ever knocked over a moose or landed a salmon. He has such appliances and means for fishing and shooting as you can find nowhere else. His sail and row-boats are tip-top ; he has plenty of live bait preserved in nets, and what is equally pleasant, his father's house is within twenty rods of the lake. By the way, let us present you to the old gentleman ; he is a resident of the county of fifty years' standing, and has killed more of feather and fin than any man in the county. He does not 'keep a public house,' but occasionally 'entertains company,' which being interpreted, means that if you look like a clever fellow, he will give you the best at his command, and if you do not, he will not have you at any price.

"Lake Piseco is about seven miles in length by two in width ; a most beautiful sheet of water, surrounded on all sides by a majestic range of hills, covered to the summit with the most magnificent forest trees. The picturesque scenes presented from many points of this seat in miniature, exhibit a savage grandeur of aspect, combined with a degree of wild romantic beauty, that would have charmed Sir Walter Scott amid his own Highlands, while Christopher North would throw away his crutch and immortalize them, after such fly-fishing as we enjoyed.

"A few more hints: do not allow your deer-hunting to break in upon your time, but drive early in the morning. If you like fin-hunting—and we hope you do not, for it is a most unsportsman-like practice,—be careful that you do not " shine the eyes " of a *panther*.

"While at Piseco do not neglect to make a trip to a large deep pool in West River, six miles from Mr. Dunning's house. The route has rarely been tracked by any thing save a moose or a panther, and you will be 'most consarnedly' tried before you reach it. Ah! but the bare sight of the place will repay a thousand ills! Our party of four took there with a fly, within an hour of our arrival, thirty-eight brook-trout, which would average two pounds each! That's what *we* call sport ! "

Mr. Porter made an agreeable excursion in August, 1843, to Stonington, to enjoy, with two friends passing the hot months there, bass and black-fishing. He gives his hints upon the subject:

"For sea-bass, if you do not stand on a rock and throw into the surf, you sail from end to end over the reef, which is far preferable for sport, though it is usually very rough. Fish for these sea-bass with a small but first-rate salmon line of a hundred yards in length; the best bait is a sort of squid, made thus: Take an eel about a foot long, and with your penknife make an incision an inch in length beneath his jaws; then carefully cut off his head without rupturing the skin, turn it over his back, and peel him entire. After turning the skin right side outwards, take your lower hook (you must have two tied on a piece of gimp) and pass it through the eel's mouth, and down his body about four inches from the head, then pull it through the skin of the belly. The upper hook, which of course is to be tied on, on the opposite side of the gimp, to the lower, you must now insert well back in the eel's mouth, and turn the point up through his head. Be careful that you place your hooks in the eel's skin at the exact distance at which they are tied on, otherwise your bait will have an unnatural appearance, and will not work well. Secure your upper hook tidily to the skin with a thread, and carefully adjust your sinker; with such a squid, provided you manage it well, you ought to take thirty bass in a single tide, that is, on the last of the ebb, and the first of the flood. You must troll across the reef selected for the sport, and Frank Blake, in twenty minutes, will put you to many 'artful dodges' to insure success.

"No thoroughbred sportsman will use any borrowed article, either for fishing or shooting, if he can possibly avoid it.

" Go to Conroy's, 52 Fulton Street, and order the following ' traps : '

1 ' New London ' hemp line, on a creel.
1 striped bass or salmon line, 100 yards.
1 doz. Hemming's or Kirby's black-fish hooks, on snells.
1 " assorted Hemming's black-fish hooks, straight and curved.
1 doz. best hemp snoods.
1 " Kirby's and Limerick assorted bass-hooks, on snells or gimp.
4 sinkers—from ¼ lb. to 1 lb.
2 squids for blue fish—bone and metal.
1 doz. cod hooks.

" With this tackle one may be considered armed all in proof for bass, blue, black or king-fish, flounders, drum, cod, haddock, or pretty much any thing else you can scare up."

ARTIFICIAL TROUT-FLIES, OCT. 12, 1844.

" We are indebted to the kindness of Robert Emmett, Esq., of this city, for one of the most acceptable presents which fortune ever ' buckled on our back ; ' a present doubly gratifying as coming from one of the most ardent and accomplished disciples of old Izaak Walton in the United States. The acquaintances of our time-honored old friend, General G., of Washington City, a veteran of the regular army, will not fail to remember his manifestations of delight upon receiving from his friend Sir Charles Vaughan, after the latter's return to England from his diplomatic mission here, a capacious book, filled with a superb

11

collection of artificial flies. With no tithe of the General's ability to express his grateful acknowledgments, we still do not yield to him in the sincerity of our appreciation of the generous impulses which prompted this characteristic token of regard from a brother angler. In the case before us we find first a dozen rare flies, dressed by the veritable hands of the renowned Paddy Kelly of Dublin, and tied on Limerick hooks of O'Shaughnessy's or Sell's bend—hooks not to be obtained for love or money in this country. Each one is worthy of a distinct engraving and a separate chapter. Next comes a dozen 'droppers,' the ex· quisite handiwork of the late lamented Father Levins, of this city, one of our most eloquent Catholic divines, among which ' the Professor,' (so named for Old Kit North, of Blackwood's Magazine,) the ' moth ' and other ' killers ' are conspicuous. In another division we find an assortment of colored gut ' leaders,' one of which, made by Kelly of Dublin, fairly ' bangs Bannagher ! ' It tapers gradually—' small by degrees, and beautifully less '—from the loop which attaches it to the ' casting-line,' to the extreme point on which *we* should tie a ' gray palmer,' or a ' green drake,' according to the state of the water. It is stained with onion juice to the delicate hue of a blush on a cheek of alabaster. Two others, colored in masterly style by Mr. Emmett himself with tea, are perfect loves in their way, and there is one more, made by Father Levins, which to our eye is as precious as the ' rich jewel in an Œthiop's ear.' Last of all, in a cover of parchment, we find an assortment of Limerick hooks of O'Shaughnessey's bend, and Kirby hooks of the ' Sneck ' bend, neither variety of which can be purchased in the United States."

In the October number of the " American Turf Register " of 1840, is given an " American Hunter's Camp " from the graphic pencil of the lamented Rindisbacher ; it is spirited and faithful to a degree. The attitudes of the hounds are full of meaning and expression, as well as those of the two hunters ; all the accessories of the sketch are in felicitous keeping.

" In the ' Backwoods ' of this country," Mr. Porter writes, " a hunter's camp is usually covered with spruce slabs or bark, while the bed is comprised of cedar sprigs, shin-hemlock or brush, over which the hunter spreads his blanket. Two years since, in a sporting trip to a remote section of the country, we frequently enjoyed the novelty of sleeping in a ' camp '—the work of half an hour—for nearly a week together, and contrived to make them warm and comfortable. First, we cut two crotched sticks, six feet long, and after sharpening their points, drove them into the ground as supporters of the fabric ; across these were laid the three string-pieces comprising the frame, the ends of two of them being securely fixed in the ground. Instead of splitting spruce planks for a roof—an opera- tion of a few minutes only—we peeled the bark of that tree, and turning the smooth side upwards, (lap- ping the pieces,) made the covering water-tight. When spruce will not peel, the balsam-fir and half a dozen other trees offer a substitute. For the sides we

interlaced the birch and witch-hopple, and afterwards
covered the whole with the tops of young trees of
luxuriant foliage. Sprigs of cedar or hemlock make
a soft, dry and fragrant bed, on which, after a good
day's sport, one can enjoy such a night's rest as Sancho
Panza never dreamed of, when he invoked blessings
on him who first invented sleep! The choice of site,
which should be near a spring, and location of the fir,
etc., depend upon circumstances. With no other
instrument than a small axe, a backwoodsman can
knock up a camp large enough to accommodate half a
dozen most comfortably in half an hour."

CHAPTER IX.

THE nineteenth volume was begun with every prospect of unsurpassed prosperity. The number of contributors had doubled within the eighteen months previous, while daily accessions were made to the already long list of subscribers in all parts of the globe. The "Spirit" at this time had a foreign circulation unequalled by any other paper in the United States; it had found its way into all the European capitals, into the East and West Indies, and was read with as much *gout* at Canton, Batavia, Sydney and the Sandwich Islands, as at home; and what is far more remarkable, among his subscribers were several of our native Indians! This volume, as was the twentieth, was stocked with an unusual variety of amusing and instructive matter, and Mr. Porter wrote:

"As for the Editor, who, being a bachelor, acknowledges to the shady side of thirty, there or thereabouts, it may not be uninteresting to some of his juvenile friends to state that he commenced this paper so long ago as the 10th of December, 1831, and has since gone on his way rejoicing," etc.

We may add that he went *out* of his way in 1849, when the preceding paragraph was penned, and varied the routine of editorial labor by a visit to Boston, where he was welcomed by enthusiastic friends to the quiet attractions of their firesides, and in due time complimented by a formal dinner at the Norfolk House. Not long after his return to New York he began to feel the first symptoms of gout, soon to become a fixed torment for the rest of his life.

All went well among the brothers, and the future looked particularly encouraging, when the telegraph announced the sad intelligence of the death of George Porter. A letter from Frank addressed to his sisters in relation to the event demands an insertion as an act of respect to the memory of those two loving brothers :

"NEW ORLEANS, *May* 26, 1849.

"To MARTHA AND SARAH:

"The wires of the telegraph have long ere this revealed to you the dreadful news that this sad letter contains.

"Our dear George rests quiet from all his toils and troubles, and his spirit is at peace. He died at the St. Charles Hotel on the morning of the 24th inst., and was buried from there in the Lafayette Cemetery the same afternoon. He complained of slight illness on the 16th, but did not finally stop work until the 18th. His disease was jaundice, caused by a morbid, bad state of the liver, producing severe bilious fever, jaundice, brain fever and death. His principal physician was Dr. McCormick, of the army, a man of the highest standing and a personal friend. Dr. Wedderburn was also called in. He was not considered in the least degree in a dangerous state by his friends until within twelve hours of his death, when a sudden change took place. He at once became highly delirious, but soon afterwards unconscious and speechless. He lay in this manner until near four o'clock

in the morning, when he quietly breathed his last. Thus suddenly passed away all of poor George. Doctors, nurses, friends,
servants and every available means were at hand, but all to no
purpose. Dr. McCormick informs me that he now thinks that
the disease from the first day of his sickness had pervaded his
system, and taken such strong and firm grasp that nothing could
have saved him. It no doubt had long before fastened upon him
its deadly grasp, and had worked its way insidiously when
he was in apparent health. His general health had been unusually good, and his friends had congratulated him upon looking better than at any time during his residence in Louisiana.
His habits were very abstemious, and though very hard at work,
he was cheerful. He at no moment, in my opinion, had the least
idea that death was near him.

"The spot where we laid him is one that would have well
suited his own taste, even if the present high water had not cut
off the route to a different one. It is in the city of Lafayette, adjoining New Orleans, and is the highest land in the neighborhood; full of trees, quiet and free from all confusion of business,
and his particular vault is the highest of a high tier. There, beneath the luxurious growth of that vegetation of which he was
so fond, and upon the very banks of the mighty river whose
swift but silent grandeur so awed his spirit, let him lie.

"The funeral was very large, and of a peculiar character. I
never before had an idea of the esteem and love so many bore
him. The Rev. Mr. Clapp officiated. He was a personal friend
and admirer of George; the publication of his sermons in the
Picayune had brought them into frequent intercourse.

"Thus all is over, and now *I am alone.* I am sitting at his
own table in the 'Picayune' office, by the side of his favorite window, in his chair, my feet on his old stool, his favorite pen in
my hand. It is wonderful that I am alive after the events of the
last few days; life to me has no aim or object. I came here to
be with him, and now he is gone. No one knew him besides
myself; I knew his outgoings and incomings. There was a tie
between us most singular, although not always apparent. It is
useless for me to explain or to add any thing."

Thus passed away another of this band of brothers, who had achieved a reputation in a path of usefulness for which he had no special attachment.

> " What now, alas ! that life-diffusing charm
> Of sprightly wit? that rapture for the muse,
> That heart of friendship, and that soul of joy,
> Which bade with softest light thy virtues smile?
> Ah ! only show'd to check our fond pursuits,
> And teach our humbled hopes that life is vain ! "

The elder sister of the family, Mrs. Paine, passed a winter in New Orleans with her brothers, and we insert a portion of one of her recent letters, which contains an especial reference to George :

" He was the cleverest of the brothers, the most scholarly, and had the most common-sense. Added to his literary tastes was an eminently practical talent, and he was capable of long-continued and intense labor. During the seven years he was editor of the ' Picayune,' he never had a week's relaxation at a time, and sometimes during the Mexican war was the only man in the office for weeks together. Besides fulfilling his duties as editor, he found time for extensive reading, and he was far advanced in modern notions of philosophy, religion and reform."

Professor S. G. Brown of Dartmouth College, a classmate of George Porter, thus writes of him to Mrs. Brinley :

" From my early boyhood, as you know, until we graduated, George was my companion and friend. Afterwards our paths separated, and I saw comparatively little of him, but always followed his course with great interest. I have indeed only this very day returned from Haverhill, where I again ran over the orchards and pastures in which we used to play together, and the hills down which we used to slide, and sat upon the very benches where more than thirty years ago we studied Virgil and Cicero under the instruction of Mr. Mack. George had a very vigorous and active mind. He was enterprising and somewhat ambitious, and successful. At Meriden, before he was thirteen, he gave an oration before a little society, of which we were members, on Eloquence. I thought it was a very good one, and I am sure it spread his fame as far as *twelve miles*, for I remember hearing it talked about in Hanover. We always met in George's room, where we had a little stage erected for the use of the orators; and I presume none of us have ever had more satisfactory triumphs than in that little room, with an audience of a dozen boys. George was very fond of speaking, and declaimed with great beauty. This was true at Haverhill. I remember now his speaking 'The Sailor Boy' at Meriden, and in college, where he carried away several prizes. He was a very good writer, and often distinguished himself by the excellence of his compositions. His mind was quick and tenacious; he learned with great facility, and had his knowledge much at command. I should think he was more fond of languages than of mathematics. He was interested in the study of history, of which, while in college, he had marked out for himself a pretty extensive course of reading. I always prophesied eminence for him in his profession, and I have no doubt that if he had devoted himself to it with half the persistency with which many pursue it, he would not only have been distinguished, but very much so. I never knew the reason of his giving it up, but it always seemed to me that in doing so he made a mistake. He must have become eminent as an advocate, and his sagacity and practical good judgment and acuteness would have found ample scope and abundant reward. His removing from New England, and still more from New York, seemed to me much like a personal loss."

There are few persons who saw and heard George speak in public at the time he won his prizes for declamation in his college days, who did not prophesy

11*

that the forum was destined to be the true sphere for the exercise of his oratorical talent; and no one with more sanguine expectation than his keen-eyed old uncle, who had watched him from the start, advising and guiding him with the tenderness and devotion of a father, selecting always the themes best suited for his elocutionary displays, and at all times forcing into vigor and breadth his youthful faculties, with a tact which it is well known few possessed in a more remarkable degree than Mr. Olcott.

The New Orleans Press was unanimous in expressions of regret at the loss of their favorite and respected associate.

"Common eulogy," writes the "Picayune," "on his merits as a gentleman and a scholar would be a faint tribute on our part. Innumerable testimonies of the exalted position he occupied in both these distinctions exist beyond the limited circle of this office, in written characters, the production of his vigorous understanding, and in sorrowing hearts that bleed spontaneously as memory recalls his polished manners, his undeviating urbanity, his warm and generous nature. Mr. Porter was a fine specimen of an American gentleman. His mind, which was richly endowed by nature, had received a careful academical training, and considerable intercourse with the world enabled him to seize character at a glance. These circumstances gave him a grasp of intellect that conspicuously displayed itself in every thing he wrote, evincing that manly vigor of thought and that accuracy of judgment which are invaluable in the journalist, who has the laudable ambition of acting up to the full dignity of his mission. As for his private virtues, we make this simple record: We have yet to know the created being that ever manifested hostility to him in word or deed. Indeed, so unobtrusive were his manners, so gentle was he in character, that the contrast between his capacity and his pretensions forced itself involuntarily on all who came within the sphere of his action. He was emphatically—to borrow a line from the beautiful record of the poet Gay—

'In wit a man, simplicity a child.'

*   *   *   *   *   *   *

"It has been said that the best monument of a writer's fame is the work of his brain. Were the labors of the journalist of a character less ephemeral, less evanescent than they necessarily are—the echo as it were of a sound borne to the ear in the passing breeze—we might, in pride of our deceased colleague's high intelligence, pure philanthropy, refined taste and sparkling wit, point to our files for the last seven years as the most lasting mementos of his worth. Peace to his manes!"

The "Crescent" thus feelingly chronicles his death:

"We were yesterday called on to consign to the grave the mortal remains of one who but a few days ago was full of life and vigor and activity. But a short time previous to his decease, the friends of Mr. Porter had no idea of his approaching death. And now that he is gone—now that the face once beaming with intelligence and fine feeling has disappeared—it is hard to realize the thought that we shall see no more of him who was but yesterday the amiable companion and the attached friend.

"To the immediate friends and acquaintances of Mr. Porter, it is useless to say how much they have lost in losing him whom they yesterday buried. To know him was to respect—nay, almost to love him. Even the casual acquaintance felt bound, by no ordinary tie, to one who carried his heart in his hand, and whose free, open, generous nature attracted the affection of whoever approached him. The friends of the deceased can appreciate those virtues which are rarely known except to a man's intimate acquaintances—the sensibility and delicacy of feeling almost feminine, joined to an elevation of sentiment and strength of will that were possessed by few men. But the New Orleans public are hardly aware of the loss they have sustained in the death of Mr. Porter. His usefulness to the community was known to but few, for his influence was of the sort which is felt and not seen.

"Mr. Porter was a native of Vermont, and had studied law in New York; but for the last seven or eight years he was a resident of New Orleans, and has been, during that time, the associate editor of the Picayune newspaper. As his name never appeared in that journal, its numerous readers were not cognizant of how much they owed to Mr. Porter's industry, energy and intelligence. With a zeal that seemed unbounded, and a will that appeared unyielding, he devoted himself to his arduous duties as if taking pleasure in labor, and seeking constant employment for the acute and active intellectual powers with which he was endowed. He never relaxed his efforts to instruct and please the public; and, with a generosity careless of praise and reward, he studied only how to make himself useful to the community in which he had cast his lot.

"He has gone!—the mind that has been so active for the good of others, has departed from our midst! But such a man cannot soon be forgotten; nor will his place be easily supplied. The heart that has so often beat in sympathy with the feelings of others is still; the brain that was so constant in its efforts for others' good, has ceased from its labors. But it will be long before the memory of George Porter will escape from the hearts and minds of his friends, and of those who, without being personally acquainted with him, were cognizant of his many virtues and extensive capacity."

The "Daily Bee," in allusion to his scholarship, says:

"He possessed enormous industry, great readiness and tact, and a capability of endurance in the ceaseless round of his labors that few men exhibit.

"There was not a particle of acerbity in his character. His pen never distilled gall, for bitterness was an element unknown in his kindly and genial organization. He has left hosts of friends to mourn his death, with a sorrow that will ever be associated with the memory of as gentle a spirit as ever toiled in the thankless travail of journalism.

"The funeral of Mr. Porter took place yesterday afternoon, and his mortal remains were attended to their earthly resting-place by a large concourse, mainly consisting of friends whose attachment had been won by the endearing qualities of the deceased. He was interred at Lafayette Cemetery, and in that receptacle of the dead there sleeps not a nobler spirit than animated the soul of him whom, with imposing and affecting ceremonies, we saw deposited in the silent habitation of the departed."

"Among the many touching and most grateful letters of condolence which we have received this week," writes the Editor of the "Spirit," "is the following from the pen of William H. Herbert:"

"MY DEAR PORTER—It is with something of reluctance that I intrude upon what some persons might consider a private matter and one unfitted for notice in your columns—I mean the death of my esteemed friend and your beloved brother GEORGE; but I have been determined not to allow any fastidious delicacy to prevent my offering my tribute of affectionate homage to the memory of one whom I truly and sincerely regarded both in a private and public capacity.

"There is the more fitness in this, that but for GEORGE PORTER there would never have been, so far as the world is concerned, any FRANK FORESTER to pen these brief lines as a testimony to his amiable qualities and his high talents.

"It was, as you well remember, I doubt not, during one of your protracted visits to the South, while George was *pro tempore* in command of the 'Spirit,' that, as much at his suggestion as in consequence of my own views on the subject, I adopted that signature as in some sort typical of the craft and character of a sportsman, in connection with a series of papers intended to popularize sportsmanship, and to divest it, in the eyes of the many, from the prestige of brutality and rudeness with which it seemed to be invested.

"How far those papers were successful this is not the time, nor am I the person, to state, but the *name* has become so far current with the readers of the 'Spirit,' that I do not fear being considered intrusive or impertinent in addressing a few lines to you on this painful subject.

"Few words have I to say beyond this, that in an acquaintance which began years ago, prior, I think, to any intimacy between you and myself, which has endured, unaltered by time, and enhanced, perhaps, rather than diminished, by absence, I have seen, heard or known no one incident of his life, no one point of his career, which I would have desired to see changed in my own brother; that all has proved him the kind, considerate, honorable gentleman, the man of energy and talent, whom none knew but to love and praise.

"Honor and respect in life he had, and now is at peace—where may we all have cause to rest as well—in the quiet repose of an honorable grave.

"Your sincere friend,　　FRANK FORESTER.

"THE CEDARS, 1st June."

At the commencement of the year 1852, both William and the "Doctor" were hard at work in their several spheres of duty, with a fair prospect of years of useful life. On New Year's Day the "Doctor" made a round of visits, and was often complimented on his fine health and exuberant spirits. It was cold and damp, and the sudden transitions from the heat of crowded drawing-rooms to the penetrating chilliness of the external air, brought on an acute illness, which soon became irremediable; and on the sixth of the month he placidly fell asleep in the arms of death, before his relatives were aware of his illness.

His funeral took place on the eighth of the month from Grace Church, from whence he was borne to Greenwood, and deposited in the lot which he had selected the year previous for the last resting-place of himself and brothers. On the Saturday following his death, an obituary notice of him appeared in " The Spirit of the Times," from the pen of his accomplished friend William Henry Herbert, who, from long acquaintance and a generous appreciation of Doctor Porter, was admirably qualified to breathe a last tribute to his memory:

> ' Quis desiderio sit pudor aut modus
> Tam cari capitis.

" On Tuesday, January 6th, died, at his residence in this city, after a very few days' illness, Dr. T. OLCOTT PORTER, in the 49th year of his age; in the fullness of his intellectual capacities and the vigor of his mature manhood, taken away from the large circle of friends, who truly loved him as a brother, by a disease so sudden and insidious, that many of those who cherished his intimacy the most closely learned only that he was indisposed at all, by the lamentable tidings that he would be indisposed no more forever.

" To descant largely upon the character and qualities of him who has been so suddenly removed from us, to the readers of this paper, would seem almost a work of supererogation, so well and widely was he known; still, there are doubtless many who will be pleased to have a brief memorial of the circumstances of his happy and blameless life, which they may preserve and lay by as something tangible and real, of one concerning whom it may be said, more truly than of almost any other mortal man—

> " ' None knew him but to love,
> None named him but to praise.'

"Again, it has been urged that to dwell long upon the praises of the dead is, in the first place, in bad taste toward the living, and, in the second, oftentimes injurious to the memory of the departed, by stirring up an envious feeling in the breast of others, like that which led the Athenian to ostracize Aristides, merely because he was aweary of hearing him ever called the Just. As to the former of these arguments, we have only to reply, that this is intended as no proud or boastful enumeration of high qualities and splendid deeds, but as an humble and sincere tribute to the calm and unobtrusive virtues of a peaceful and well-spent private life, endearing the deceased to all who came within the sphere of his attraction. As to the latter, the writer of this unpretending record has no fears, for of the late Dr. PORTER alone, of all the men he has ever seen or heard of, it may be emphatically asserted, that he never had an enemy. In a close and uninterrupted friendship of above eighteen years, he who writes this, not as a labored eulogy, but as the simple outpouring of a wounded heart, never once heard one unkind or uncharitable expression concerning any living being fall from those lips, now so cold and silent, which, while life warmed them, were ever literally overflowing with the milk of human kindness.

"Dr. Porter was born in the town of Newbury, in Vermont; was educated at Dartmouth College, in New Hampshire, where he graduated with distinction and high promise in the Humanities. He afterward studied and practised medicine for some short space of time, but subsequently retiring from his profession, devoted the last eighteen years of his life to literary pursuits in this city, during the whole of which period the writer has known and loved him as a brother, and received from him all a brother's kindness. Many readers will remember him as connected with Mr. N. P. WILLIS in the conduct of the 'Corsair '—probably the best literary journal ever published in New York—which was in fact wholly under his editorial control, owing its excellence to his unassisted abilities; since his co-editor was absent in Europe during nearly the whole term of its existence. He was, moreover, for many years an occasional contributor to the columns of this paper, and as such was well known generally to all its readers, and personally to nearly all its correspondents and contributors. For many years he had been connected with Mons. COUDERT, in the management of a large and excellent school in this city, patiently practising a thankless and ill-rewarded profession, for which the clear sincerity of his mind, his equable and foresighted intellect, his fine taste and large reading, and, above all, his imperturbable good temper and unvarying kindness of heart, singularly qualified him.*

"He was a man who might have been great by the exertion and display of his talents, which were of a high order, but that he was one who preferred being loved to being admired; who was born to be the idol of a circle, rather than the wonder of a sphere. His reading was varied and extensive; and, particularly in the ancient English authors, he was an elegant and finished scholar; an excellent classic, a thorough and judicious historian, his criticism, for which his independence, clearness of perception, and candor, rarely qualified him, was of the highest order; and we can say sincerely that there were few men living to whose judgment we would more readily have resigned our own, as to the merits or defects of a new book, a new actor or a new drama—nor any by whom we should have been more proud to be praised, than he whom we now deplore.

"The characteristics of his intellectual abilities were elegance, ease and polish, clear judgment, fine taste, and high appreciation of all that is beautiful and true, in letters, art and science.

* Mr. Coudert had been ill for several weeks previous to the sickness of the Doctor, and the anxieties of the latter concerning the school when he too became confined to his chamber, were very much increased. The day before the death of Dr. Porter, Mr. Coudert sent his eldest son with a kind message concerning his health; to his surprise, he found the Doctor up, and partly dressed, feeble as he was. He was greatly attached to the Doctor, and perceiving his extreme prostration, urged him to return to his bed. "No," rejoined the Doctor, "tell your father that I do not intend to shirk my duty." But he was exhausted by the effort, and from sheer debility was reluctantly obliged to follow the advice of his young friend.

Of his moral qualities the most remarkable were, that regular benignity, which was written on his fine face by the hand of God, as if by the fingers of man in a book, that perfect truthfulness, candor, affection to his friends, and charity—in its most extended sense—toward all mankind, which literally caused every one who knew him to love him, and which will call tears from many an eye unused to weep, and awaken regrets in many a far-distant heart. Woe! woe! for thee, my brother and my friend!   He died, as he had lived, so placidly and easily, that the change from time to eternity was scarce perceptible to those who watched beside him, probably scarce perceived by himself, until he awoke from the sleep of life to know himself immortal.

"He is one of the few, the very few, for whom there is no fear —for whom Hope is all—Hope alone—certain as truth and Heaven.

"To say that he never *did* evil to a living thing, is to say nothing!   For we verily believe, if it may be believed of any mortal man, that he never even *thought* evil of his neighbor. Rest is for the dead, and peace and happiness immortal: for those who remain behind, the weariness of memory, the loneliness of regret, the yearning for the untimely lost, which will not pass away until life itself shall have passed through the darkness of the grave, into the light of immortality.

"Happy they who live as he lived—who shall die as he died —for if many a greater and many a wiser man has blazed upon the world, and died and been forgotten—none kinder, or better, or more beloved, ever adorned or charmed a circle.   None ever left behind a fame more pure, a memory more fondly cherished, or longer to be remembered.

"For him we do not pray for peace, since wherefore should we doubt that he, whose whole life was peacefulness, hath, by what we call death, been removed only from this mortal turmoil into the exceeding peace of the Lord?   *Valeat in æternum valeat!* "

In a letter from William to Mrs. Brinley of this

date he says : " The dear old Doctor is gone from me. I can do nothing to realize it. His kindness, his love, his counsels, his very being, were so interwoven and incorporated into all my life and thoughts, that I am bewildered and crushed to find him gone. The main defence that has stood by me from boyhood, which seemed so stable and so necessary to my well-being, is now laid level forever! Frank and I are now left alone to battle on as best we can for the rest of our journey."

We come down to the year 1855, as the volumes of the immediately preceding years, though sparkling with items and amusing paragraphs from the old mint, do not contain any very salient articles by the Editor. His previous work had been never-ending, and a time had now come when he felt relieved from the duty of getting up elaborate leaders, by the continual flow of admirable contributions from gifted correspondents ; and never was mental repose so necessary and so grateful to him, for the bright advent of the New Year was soon shrouded by the death of Frank, the youngest and the pet of the brothers, and who had been attached to the " New Orleans Picayune " for some seven years, during all which time his course was marked by signal and ever-increasing ability. His labors were exceedingly onerous, in view of his impaired health, and though scrupulously performed, his heart was not in them after the death of George. A voyage to Europe was recommended to him, and through the affectionate interest of Mr. Holbrook, the chief of the Picayune, it was accomplished, but without material advantage to the invalid. We extract a few passages from his letter, dated New Orleans, the 1st of May, 1854:

"I am off for Europe this evening, on board of the clipper ship 'Bostonian,' Capt. King. She is a most beautiful vessel, of 1098 tons, entirely new, superb accommodations, and I am the only passenger, with a large parlor state-room to myself. * * * My present intention is to be absent five or six months, and to visit Liverpool, London, Paris, Marseilles, perhaps Naples, Venice, Vienna, Hamburg, &c., &c.; but much will depend on my health, time, expense, and other matters. I will more fully write you of my intended movements when in London or Paris. Should my health be so bad in the autumn that I think I should not be able to work if I returned home, I may, if I can make suitable arrangements, spend the winter in the south of Europe, and visit Constantinople, &c., which I much wish. Our paper has now several European correspondents, and Mr. Kendall, who lives with his family in Paris, thinks of going to Constantinople; still I shall probably write some, and over my old signature of 'Gleaner.'

"My health and spirits are to-day good, for me; my friends have been most kind and generous to me in all fashions, and lots of little 'fixins' have been sent on board the ship for my comfort on the voyage. I have worked long and faithfully for the 'Pic' office, and my services have been appreciated and generously repaid. The attachment of Mr. Holbrook, the principal manager of the paper, to George, was strong, and is so to myself, and I have no other such firm friend for life, who has the means, as himself. * * * I visited dear George's grave a few days ago, as is my frequent pleasure. My purest, dearest, and holiest recollections of life are connected therewith, and I trust it may be permitted me to lay my bones beside him. Remembrance of him and of our sainted mother is much oftener in my thoughts latterly than ever before."

After his return from Europe, he wrote from New Orleans, January 1st, 1855 :

"I owe you many apologies for sins of omission in not visiting or writing you, but I so dislike to be the bearer of bad news, that I have omitted even writing—putting it off from day to day.

"My situation is now truly sad, as my health and strength seem entirely to have forsaken me, and I am now constantly confined to my room, with what I have too much reason to believe is a confirmed consumption. My trip abroad did me no good, and as I was laid up in Paris for three weeks, I was weakened very much. Before I went away, my physicians were somewhat divided as to my disease, and my Paris physician assured me that I only had a very bad chronic disorder of the bronchial tubes. To this idea I clung until facts proved its incorrectness, and I find myself totally prostrate.

"I hastened home to renew my labors, but I found on my arrival here, that my strength was not equal to their performance, and I gave a portion of them up, retaining such as would call for the least physical exertion. One month's work used me up. * * *

"My physician is Dr. Wedderstrandt, as eminent a man, particularly in diseases of the lungs, as any in the country. For fourteen years he was the principal physician in our great Charity Hospital, and has of course had great experience. He is also a particular friend of mine, and has taken much interest in my case. He has examined me critically, and has pronounced my lungs badly affected, as indeed my constant and shocking cough now too clearly attests. * * The Doctor says: 'Follow my advice strictly, and you will be able to meet the warm spring weather, when I hope you will improve, and obtain strength enough to move about in the open air.' I am too much a man of the world not to know what all this means. *It is a mere question of time, with me. No cough like mine can ever be cured.* To be thus confined in the house, deprived of work, air, society and excitement, tasks my fortitude, while the prospect for the future is gloomy. I am now living in the family of my old friend, Madame Hall, where I am well nursed and cared for; which I could not be at the St. Charles Hotel, my former home. I have a thousand minor ills and troubles; but I will not worry you by relating them. I feel, however, that I ought to let you know of my feeble and sad condition. * * *

"My trip, had my health and strength not failed me, would have been delightful. As it was, I worked hard, and saw much that interested me. Scarcely a place of 'high or low degree,' in London or Paris, that was famous, that I did not visit. I wrote nothing while I was absent, as I was too busily employed in sight-seeing; but I came home with my mind well stored with that which would have interested my friends, and been a source of pleasing remembrance to me during a long life. My power of observation and comparison never had full scope before, and I improved the opportunity. * * * I saw all of high life I wished—I brought home many little trifles as souvenirs of some of the places I visited, which I should have been pleased to show you, had an opportunity offered. Many of my most pleasant days were spent in the galleries of art; but I thrust myself into every species of amusement, gayety, sumptuous living, curiosity shop, palace and *stable* that promised to repay me. In fact, what I saw and learned, would be of more use to me could I live to manage it, than all I ever learned before. I never weary in talking over my adventures to my friends. * * * *

"You may think that I write despondingly, but it is always better to look trouble full in the face. I know my own situation better than I can tell you, and I feel assured that I can only linger out a painful and troubled life, be the time long or short. I could fill pages did I dare to trust myself to speak of my thoughts and feelings, but it would be useless.

"The merciful God who has thus far watched over me in my wanderings and vicissitudes, will not, I sincerely trust, forsake me in my hour of need; that he may cherish and protect you both, is the fervent wish of your brother

"FRANK."

In due course of mail, the following letter was received, all but the last sentence and signature being in the handwriting of a friend :

"NEW ORLEANS, *February 8th,* 1855.

"To MY SISTERS—I am too feeble to write to-day, and have availed myself of the kindness of a friend, to communicate to you. It was a long and dreary suspense from the first of January till to-day, when I received Sarah's letter; Martha's and William's letters having reached me two days previously. But my confidence in her love and sympathy never forsook me; I knew that some accident must have prevented an earlier reply.

"My health and strength have rapidly failed me since I last wrote you, and I am now confined to my bed by the orders of my physician. My cough of itself is not very troublesome, although getting worse constantly; but the many ills and diseases brought on by sympathy with the lungs, are very annoying.

"I am surrounded by kind friends, who do all in their power to make me comfortable. If I am not able to write myself, some one else will write you very soon. Your letters have afforded me great consolation, and your mention of domestic matters has carried me back to the days of childhood. I still anticipate great pleasure from letters which must now be on their way from you."

(The closing lines are in Frank's trembling hand, and were the very last ever written by him :)

"God bless you, my dear sisters; this is probably the last time I shall be able to say so to you. My last thoughts shall be of our mother and of you.

"As ever, yours,
"FRANCIS T. PORTER."

The next intelligence was of his death, on the 28th of February. He was conscious to the last moment, the almost inaudible prayer, "May God receive my soul," trembling on his lips as his spirit took flight. He sleeps, as he desired, by the side of his brother George.

When we consider that his academic education terminated by his own choice when he was quite young, and that his subsequent pursuits were not favorable to mental cultivation, we marvel at the extent of his attainments, and recognize in his manner and style of composition the evidence of no ordinary degree of natural ability.

From the numerous testimonials of respect to his memory in our possession, we make but a single extract, and that from an obituary in the " Picayune : "

"Francis Porter was a man of many fine traits of character, one of which was eminently distinctive—his innate sense of what constitutes true manly honor. We never knew a man whose instincts were more unerring in the detection of aught that was mean, sordid or unworthy in the characters of those with whom he was thrown in contact; and he was never so earnest and decided in the expression of his opinions, as he was when denouncing or satirizing such traits. At the same time he was one of the most affectionate and attachable of friends and companions. His perceptions were quick, and his impulses generous and noble. His temperament was of a character that, added to disappointments and private griefs, ' with which the stranger intermeddleth not,' occasionally clouded his mind with fits of morbid gloominess and abstraction. But the general course of his life, like the predominant tone in his character, was manly, consistent and innocent ; and now,

' After life's fitful fever, he sleeps well.' "

By Frank's death William was thoroughly deso-
lated. The attacks of gout for the rest of his life were
frequent and severe, with little or no alleviation, from
Sydney Smith's idea that it must have taken five or
six generations of gentlemen to have given it such
frightful vigor. It sometimes took French leave of
him for months together, when he would resume his
old desk with something of revived interest. But the
main-spring was gone, and he soon returned to the
solitude of his home in Bleecker Street ; or taking his
trout-rod, solaced his weary spirits with an occasional
easy drive out of the city. His benignant smile continued unaltered, and those who casually met him
during the year succeeding his last bereavement could
not have suspected from his manner that he had to
all intents and purposes about done with life. It was
fame enough for him that the life-scheme which
swelled in his heart the morning he left in the mail-
stage for Andover, was already a fixed fact among the
things of Time. The seed had been good and honest,
and was planted by his own hand, when his tears and
some brave hopes were about all he had to help to
moisten and quicken it into life. He had waited long
and patiently for its first small, humble shoot to strike
through the hard, unyielding clod into the air and
light, and had had the full satisfaction of seeing it ex-
pand by his own bounteous and lavish culture, until
its spreading branches sparkled in the sunshine of a
generous and loving patronage, its roots all abroad to
resist the battling of a century's storms.

The " Salutatory" for the year 1856 has a flavor of

12

the humor that for a quarter of a century had charmed and cheered the readers of the "Spirit." But from the day of the "Doctor's" death, he was unlike his former self; even his interest in the "Old Spirit" was much diminished. Up to this time no intimation had fallen from him that he could be induced to sever his connection with it; yet most unexpectedly to his friends, on the 26th of September he permitted his name to be associated in the publication of another weekly Sporting Journal, called "Porter's Spirit of the Times." Old friends and old correspondents rallied round him, and the enterprise started with flying colors; its success was unprecedented in the annals of the newspaper press, for as early as the eighth number it was "backed by a circulation of 40,000 copies"! To what extent Mr. Porter contributed to the literary portion of the paper, the writer will not assume the province of determining; the probability is, that he did not compose any elaborate articles, except those to which his initials or other sure signs of paternity are attached. Care, disappointment, and that sickness of heart which he concealed from the world, began to tell on face and form and mental activity, and he availed himself of a stipulated privilege to spare himself much of the labor that even to a recent day had been his delight and pride. The last articles which he furnished of any great consequence were obituary notices of his old and respected friends John C. Stevens, Esq., of New Jersey, and Colonel Wade Hampton, of South Carolina; and they bear the stamp of that keen analysis and generous appreciation of character which marked his numerous essays in that difficult form of composition. It has been stated, and no doubt correctly, that just before his death he was engaged in an elaborate biography of the late William Henry Herbert, whose untimely end was a source of universal and painful sorrow.

Mr. Porter passed most of the last winter of his life at home, with books for companions when not receiving the kind attention of his friends. His thoughts and conversation were often occupied with those divine truths which were stamped upon his soul in childhood at the knee of his mother :

> " Shadowy recollections,
> Which, be they what they may,
> Are yet a master-light of all our seeing ;
> Uphold us, cherish, and have power to make
> Our noisy years seem moments in the being
> Of the Eternal Silence ; truths that wake
> To perish never ;
> Which neither bitterness nor mad endeavor,
> Nor man nor boy,
> Nor all that is at enmity with joy,
> Can utterly abolish or destroy ! "

For two months before his death he had been unusually well and cheerful. On the night of Tuesday, July 13th, by imprudently leaving open a window in his sleeping-room, he took a severe cold, which resulted in congestion of the lungs, and terminated his earthly career at half after nine on the morning of the following Monday. He was from the first impressed with the idea that it was his last illness, and with clear mind and firm serenity expressed his satisfaction that the end was near at hand. The same urbanity, gentle patience, and thoughtfulness for others which marked his whole previous life, were equally conspicuous during these last days of mortal suffering. Just before the closing moment he requested to have the curtain of a window near his bed raised, that he might once more see the light of day. "How beautiful!" he fervently murmured, as the sun broke into the room; and as if he at that moment caught sight of the blue hills of Newbury, and the white paling of the cottage where he was born, or heard the far away toll of the village bell, which brought back to his fading memory the objects which surrounded his boyhood, he breathed the names of mother and father and brothers, adding with a last effort, "I want to go home," just as the veil which separates the things of Time from the Infinite Unseen, parted to admit him, as we fondly believe, to their embrace.

The intelligence of his death spread with electric rapidity throughout the land, and the melancholy response of the universal newspaper press told how sincere was the grief felt at the loss of one of its distinguished ornaments. The funeral ceremonies took place at St. Thomas' Church, in the presence of a large audience of sympathizing friends. At their conclusion, the lid of the coffin, which rested between the reading-desk and the pulpit, was opened, and such of the congregation as desired to take a last view of his manly features, to which death had imparted a more than earthly beauty, were informed that they might do so. The whole congregation embraced the offer, and passed round as indicated.

A generous tribute to his memory appeared in the
" Old Spirit," from the pen and from the heart of
that sterling gentleman, James Oakes, Esq., of Boston, who over the signature of " Acorn " has for so
many years contributed to the value of its columns :

" For more than twenty-five years have William T. Porter and
myself battled our way on the banks of the river of life, as it
were hand in hand, but in different professions. During that
time I have never known him to wilfully commit an unmanly,
ungenerous, unkind, dishonorable or even discourteous act, to
his fellow-man. He, it is true, had his weaknesses, but they
were those that did injustice to himself only—no wrong to
others. It was his nature to be as gentle and as kind as a child,
and so made up, and so harmoniously mingled in him were all
those rare and extraordinary characteristics which go to make
the high-toned, high-bred gentleman, that he possessed the power
to fascinate every one with whom he came in contact, whether
it were the little girl whom he trotted on his knee, the boy with
whom he played, or the thoroughbred sporting gentleman. His
mind was comprehensive, his perception keen, his deductions
clear and concise ; whilst his judgment and decisions in all
sporting matters were more reliable and more respected than
any other man's in this country. He was the father of a school
of American sporting literature, which is no less a credit to his
name than it is an honor to the land that gave him birth. Many
of his decisions and sporting reports will be quoted as authority
for generations to come. He possessed a fund of sporting statis-
tics unequalled by any other man in America. While living, he
was respected and beloved by every one, no less for his child-
like simplicity of nature, than for those high and manly characteristics which so strongly marked him as a journalist. His
death will be deeply and sincerely mourned by every person who
knew him. With much truth can it be said :

> ' 'Thou art the ruin of the noblest man
> That ever lived in the tide of times.' '

George Wilkes, Esq., associate editor of " Porter's Spirit of the Times," furnished for that paper a tribute to his memory, from which we make the following extract :

"Loftiest among them all—with a gentleness and grace that so mingled man and woman in his nature that his own sex might love him even to tenderness, and not feel ashamed—WILLIAM PORTER moved among the LIVINGSTONS, HAMPTONS, STEVENSES, STOCKTONS, JONESES, WADDELLS, LONGS, &c., making all happy by his cheerful spirit, and distributing favor by his presence, rather than receiving patronage. The merit of his paper, and the high character of these voluntary associations, not only drew around him the most distinguished writers and correspondents of the time, both at home and from foreign lands, but brought out a new class of writers, and created a style which may be denominated an American literature—not the august, stale, didactic, pompous, bloodless method of the magazine pages of that day ; but a fresh, crisp, vigorous, elastic, graphic literature, full of force, readiness, actuality and point, which has walked up to the telegraph, and hardly been invigorated or improved by even the terse and emphatic lightning. This literature was not stewed in the closet, or fretted out at some pale pensioned laborer's desk, but sparkled from the cheerful leisure of the easy scholar—poured in from the emulous officer in the barracks, or at sea—emanated spontaneously from the jocund poet—and flowed from every mead, or lake, or mountain—in the land where the rifle or the rod was known. Of this literature, which is better known as 'American Sporting Literature,' Mr. PORTER may be said to be the founder and the head ; and for its creation and thousands of happy hours the people of the United States owe him as great a debt of gratitude as they do for that stimulation to the improvement of the breed of horses, which has made us already foremost of all the world in the production of the most valuable species of working and pleasure stock.

" The life of Mr. PORTER, for the thirty years which terminated with his management of this paper, was not marked by any striking incidents. His life flowed equably from day to day; and year by year parted company with him, without taking on its record a single quarrel or scarcely a ruffled feeling against any being in the world.

"He was peculiarly qualified to be endeared to every thing that came within his presence; and his kind nature was so justly balanced and so free from all invidious inclination, that, by common consent, he was received throughout the country as the umpire of all controverted points, not only in matters growing out of the specialities of his paper, but in all questions of friendly argument, which would not take parties into court. During his editorial career, he has probably decided more disputes, involving the award of money, than any judge who ever sat upon a bench; and what is most remarkable in this connection is, that his decisions were always cheerfully acquiesced in, and never were made the subject of appeal. To use the language of a contemporary: 'He seemed to live without an enemy; and at the time of his death, he was probably the best known of any man in New York who had never filled an official place!'"

In the same paper appeared these stanzas by R. S. Chilton, Esq., of Washington, which were republished in the "Knickerbocker" of February last:

IN MEMORY OF WILLIAM T. PORTER.

A heart where kindly words and deeds
  The founts were still unsealing,
Whence flowed, unchecked through all their course,
  The streams of generous feeling;
A kind, true heart, that with the joys,
  Could share the griefs of others;
And ne'er forsook the grand old faith
  That all mankind are brothers.

A soul in which the manlier traits,
  And gentler, were so blended,
That none could say where these began,
  Or where the others ended :
Alas ! to fitly speak his worth
  All words seem poor and common,
In whose large spirit Nature fused　.
  The tenderness of Woman !

Enough ! his heart has ceased to beat ;
  His soul has passed the portal
That shuts the other world from this,
  And what remains is mortal.
But long as brave and gentle hearts
  Are held in memory's keeping,
Our fond and sorrowing thoughts will haunt
  The grave where he is sleeping.

                                    R. S. C.

Similar testimonials from all parts of the Union
are before us. The "London Times" appropriately
noticed his death, and referred to him as "a man
known world-wide." These we lay aside for our private gratification, with the conviction that " this post-
humous esteem reached no higher attitude," to use the
words of a contemporary editor, "than that which
was felt and uttered for the living man."

In bringing this volume to a close, we take the
highest satisfaction in the reflection that the design
of compiling a Memoir of William T. Porter did not
originate in an exaggerated estimate of his genial and
beneficent nature, of his magical power to attract and
secure the warmest affection of all who were brought
within its influence, of that rare combination of child-
like confidence and sagacious self-reliance in his in-

tercourse with the world, or of that large-heartedness which made him, perhaps, too much given to hospitality, a failing so near akin to a Christian virtue ; by neither of these considerations were we stirred, but rather by an admiration of that indomitable energy which enabled him to carry out from its first and discouraging inception to a successful issue, the fixed, definite, precise, great idea of his youth, the introduction and advancement of a fresh, original and captivating department of letters, and by the conviction that his editorial progress illustrated a truth which there is a tendency in youth to disregard, that vague and loose application will be barren of fruitful results, while courage and constancy are but equivalents to success and fame.

> " Who is the happy warrior ? who is he,
> That every man in arms should wish to be ?
> It is the generous spirit who, when brought
> Among the tasks of real life, bath wrought
> Upon the plan that pleased his boyish thought :
> Whose high endeavors are an inward light
> That makes the path before him always bright :
> Who, with a natural instinct to discern
> What knowledge can perform, is diligent to learn ! "

So long as a love of recreation is recognized as " one of the features impressed on man's spirit by the Divine Creator," so long we venture to believe the name of William T. Porter will live.

www.ingramcontent.com/pod-product-compliance
Lightning Source LLC
Chambersburg PA
CBHW060606030726
47498CB00005B/1568